Sugar Among the Freaks

Lewis Nordan

Sugar

Among the

Freaks

Selected Stories

Algonquin Books

of Chapel Hill • 1996

Grateful acknowledgment is made to the magazines where these stories were first published: to *Harper's* for "Rat Song," "Welcome to the Arrow-Catcher Fair," "Sugar Among the Freaks," and "Sugar Among the Chickens"; to *Redbook* for "The Sin Eater"; to *The Southern Review* for "Sugar, the Eunuchs, and Big G.B.," and "A Hank of Hair, a Piece of Bone"; to *The Greensboro Review* for "The Talker at the Freak-Show"; to *The Arkansas Times Magazine* for "Wheelchair"; and to *Playgirl* for "John Thomas Bird."

The barker's spiel and some of the preceding images of freaks in the story "Talker at the Freak-Show" are from the poem "Side Show" by Miller Williams © 1970 by Miller Williams and are used by permission of the author.

Published by
Algonquin Books of Chapel Hill
Post Office Box 2225
Chapel Hill, North Carolina 27515-2225

a division of
WORKMAN PUBLISHING
708 Broadway
New York, New York 10003

First Front Porch Paperback Edition, May 1996. Originally published in two collections, *Welcome to the Arrow-Catcher Fair* (1983) and *The All-Girl Football Team* (1986), by LSU Press, both reprinted by Vintage in 1989.

Library of Congress Cataloging-in-Publication Data
Nordan, Lewis.
      Sugar among the freaks : selected stories / by Lewis Nordan.
          p.   cm.
      ISBN 1-56512-131-7
      1. Mississippi—Social life and customs—Fiction.   2. City and town
life—Mississippi—Fiction.   I. Title.
      PS3564.O55A6   1996
      813'.54—dc20   95-42309
                                                                                CIP

10 9 8 7 6 5 4 3 2 1
First Edition

For Joe Kelly

Contents

Introduction by Richard Howorth   ix
Foreword by Lewis Nordan   xix

Part I

Storyteller   3
The Sears and Roebuck Catalog Game   15
John Thomas Bird   30
The Sin Eater   49
Wild Dog   67
One-Man Band   81
Rat Song   97
Welcome to the Arrow-Catcher Fair   118

Part II

The Attendant   143
Wheelchair   163

Part III

Sugar Among the Chickens   179
The Talker at the Freak-Show   199
Sugar, the Eunuchs, and Big G.B.   217
The All-Girl Football Team   243
Sugar Among the Freaks   261

Sugar's Buddy: An Introduction

Once at a gathering of regional booksellers it was my job to find a writer to speak at a breakfast assembly, and I was able to get Lewis Nordan to appear. This was before I had met him, and he called me shortly before the time he was to speak and asked if there was anything in particular he should say or read. I told him he could say whatever he liked. He was silent for a moment, so I added that it certainly was not necessary to say how much he loved booksellers or bookstores. At the breakfast, when he began to speak, he explained to the audience that he planned to go against my advice, *which was to say how much he loved booksellers*, and that he would simply read one of his stories.

Only a few days later I was to become again the only person in an audience to "get" a Lewis Nordan joke of which I was also the sole butt, when he came to read in our store. He asked what I would like him to read, and again I said the matter was up to him, but, if I had my druthers, I would like him to read something long—not generally my request with readers. As he prepared to read to the crowd, he explained that, although *I had asked him to please read a very short story,* he had decided to read instead a long one.

I don't know whether inverted truth is a device Lewis Nordan employs in writing and therefore plays around with in life, or if it's a part of his character that ineluctably comes out in his fiction. But if you asked him, I am certain you could not rely on his answer.

"I've got this mythology," Lewis—Buddy, as he is known around home—Nordan says, "the Delta *earth* is part of everybody who's ever walked across it." To understand the Mississippi Delta, the "South's South," as Richard Ford once called it, is to understand America, America's economic, social, racial, and political extremes in their most ambivalent state, perhaps the whole miserable and joyous human condition.

The Delta is not a typical river delta. It is an ancient floodplain, a flat crescent of land two hundred miles long and eighty miles wide, incorporating the plantations and crossroads of the great Delta blues musicians and Buddy Nordan's hometown, Itta Bena. As recently as a hundred years ago, it was a vast, swampy wilderness, much of it cleared out first by slaves, then by cheap black labor, "the richest land this side of the Nile," as Big Daddy says in *Cat on a Hot Tin Roof*, a hot, humid, mosquito-plagued, snake-infested farmland known to kill a dog in five years, a mule in ten, and a man in twenty.

Buddy Nordan's Itta Bena is down the road from Money, the town where Emmett Till was murdered, an event that Nordan finally felt he could write about in his fourth book, *Wolf Whistle* (1993). In his early stories collected here, however, race is peculiarly absent, with the exception of one black character, Floyd, who remains invisible for most of the title story, "Sugar Among the Freaks." "It's the truth, I couldn't see him," says Sugar, sounding much like Nordan who, when asked whether at that time he was intentionally avoiding racial themes, answered, "At the time I didn't know I was avoiding it, which I was. I was traumatized by racial violence . . . I also didn't know how to write about sex, either, though I'd had plenty of experience with both."

It is also true, particularly in these early stories, that Nordan maintains a sort of distance from outright reference to his relationship with Mississippi. And Mississippi has kept an odd distance from Nordan. Bewilderingly, he is seldom mentioned in numerous articles about Delta or Mississippi writers or artists. Although he won a Mississippi Arts and Letters Institute prize in 1992 for his beautiful novel-in-stories, *Music of the Swamp,* he is represented in the Mississippi Writers Room of the Eudora Welty Library in Jackson by only two of his five books, and his photograph is noticeably missing from the walls. He rarely appears in adoring articles in the state press the way Miss Welty and Willie Morris do, where one can read weekly, it seems, what's up with John Grisham.

This likely is owing to the fact that his stories are emotionally complex and literally bizarre. Many reviewers and small-town paper editors might reasonably have a hard time glamorizing Nordan's stories of fishing for roosters, adolescent cross-dressing, swamp elves, administering suppositories, eunuchs (who never really show up) in a small Mississippi town, or the likes of a lake-water lamprey eel, or a mother who attempts suicide in her son's presence, stories where "doom is domestic and purrs like a cat."

Sugar Among the Freaks is, with the exception of three omitted stories, a complete but rearranged collection of Lewis Nordan's first two books, both story collections: *Welcome to the Arrow-Catcher Fair* (1983) and *The All-Girl Football Team* (1986). *Welcome to the Arrow-Catcher Fair* was published by the Louisiana State University Press after it had come in over the transom and found editor Martha Lacy Hall, who was "arrested by those stories as soon as I saw them," and who now, upon picking up the book more than a dozen years later, "remember[s] each one vividly." Hall had edited a good bit of fiction for LSU Press, most famously John Kennedy Toole's *A Confederacy of Dunces*, in 1980, the novel that had been turned down by numerous New York houses and whose author killed himself, due in part, many say, to the initial failure of the manuscript, which was finally tossed to LSU by Walker Percy, where it went on to sell exceedingly well and win the Pulitzer Prize.

LSU Press fiction was capable, then, three years later, of getting reviewers' attention, and *Arrow-Catcher* fared well in the January 15, 1984, *New York Times Book Review*. It was reviewed with two other books of short fiction, all first books by their authors. Edith Milton said that all three "add up to something of a celebration of the variety of which the short story is capable," singling out *Arrow-Catcher* by saying, "in fact, Lewis Nordan's *Arrow-Catcher* nicely illustrates the diversity all by itself." Her favorite stories were "Storyteller," the first one in this collection, and "The Sin Eater."

Many of the stories that eventually were published in the second collection, *The All-Girl Football Team*, never saw magazine publication. *Harper's* rejected the title story, writing back to Nordan, "Dear Mr. Newman, Thank you for your article on football" and explaining that it did not publish sports pieces. In a short, favorable review in *The New York Times Book Review*, Ursula Hegi said that, in *The All-Girl Football Team*, "Lewis Nordan questions the line between inner and outer reality again and again in this stunning collection of short stories."

As it turned out, neither book sold very well for LSU Press, although Martha Lacy Hall said that they sold well enough "for university press fiction"—a figure one could guess to be about 2,500 copies. As is the pattern with much lasting literature, most of the attention Nordan's stories received was from other writers.

Pat Mulcahy was an editor at Vintage Books, the prestigious Random House paperback imprint, when she went to LSU Press shopping for James Lee Burke's *The Lost Get Back Boogie*, a book that rescued that author from obscurity. Mulcahy lost the auction for Burke's book, but in the process discovered from Martha Lacy Hall the work of Lewis Nordan. "I was looking for an original voice . . . something fresh," Mulcahy said, and found Nordan brilliant "primarily as a storyteller"; plus, she could not resist, she said, "Sugar—who is a little Huck Finn-ish."

The All-Girl Football Team was reprinted first by Vintage (probably because its title was thought to be more marketable), then *Welcome to the Arrow-Catcher Fair* a few months later, in 1989, under the Vintage Contemporaries imprint. The VCs had rocked the publishing world with a combination of paperback originals—such as *Bright Lights, Big City* and *The Sportswriter*—and modern classic reprints—such as *Suttree* and *A Fan's Notes*. They were hot . . . for a while. But by the time *Arrow-Catcher* came out under the VC imprint, now six years after its original hardcover publication, the list had grown to some seventy-odd titles and "lost its sheen among hip writing," as Mulcahy said. Sugar was late to the ball and didn't get the marketing attention accorded earlier VC titles.

By late 1989, Mulcahy had left Vintage for Little, Brown. Meanwhile, Shannon Ravenel, who had encountered Nordan's stories in the literary magazines she read as series editor of *The Best American Short Stories*, had joined Louis Rubin in founding the upstart publishing house, Algonquin Books of Chapel Hill. When she heard that Nordan and his agent were looking for a new publisher, she opened Algonquin's door. "To my mind, Lewis Nordan's writing was so extraordinary that I was not very hopeful about asking to be added to what I was sure was a long list of publishers lined up for his new book. To my endless delight, Buddy and his agent thought Algonquin was the right place for his work." Algonquin has published all of Nordan's subsequent books—*Music of the Swamp* (1991), *Wolf Whistle* (1993), and *The Sharpshooter Blues* (1995)—and has acquired the rights to the now out-of-print LSU collections. Said Ravenel, "We see Lewis Nordan as an important American fiction writer and we want to try to keep all of his best work in print—hence, and I might add, especially, *Sugar Among the Freaks*."

The Sugar (Mecklin is his surname) who appears in so many of these stories is as complex a character as the "freaks" around him. His creator is not a simple writer, either, having more than a little in common with Sugar. If the publication history, while short at this point, seems peculiar, it's a lot like so much of Lewis Nordan's life and writing career, and Sugar's world as well—fraught with fortuity.

As an infant, Nordan lost his father. "My stepfather was good, but there was a space there. Naturally," he said, "I was attracted to lost father themes," which have become one of the more forceful, arresting characteristics of Nordan's work. In "Sugar, the Eunuchs, and Big G.B.," the story in which Sugar struggles with his love for his father intensely and violently, Sugar fires a pistol into his house knowing his father is inside and says that at one point he "believed that my daddy and I were somehow the same person." In "The Talker at the Freak-Show," a story that swims with Nordan's satisfying ambiguities, we see through Nordan's eyes just as Sugar sees through his daddy's, that "belief and disbelief were the same creature in me." Nordan credits among his early literary influences comic books, yes, especially Superman. "I identified with Superman, who was separated from his parents." Superman's heroics, his death-defying feats meant nothing to Nordan. "I identified with him as an alien . . . I was an alien on my *own* planet."

"As a young man I thought I'd been 'cheated' by being raised in the Delta," he says. "I thought I'd be better off if I'd gone to Harvard, or been raised in New York." But Nordan acknowledges he never could have written what he has without the Delta, a place where he *does* know "shit from shinola," as the expression there goes. When Nordan was 35 he moved his family to Fayetteville, Arkansas, to attend the writing program at the University of Arkansas. He had got his Ph.D.—Shakespeare—at Auburn, but became "hopeless about Shakespeare" when he could not get one of the 250 teaching jobs he had applied for.

When Nordan first began to write at Arkansas, he "had no sense of what [he] wanted to write about." Over lunch one day he told this to William Harrison, one of his teachers there, and Harrison said, "'I don't know?' That sounds like what a sophomore in college would say." "I felt terrible," Nordan said. "By the end of lunch I told him, 'I think I want to write about love and death in a comic way.' I said this without knowing what exactly that meant."

Although he dropped out of Arkansas after a year, he was productive there, placing stories in such literary magazines as the *Greensboro Review* and the *New Orleans Review*. *Harper's* eventually published several early Nordan stories, the first being "Rat Song," the seventh story in Part I here.

"Rat Song" was recommended to *Harper's* by an editor at *The New Yorker* who loved it but could not persuade the magazine to publish it. The story is about love and lust and a man who takes in as pets two rats from his daughter Missy's class and says "Godamnit" at least once—not your typical *New Yorker* fare, not of those days, anyway.

The first four of the five stories in Part III all appeared originally in *The All-Girl Football Team*, the second story collection. Most of the stories were written in Pittsburgh, where Nordan had been offered a position teaching creative writing at the University of Pittsburgh. Shortly after moving there, one of Nordan's sons committed suicide (another son had died earlier, at birth), and Nordan "wrote in a frenzy," as this book became for him "a cathartic experience." It is logical that we find young Sugar Mecklin in these stories, and that the fulcrum for them is the relationship between Sugar and his father, Gilbert, for Nordan must have written out of complete emptiness—"that diamond of pain and emptiness," as loss by death is described in "The Sin Eater."

There is a story about Buddy—I don't know whether it's true—that he drank hard for a number of years before he straightened himself up, climbed on the wagon, and put together a résumé in order to find a job. The period of several years when he was drinking vodka was left blank, and when he interviewed for a job, the interviewer said, "Mr. Nordan, I notice that the years from 19-- until now, you appear not to have been employed. Can you tell me what you were doing those years?" "Well," Nordan is said to have replied, "I wasn't just sitting around drinking vodka." Supposedly, he got the job.

"I was a storyteller a long time before I became a writer," Nordan has said. "Everyone in my family is a storyteller, though none of the others are writers. For a long time I thought I was somehow defective for not being able to tell the truth—the 'truth,' I should say—without changing it, amplifying it, or romanticizing it. This seemed to be a flaw in my character. Now I think that it may be a flaw, but it is also a gift for which I am grateful."

That Lewis Nordan succeeded in "writing about love and death in a comic way" was never an accident, not his accident, anyway. Only a person from his time, from his place, with his own sweet and tragic life, with his artistic sensibilities and a propensity to reinvent truth, steeped in Shakespeare, brought up in the Delta and taught to write in Arkansas, only Lewis Nordan could have written these thrilling, fabulous stories.

—Richard Howorth
Oxford, Mississippi

Foreword

In the summer of 1981, I was a part of the small, lively writing community of Fayetteville, Arkansas, centered around the university's Creative Writing Program, where I had been a student a few years previously. Ellen Gilchrist, Jack Butler, Steve Stern, Lee K. Abbott, John Dufresne, Carl Launius, and Otto Salassi were a few of the other youngish writers just beginning to publish their work. There were a dozen or more others. I had placed a few short stories in small magazines, and a couple of times had sold stories to *Harper's*, so my situation was similar to everyone else's. Though publication was always on our minds, we drew our real strength as writers from the constant conversations we had about writing, the late-night talking and drinking and reading sessions. We sometimes stayed up all night reading aloud scenes from Shakespeare, and no one was ever shy to read his or her own work. This was a formative and scary time for all of us, and it is fair to say that we were using one another to seek out— or at least to talk out—our own identities as writers.

I am remembering a particular evening when the title story of the present collection rose up before me, out of the summer mist, or seemed to do so, I swear.

As in many writing communities, there were a couple of bars in town that were receptive to our presence. The Deluxe Rathskeller (pronounced "Dee Lux Rat Cellar") and George's Majestic Lounge (then catering to gays but also friendly to artsy types like ourselves) were among them. I have not visited these establishments in many years now, but then both were bare-boned, hard-core bars, smelly with stale beer and dark as graves.

One suffocatingly humid summer evening I was scheduled to read from my work in an outdoor courtyard behind George's Majestic Lounge. I was to appear on a bill with an amazing young poet named John Stoss, of whom there are enough stories to fill many books. The only problem was that the story I was supposed to read had not yet been written. I had begun writing the story, but only barely, and what was written was a complete mess and not working at all. At this time I was still writing everything out in longhand on a yellow legal pad.

Several hours before the reading was to begin, I took the miserable legal pad and its failed fiction with me to George's and sat alone at the bar. I ordered refreshments for myself and, in the dim half-light of a revolving beer sign, began to try to salvage the story I had begun to scrawl there. The story purported to give a more-or-less straightforward account of a trip to Oklahoma with two friends, one of them the poet and memoirist Carl Launius, a quadriplegic paralyzed years before in a high school football game, and the other a man afflicted with the condition popularly known as Elephant Man's disease. For some reason I had imagined that the extravagant health problems of my friends constituted an interesting story, in and of itself. This was ridiculous, of course.

I sat at the bar, I drank, I stared at the paragraphs I had written. The story was not interesting. Something was wrong, but I didn't know what. I knew that my friends were interesting people. I knew that I was interested in them and in their courageous struggles in life. And yet the story was flat.

So I took a red pen from my pocket and went down the first page of the piece, circling in red everything I did find interesting on that page, each image, detail, idea, turn of phrase. When I had finished, there was a bare scattering of red circles. I sat and looked at how few there were, and in this way had a sort of objective picture of my dullness. By doing this, I developed in that moment a technique that still serves me, and that, in fact, is the basis for the prose style that I now claim as my own. I said, "All I need is more red circles."

I went back to the first paragraph. The character was sitting at the counter of a truck-stop restaurant. A bland, third-person narrator—myself, I mean—told the reader this. So in a way I already knew what was uninteresting about the story. I was the wrong person to tell the story, for some reason. So I changed the narration to first person. I didn't know who this new speaker was, but he had to be more interesting than me. He sat at his counter for only a moment before he noticed what I had not. He saw a pie case behind the counter. He looked into the case and saw the pies. He noticed that the meringue was "real dilapidated." Then he noticed the detail that made this story possible, and easy, and fun to write. He saw a couple of flies on the inside of the glass pie case.

I don't know why those flies changed this story for me, but they did. As if a key had been inserted into a lock, a door was flung wide open and my imagination was allowed to get out, escape, and run laughing and wacky into the daylight. Later, after I had finished writing, I went back and covered this page with red circles, but not right away. I kept writing. No one could have stopped me. I wrote and wrote and wrote, filling the legal pad. The bar started to fill up with people, regular customers at first, then people coming to the reading. I kept on writing. Eventually the crowd moved to the outdoor area, and I stayed at the bar with my pen and legal pad. The reading started without me—John Stoss, big as a gentle bear, reciting those delicate, sweet poems.

I wanted to be out there, among those people I loved, listening to those lovely lines, but—to say this only slightly more dramatically than I felt it at the time—Sugar Mecklin and his whole strange family were being born beneath my hand.

I finished the last lines of the story before John Stoss finished reading his final poems. I stepped out of the bar, into the audience, and took my place at a table in the dark, beneath the stars, and listened until he was done. There was a break. Waiters came around. I made myself a part of the crowd I had shunned for a few hours. I rewarded myself with extra beers. Later I read to this receptive crowd the story I had just written and was pleased by their laughter and applause. The story, of course, was "Sugar Among the Freaks."

I was also pleased at a deeper level, as I have said. I knew I had just invented a boy whom I loved and wanted to know better. I knew that if I was lucky and worked hard, I might be able to write more stories about him. He was surely a part of me, and yet when he spoke of his parents, it was clear they were equal parts of me as well. Sugar Mecklin was not me—no more or less than Gilbert Mecklin was—but he could speak for me, for all my contradictory parts, and now he seemed free to do so. I think of this moment as a particular turning point in the process of my finding what I meant to write and how I meant to write it.

"Sugar Among the Freaks" is the only story in *Welcome to the Arrow-Catcher Fair* (LSU Press, 1983) in which Sugar himself appears, and it was the last I wrote before putting together that collection. Even then I was suspicious that "Sugar Among the Freaks" was slightly misplaced in that book, but I knew that in this story I had turned a corner of some kind. In my second collection, *The All-Girl Football Team* (LSU Press, 1986), Sugar appears as himself, or in barely disguised form, in most of the stories. He is the central figure in a later novel-in-stories, *Music of the Swamp* (Algonquin Books,1991). And now as I look back over the early stories in those first two collections, from which these fifteen stories are drawn, I see clearly how the town of Arrow Catcher, Mississippi, its geography and its inhabitants—not just the Mecklins but also many others—were slowly taking form and shape and moral dimension, a little like a photograph in a developing tray, appearing first in dim and fuzzy outline and then becoming crisper in the details, sharper at the edges.

The grown-up Sugar, who narrates much of his biography in these stories and in the third book as well, would seem to have an unreliable memory, at best. He tells two versions of his father's death; he seems confused about when he knew of the existence of the Rock 'n' Roll suit; and isn't it unlikely that Sugar's mother ever made a dramatic, semisexual suicide attempt right in front of Sugar, as the mother does in "The Sears and Roebuck Catalog Game"? Sugar seems a little crazier in "Sugar Among the Freaks" than the child of the same name in the later stories.

The third-person narrator of other stories makes as many mistakes as the unreliable Sugar. He reports, without blinking, Hydro's double or triple parentage and his life in both Arkansas and Mississippi. By this narrator's account Sugar once went by the name of Harris, as in "The Attendant." Arrow Catcher itself seems formerly to have been named Big Ugly, a corruption of some strange Native American word meaning Home in the Woods. And what is Sugar's mother's name, for heaven's sake? What exactly do eunuchs do at Episcopal baptizings? What is a swamp elf?

There is no use pretending that there is any design in all this confusion. There isn't. In many of the stories collected here I was, without knowing this at the time, painting details that I would later reimagine, revise, repaint, when it came time to add them to the broader canvas. That afternoon and evening in George's Majestic Lounge, when the door of my imagination was flung open, I knew that one way to close it again, maybe forever, was to entertain a foolish belief that consistency and good sense are as important as invention. They are not.

I hold a special affection for the stories collected here. They cause me to remember the young writer that I was, twenty or more years ago, as I wrote the stories included in the present volume—frightened, compulsive, ambitious, driven, with nothing to lose. I learned how to write alongside friends who were also teaching themselves to write. I used to complain, back then, that I didn't have a "generation" to identify myself with—lost, beat, silent, angry, agrarian, whatever—and that if I did, I'd be a better writer. Well, who knows. Here are the stories. They feel like old friends themselves, one of that number that I stayed up all night with, so many nights, talking, talking, talking, telling the tales that would make me, make all of us, ready to write the ones that needed to be written.

—Lewis Nordan
Pittsburgh, 1995

Sugar Among the Freaks

Part 1

Storyteller

It was Wiley Heard talking and cooling his coffee at the same time. "You heard about all them grain elevators blowing up in Kansas, didn't you?" Wiley was a short, wiry one-legged man with a red face and white eyebrows. He was retired head coach of the local football team. He stopped blowing across his coffee and took a long, slurping pull, then held up the heavy cup, like evidence, so everybody could see. One or two of those standing around moved in closer to the marble counter and were careful not to overturn a spittoon. They poured cups for themselves and laid their change on the cash register. "See this?" he said. "It's the best cup of coffee in the entire state of Arkansas. Right here in Hassell's Blank Store. Used to be called Hassell's Drug Store, long time ago. Back before any you boys would remember." They tried not to notice Coach Wiley pour a nip of Early Times into his coffee from a flat bottle he slipped out of his jacket pocket. "Yessir," he said, "Gene Hassell sold the wrong drugs to the wrong man. Two men, in fact. Federal agents pretending to work on a truck for two days across the street, out yonder by the railroad tracks, before they come in for pills. On account of which old Gene's pharmacy license got taken away. And so

did Gene, come to think of it, down to the Cummins peni-
tentiary. Couldn't get him in Atlanta. It was all full up that
year, I think was the trouble. His wife, poor thing, Miss Eva,
I swan. She just painted out the word *Drug* on the sign and
held a shotgun up under her chin, bless her time. It was that
old twelve-gauge of Gene's that kicked so bad, real old gun,
belonged to his daddy and ejected shells out the bottom.
Remington, I think it was. She pulled the trigger and shot off
her face. The whole damn thing from the bottom up, jaw,
teeth, nose, and eyes, and broke both her eardrums. Terrible
sight to see, even after the skin grafts. No face at all. Can't
see, hear, smell, or taste, just keep her alive in a nursing
home down in Arkadelphia, feeding her through tubes, and
not one pellet touched her brain. It's a sad case, boys. It
would break your heart. We been calling it Hassell's Blank
Store ever since, and him still in jail, I guess, or dead, but
you say you did hear about them grain elevators, didn't you?"

Somebody said he had. Everybody else agreed.

"I know you did," said the coach. "You heard about it on
the Walter Cronkite Show, didn't you? They had it on the TV
every night for a month, seem like. But I bet you forty dollars
you didn't hear what happened the other day over in El
Dorado, did you? Just outside El Dorado, I ought to say, over
close to Smackover. A dog food factory blew up. That's about
like El Dorado, ain't it? Ain't nowhere but El Dorado, and
maybe parts of north Mississippi, they going to blow up a
dog food factory. But you never will hear that one on the
Walter Cronkite Show, nayo-siree, and don't need to. The
longer they can keep El Dorado, Arkansas, off the national

news, or Smackover either one, the better for everybody, is what I say. Hound Dog dog food factory—and three men are missing, so they tell me. Might of been mule skinners, mightn't they? I think they was, in fact. If any you boys are looking for work they going to need somebody to skin them miserable old horses before they can put them in a can. Over this side of El Dorado actually, up close to Smackover. But that was years ago Gene Hassell went to jail. You boys wouldn't remember him, years ago. Hell, he may not be dead now, all I know. Probably is, though. Probably is dead now he can't drink no more of that paregoric. He probably died his second day off that paregoric, didn't he? He'd been drinking it for twenty years. He's been constipated that long. He probably didn't know what to think, did he, down there in Cummins behind them bars, or out on that hot scrabble farm chopping him some prison cotton, when he felt that first urge to go to the bathroom. Hell, he probably died right off, didn't he? Didn't even have to call the dispensary. He probably got him a shit fit and the blind staggers and keeled over with his eyes rolled up. His old crazy paregoric eyes probably looked like the rolled-up window shades of Miss Dee's whorehouse on Sunday morning, he was so happy. But not Miss Eva, that's his wife, she's not dead. She's still over to Arkadelphia at the Wee Care Nursing Home, got a married daughter out in California, or is it granddaughter, pays the bills. That little redbrick building with the neon sign saying *Wee Care* out on the old airport road, real nice place, and expensive too. But Jerry Rich down in Prescott, out beyond Prescott really, just this side of Delight, he's the one owns this place now, Hassell's Blank Store. He's owned it for years. Poor old woman had to sell out right away, of course, after she lost so much face here in town trying to kill herself, and her husband in the pokey. The daughter had to sell, I mean. And no face at all, Miss Eva, and never did have much personality to speak of. But old Jerry, he doesn't get up here much anymore, long as there's a quail in them cornfields and one old sorry dog in the pen. Not even to change the name on the front of the store. Painting out Gene's name would be a piss-poor way to remember a good man, though now wouldn't it? Lord, but his wife was a boring woman, even back when she had a face. It was three of them missing, though, three skinners, all of them white men, I believe it was, I'm not real sure about that. Dog food factory over in El Dorado, outside El Dorado really, out close to Smackover, Hound Dog dog food factory."

*W*iley was still talking. "They used to feed dog food to circus animals. Sounds awful, don't it? But it's true. It'd make them crazy, too. It'd make a trained beast turn on his master, so I hear. Nothing to be done about a bitch elephant once they turn on their keeper. Bull elephant's a different story, trustworthiest old wrinkled buggers you ever want to meet, but not a bitch, you can't trust one with a nickel change once she gets sour on life, might as well save yourself the trouble."

"Why's that, Coach Wiley?" The coffee drinkers turned and looked. It was Hydro, a gawky young man with a broom and a large head.

"Nobody knows," said the coach, "and don't ask no more

questions, Hydro. Godamighty. You get on done with that sweeping before you start asking so many questions. But it happened one time over in Pocahontas. One two y'all might be old enough to remember it. Your daddies'd be old enough. Some little off-brand circus or other. Clyde Beatty or something. Naw, not even that good. They had two old scrawny lions that hollered half the night they was so hungry from eating that dried dog food they give them. Probably Hound Dog dog food, when they was looking for meat, like that place blew up over past El Dorado, except that factory wasn't there till ten years ago, so it must have been some other brand the lions had to eat, but nobody ought to feed dog food to a lion and get away with it. King Jesus jump down. It'd take a worthless sumbitch to do that, now wouldn't it? Worthless as a whistle on a plow, as my poor old dead daddy used to say. Daddy he was a funny little quiet man with rusty hair and deep eyes. Housepainter and paperhanger, and a good one too, and a handful of elephants with their nose up each other's ass like a parade and some scrawny old woman in a little white dress and bleached-out hair riding on top of the first elephant, when this baggy old gray African elephant went kind of crazy. *Commercial-Appeal* said she was in heat and real nervous. That's when they dangerous. Some old boy name of Orwell, from West Memphis or Forrest City or somewhere, was quoted as saying that was right. He claimed to know all about elephants, though I can't say I ever knew a family of Arkansas Orwells. Plenty of them in Mississippi, of course, Delta people, but none to my memory in Arkansas. Unless, of course, they come here since the

World War, but I think she was just sick of Pocahontas and circus food. That'd be me. Best thing ever happened to Pocahontas was that tornado in 1957, tore down half the town. They just about due another one, if you want my personal opinion. Didn't have many teeth, my daddy, and had fainting spells on top of that, because you notice she didn't bother to pick out her own trainer to step on. That'd be too easy. She had to bring down all hell and her left front foot on another African, one of her own people, you might say. She had to step on some little local boy hired on as a handler. Plez Holloman's grandson is who it was, in case some y'all are old enough to remember Plez. Course my daddy always did love his whiskey and had a heart enlarged up the size of a basketball, but the fainting spells commenced long before that come to pass, who I always liked, Plez I'm talking about, and hated to see anything bad come to him in spite of not especially blaming the elephant and never could straighten up his back, Plez, on account of getting syphilis when he was just a boy, stepped right on that poor little child and flattened him out like one them cartoon pictures when a steamroller runs over somebody. He looked like a pitiful little black shadow some child lost. But you couldn't blame the elephant, I couldn't, having to live cooped up in Pocahontas all week and that terrible sawed-off circus. It wouldn't do, though, but they had to kill the elephant, and you can see their point, especially if that Orwell boy from West Memphis knew what he's talking about, though I still think he was from somewhere over in Mississippi.

"Anyhow, that's what the mayor and aldermen said, got to

destroy the elephant. They was agreed with by the Colored Ministers Association, which has now got some other name and is joined up with the NAACP. They was quickly agreed with, I might add, which was the first and last time the Pocahontas town officials and the colored ministers ever agreed on anything, except maybe last year when Horace Mayhan —you remember him playing football right here in town and always stunk real bad, before old man Mayhan moved them all to Pocahontas where they'd belonged all along and fit in so good with the paper mill—last year when old Horace won a free trip, so to speak, to Washington, D.C. He had to testify before a Senate subcommittee on the subject of who cut them eyeholes into the sheets the FBI found in the trunk of Horace's car, that cream-colored Mustang with the rusted top and STP stickers on the front bumper. That boy gave new meaning to the word *white-trash*, not to mention who sawed the stocks and barrels off all his shotguns and enough dynamite to provide every man, woman, and child in Arkansas fish dinner every night for a week. But the trouble was, of course, that nobody in Pocahontas had a gun big enough to kill an elephant, not even a hungry old scrawny elephant that probably needed killing."

"Shoot him in the eye." The words were totally unexpected, but the minute they were in the air everybody knew it was Hydro again and that he was in trouble. He had forgotten that the coach told him to stay quiet. It was obvious from his enormous face that he thought he had made a good suggestion. The coach stopped talking and looked at him. Everybody else looked at the floor and tried not to breathe.

They wanted to become invisible. "Hydro, my man," Coach Wiley said, with a chill in his voice that galvanized every gaze upon the floor, "I always kind of liked you, boy. And I know you got your own problems. But listen here. Don't you never interrupt me again. Not now, and not never. Not till you get smart enough to know a whole hell of a lot more about elephants than shoot him in the eye."

"Or," said a voice with an unnatural cheeriness, "maybe you could just shoot him up the butt." It was Hydro again, and he had missed the fury underlying the coach's tone. If any of those standing around the coach in the Blank Store had not been too embarrassed to think of it, they might have hated Hydro, and themselves, and they might have hated God for making Hydro so damn dumb. Nobody thought of it. Nobody knew why they depended on Wiley Heard's approval, and dreaded his disapproval. "It's bound to bust something loose up in there," Hydro said, still pleased as he could be to help.

The coach became more deliberate. For everybody but Hydro, breathing was out of the question. Some of this began to dawn on Hydro.

"Hydro," said Coach Wiley Heard, "I am going to say this one more time. Now, boy, I mean for you to listen. Are you listening?" There was no need for Hydro to answer. He had caught on now. "Shoot him in the eye and shoot him up the butt will not do. Not to interrupt me telling a story, nawsir. And neither will anything else do, to interrupt me telling a story. Are you listening, Hydro? Not nothing that you or anybody else that's going to come into Hassell's Blank Store is likely to think up is going to do to interrupt me. So just forget about interrupting me, boy. At any time, or for any reason whatsoever, with shoot him in the eye or shoot him up the butt or anything else. Now do you understand what I am saying?"

Hydro was quiet and miserable. He said "Yessir" in a tiny whispery voice. He recognized his chastisement. The act of breathing started up again. Throats got cleared, and feet were shifted. Some of the little crowd looked up.

*W*hen the coach finally spoke again, it was not to them, not at first, not exactly. His voice was low and deep and coarse and gravelly, and there was a snort of a humorless laugh behind it. "Shoot him up the butt," they heard him say, almost soundless, and they heard the low, snorting laugh. A few of them laughed a little too; they tried it anyway, the laughter, not loud and not self-confident, and when they heard it, they found no pleasure in its sound. For a few more seconds he let the silence continue. He sweetened his coffee again with Early Times, and they made sure they didn't notice.

When he began again, the tone of his story was immeasurably darker. There were no more self-interruptions, there was no more marshaling of irrelevant detail. The story had become deadly serious and even most of the errors of grammar had disappeared from his speech. If the story were told again, or if it had been told without Hydro's interruption, each person in the store could have imagined it as wonderfully comic, the dark, laughing comedy that underlay every

11

tale he told. But it was not comic now. The elephant he said, would have to be killed. It would have to be killed by hanging. Some let out sounds that might have passed for laughs, but none of them were proud to have done so.

"By now the elephant was quiet," he said. "I saw her led to town by her trainer, a dirty man and sad-faced. The bleach-haired woman was with them too, wearing a maroon suit and low-heeled shoes, the one who rode the elephant in the parade. The railroad crane and log-chain were on a flatcar. The chain was made into a noose and put around its neck. The giant gears started creaking, the crane was lifting. I remember a blind fiddler was in the crowd and a little Indian boy with blue short pants and no shirt high up on the top of a locomotive. The elephant's feet were like the feet of a great turtle. The hind feet brushed the air a scant inch above the cinders in the station yard. When she was up, hanging there, choking, she lifted the wrinkled old trunk straight up and trumpeted one time, one blast to heaven, before she was choked dead. Her back feet, her gray old big turtle feet, were just an inch above the cinders, a little inch."

Those who listened stood, silent, and held their coffee cups without drinking. One man, whose son stood beside him, laid an unconscious hand on the boy's arm and pulled him a little closer to his side. No one knew what to say, or do. For a moment, during the silence, they forgot that Coach Wiley Heard was in charge, in control of the pause. He allowed a few more seconds to pass. They thought of the beast's trumpeting. They did not imagine, even for a second, that the coach's story might be untrue, that he might have made it all up, or adapted it from an older tale, and now maybe even believed it was all true, that it had all really happened on a certain day, to a certain people with bleached hair or sad faces or blind eyes or Indian blood, or any other hair and face and eyes and blood he chose to give them, and that it all happened in a station yard in eastern Arkansas, in a town called Pocahontas. If disbelief crept in, it came like a welcome brother into their company. They poured it a cup of coffee and showed it the sugar bowl and treated it like a friend too familiar to notice. They thought only of the gray feet and the cinders, the little inch between.

Then it was over. The coach released them. With a sudden, unexpected cheeriness, and maybe even a wink, he said, "You not going to forget what I told you, now are you, Hydro?"

"No sir," Hydro said, certain he would not, but still a little uncertain how to act. The coffee drinkers were able to love Hydro again, and pity him and feel superior to him. He shifted his broom and looked at its bristles. Everybody felt confident and happy. Everybody smiled at Hydro's innocence and at his need for forgiveness.

"Shoot him up the butt!" the coach roared suddenly, merry and hilarious and slapping his good leg. "Shoot him up the butt! Great godamighty!" Now they could laugh. They did laugh, uproarious and long. The coach slapped Hydro on the back and called him son and hugged him roughly against him and shook him by the shoulders. "Shoot him up the butt!" he said again. "Got damn, Hydro, I'm going to have to tell that one on you, now ain't I!"

13

When the laughter was over and the coach had wiped a tear from each eye with a clean handkerchief, he spoke to Hydro in a voice a little different from the one they had been listening to for most of the day. He said, "Let me tell you about my daddy, son. You'd of liked him. He had to walk on crutches all one winter, he had tonsillitis so bad." They knew now that they could stay and hear this story if they wished, but they knew also that it would not be told to them. They envied Hydro. They wished they were Hydro. They wished they were holding his broom and feeling the coach's warm, alcoholic breath on their faces. "Daddy always smelled like turpentine and Fitch's shampoo," they heard the coach say, as if from a distance. "It's the only place I ever smelled the two in combination. It breaks my heart to remember." There was a pause, a silence of a few seconds. "He carried this little nickel pistol with him," the coach said, thoughtful. "I'll show it to you sometime. A little nickel pistol, with walnut handle-grips."

Hydro was happy. Everybody could see that. There was no reason for anybody else to hang around, though. They eased out by ones and twos.

The Sears and Roebuck Catalog Game

I had known for a long time that my mother was not a happy woman. When I was a young child in Mississippi, the stories she read to me at bedtime were always tales of Wonderland—of little worlds into which one might escape through rabbit holes or looking glasses or magic wardrobes. The same was true of the games she and I played together.

My favorite game was to open a Sears and Roebuck catalog and to sit with my mother on the floor or in her lap in a chair and to point to each model on the page and to say, What does this one do?—where does this one live?—which one is her boyfriend?

My mother was wonderful at this game. She made up elaborate dossiers on each of the characters I asked her to invent. She found names and occupations and addresses and proper mates for each. Sears and Roebuck was a real world to me, with lakes and cities and operas and noisy streets and farmlands and neighborhoods.

There was even death. Mother shocked me when I was ten by reporting a suicide among the inhabitants of Sporting Goods. I loved and was terrified by the unpredictable drama and pain.

15

My father had no imagination. He disapproved of the game. It is more fair to say that he was baffled by it, as he was by all forms of imaginative invention. He did not forbid games or movies or books or Bible stories; he simply did not understand what use they could be to anyone. At night when my mother had finished saying my bedtime nursery rhymes to me, he would sometimes say to her, "Why do you do that?"

The summer I was fourteen I had occasion to think of the catalog game again.

I had taken a job working for my father on a painting site at the county high school. The local swimming pool was directly behind one wing of the schoolhouse, so while I should have been carrying ladders or washing brushes or wiping up paint drippings, I was usually hanging out the window watching the swimmers in the pool.

That's what I was doing one Friday afternoon, when I happened to see a child drowning. I don't know how I happened to see her. Even the lifeguard had not noticed yet. It was a gangly retarded girl with long arms and stringy hair plastered to her face.

I watched her rise up out of the water, far up, so that half her body showed above the surface, then she sank out of sight. Once more she came back up, and then she sank again.

By now the lifeguard was in the water and the other swimmers were boiling up onto the sides of the pool to get out of his way.

After a while the child's body was retrieved, slick and terrible.

We stopped work for the day. Nobody said anything, we just stopped and loaded the van and drove away.

That evening Father sat in his room in his overstuffed chair and drank glass after glass of whiskey until he slept. He was not grieving the death of the child. Death sparked no tragic thoughts for him, no memories, he drew no tragic conclusions. He felt the shock of its initial impact, and then he forgot about it.

The reason he was drinking had to do with my mother. He was preparing himself for whatever drama was certain to develop now that she knew of the death. Drama was the thing for my mother. When there was none she invented it. When one came along she milked it for its every effect.

My mother went into the guest bedroom—the room she called the guest bedroom, because she loved the sound of the phrase, which suggested to her the possibility of unexpected visitors, long-term guests, though actually it was her own room. It had her bobbypins on the dresser, her facial creams, a hairbrush, her underwear in a drawer. She closed the door.

Down the hall my father was drunk and snoring in his chair.

I went into my father's room and watched him snore. I opened the drawer of his bedside table, as I had many times when I was alone in the house. I took his pistol from the drawer and found the clip. I shoved the clip into the handle and shucked a cartridge into the chamber. I flicked the safety on and off, clickety-click. I unloaded the pistol again and put everything back where it belonged.

My mother was standing in the doorway of the bedroom. My insides leaped when I saw her there in her nightgown. She said, "You are your mother's child."

We walked together to her room, her arm around me, my arms stiff at my sides. We sat on the edge of her bed together. She told me she understood why I wanted to kill my father. She said, "It's natural. Every son wants his father to die."

I wanted to say, "I don't want him to die," but I knew this would disappoint her, would spoil the drama of her pronouncement.

She said, "Death is a beautiful thing. Death is the mother of beauty."

I said, "I guess so."

She said, "Do you love me?"

I said, "Yes."

She said, "I love you, too."

She said, "How much do you love me?"

I wished I was in my father's room watching him snore.

She smiled when I didn't answer. It was a very cute smile. She seemed younger than she was. Younger than me, even. She said, "If I asked you to—oh, let me see now, what could I ask my young man to do for me?—if I asked you to, well, to *kill me*"—here she laughed a silvery little-girl laugh with silvery bright eyes—"if I asked you to do that, honey, would you do it?"

I was terrified and sick. I thought I might vomit. And yet

in a way I thought she might be joking with me, that there was a grown-up joke here that I didn't understand. I said nothing, I couldn't speak.

She looked at me and suddenly her face changed. Her voice changed.

She said, "I just want you to know, there is no reason to be ashamed of discussing the subject of death. Death is a natural part of the whole life process."

She propped two pillows against the headboard and leaned against them. She motioned for me to sit beside her, but I stayed where I was, on the edge of the bed.

She said, "Do you want to talk about the drowning?"

I couldn't answer.

She said, "After an incident of this kind, the healthiest thing in the world is to talk about it. I'm interested in your feelings about death."

I said, "I saw her drowning before anybody else. Before the lifeguard."

She told me the strangest story. It was exactly like a story she might make up about the Sears and Roebuck people, except that it was about herself; there was no catalog. She told me she was born in Saskatchewan. (Remember that not a word of this is true. She was born in Mississippi and had lived nowhere else in her life.) She said that her family had lived in a four-room fifth-floor walk-up with cold Canadian winds whistling through the chinks in the thin walls. "Cold Canadian winds," she actually said. "The thin walls."

I wanted to call out to my father, but I knew he was too drunk to wake up. I knew I could not call out anyway, because it would say the truth to her, it would say, "You are insane, you are ruining my life." I wanted to protect her from that embarrassment.

She said that her mother had earned a pitiful living for their entire family by beading bags for rich women. (Where on earth did she come up with occupations for her characters? One of her catalog people was a crowd estimator. Another was a pigeon trainer.) "My mother," she went on, tearful, "sat huddled over her georgette-stretched beading frame, her fingers feeding beads and thread to her crochet needle like lightning." I was torn between the wonderful melodrama of the story and the dangerous madness of it. "My cruel Canadian father," she said (her father was a man from Tennessee with a white mustache and stooped shoulders and a brace on one leg), "my cruel father spent every penny of my mother's hard-earned money on a mahogany gold-handled walking cane and sunglasses and pointy-toed shoes made of kangaroo skin."

She stopped suddenly and swung her legs off the bed and stood up. She sent me from the room and closed the door hard behind me, as if she were annoyed.

I was relieved to be set free. I got undressed in my room upstairs and slipped into bed and lay still. I thought of the things she said: the beaded bags, the kangaroo-skin shoes.

I never mentioned this incident to my father. I was afraid he would find out I had been playing with his pistol.

In many ways, despite my mother's lapse into madness, I remember this as the happiest summer of my life. There were quiet times and funny times. Mother sewed in the dining room on the portable Kenmore. Father went to work and came home smelling of paint and turpentine and whiskey. He fed the chickens in the backyard.

Mother redecorated the living room. It was not a big project, but not small either. The sofa was reupholstered, there were new pictures for the walls (one, I remember, was a bright poster with parrots). A white-painted wicker chair was brought in, the old rug was replaced. There was a tropical theme, I would say, with a couple of large ferns and hanging baskets.

Who knows what the decoration of this room meant to my mother. Something from a Bogart movie, a Graham Greene novel.

I continued to work (to loaf!) at the schoolhouse. I fetched and toted, I cleaned up paint drippings. I collected my weekly paycheck.

Though I worked six days a week, my time seemed my own. I swam in Roebuck Lake—a lake that, according to one of my mother's stories, was created by an earthquake and was "bottomless." I dived into it and brought up its stinking mud in my hand. I tasted whiskey for the first time, with two other boys at a dance. A girl named Alice Blessing let me take off her bra. The summer was golden and filled with new joys.

The schoolhouse job was nearly completed. Summer was almost over. One day late in August, my father sent me home from work early. Later he said he sent me to check on my mother, though I didn't know this at the time.

I walked into the living room and found Mother sitting naked in a wicker chair. I had not seen her naked since I was a small child.

She was holding a razor blade in the air above the veins of her left arm. She did not press the blade to her flesh, only held it and pretended to draw it along her arm. A pantomime of suicide. The skin was untouched.

When she was done, she placed the blade on the glass-topped table in front of her and slipped into a silk robe that lay across the arm of her chair.

She sat back and looked at me. It was a brazen look, without apology.

And then—this sounds as if it is a dream, but it is not—my mother picked up the razor blade again and put it to her left arm and opened an artery.

I couldn't move. The blood soaked her robe to the armpit. It spilled through the wicker. I watched my mother's face become the face of a child and then of an old woman and then a hag-witch, unrecognizable.

I saw all her life in her shattered face—the hidden tyranny of her father, her frightened acquiescent mother, a drunken husband she never loved, a child she never wanted—and at the same time a sad dream of dances with the governor's son on someone's cypress-shaded veranda, the wisteria and jonquils and lanterns and laughter and music.

I moved toward my mother, one step, another, until I had

crossed the room. I stood in her slick blood and clamped her arm in my hands.

I pressed hard, with such a fierceness of anger and love that the near-lifeless arm rose up at the elbow as if it had life of its own.

I let go with one hand and stripped a shoelace from my shoe and brought it up as a tourniquet. I picked up a brass letter opener from the table beside her and slipped it into the tourniquet and twisted it like an airplane propeller. The shoestring bit into my mother's arm. I twisted and twisted until I thought the shoestring would break.

I held the tourniquet tight and did not faint.

My father came home and found us there, statue that we made together, pale as marble.

My mother lived longer than my father, it turned out. She is alive today, in Mississippi, where she is friend to a woman I once loved and was married to. My mother is an attentive grandmother to my children—two sons, whom I no longer see. She plays charades and board games with them on her porch and offers them Coca-Colas from her refrigerator. She makes shadow-shows for them on her bedroom wall at night. She is gray-haired and serene and funny.

She calls me on the phone occasionally and laughs that she is not much of a letter-writer.

The scars on my mother's forearm are pale and scarcely noticeable. Nobody seems to care what happened so long ago.

But the afternoon my mother opened her arm and was taken to the hospital, I believed my father would live forever and that the world would always be as manageable as it seemed then. I had saved my mother's life—there was a practical fact that could not be changed. It was the kind of simple, necessary thing that my father could understand and appreciate, and now I could appreciate it too. I could do it and then go on living, with no replays of the event in dreams, no additions or corrections, no added details, no conclusions about life. I was my father's son.

While Mother was still sick, we spent our days alone together doing man's work—the paint and the ladders. Afternoons, we spent beside Mother's hospital bed. We adjusted the IV bottles, we saw the stitches, we heard the doctor's suggestion that Mother go into therapy.

Nights we spent in the kitchen of our home. We boiled potatoes, we floured and fried cubed steaks, we made milk-gravy in the grease. It was a simple, manageable life. It required no imagination.

Many years later, when I was grown and my mother had learned to live her life, I would travel back to Mississippi to wait out my father's last days. His liver was large and hard and showed through his clothing. His eyes were as yellow as gold, his face was swollen.

One afternoon of the visit, I took my eyes off him for a few minutes and, sick as he was, he escaped from the house and, with the last of his strength, crawled far back under the house and died there in a corner, beneath the low water pipes. I crawled on my belly, back where his body lay, and tied a length of rope around his feet and pulled out the jaundiced corpse dressed in pajamas. A retarded woman named Mavis Mitchum, who lived next door, watched the whole operation while sucking on the hem of her skirt.

At my father's funeral the minister said, "He brightened many a corner." It was hard to know whether to laugh or cry.

But at our kitchen table those late nights when my mother's life was so recently out of danger, we were alive and beautiful together, two men in the fullness of our need and love. Each night my father was fragrant with whiskey, and each night I relinquished more of my heart to his care.

I joked with him, knowing how he would respond. "So Roebuck Lake has no bottom—is that the story?"

He said, "You'll never get me to believe it."

We laughed, without guilt, at my mother's expense.

I said, "I can dive down and bring up mud."

He said, "Well, there you are. No two ways about it."

He poured Aunt Jemima syrup over the last of his cornbread. He was ripe and wonderful with alcohol.

I don't remember now, these many years later, who suggested that we play the Sears and Roebuck catalog game. I must have suggested it. I must have wanted to tease him in some way, by suggesting a thing so antithetical to his nature. I must have thought it would make him laugh. Or maybe I thought to dispel more of the influence of my mother's bad magic, the strength of imagination that had brought her to madness and near death. The game must have been my idea.

And yet I think I remember that it was my father who wanted to play. I think I remember that he pushed back from

25

the table, contented and tired from the day's work, happy with a stomachful of cornbread, and that when he had wiped his mouth on his napkin, he said to me, "You know what we ought to do? You know what might be fun, now that Mama's all better and coming home soon? We ought to play us a little game of Sears and Roebuck."

Anyway, I got the catalog and brought it to the kitchen table. We opened it at random and sat and stared into its pages and waited for the game to happen. It was not easy to do this without Mother.

We were awkward at first, embarrassed. We looked up at each other and laughed. We looked at the catalog again.

Nothing.

We were in Women's Clothing. There were models: one woman stood alone and looked off into the distance, as if she were expecting someone. The wind seemed to be blowing. I said, "Who is she waiting for?"

My father stared at her for a long time. He was serious. I could see the strain in his face. He was trying to read the mind of the model in the picture, trying to imagine what on earth she might be doing there.

My father had no experience in this. It was painful for him. Despite his efforts, he was drawing a blank. He began to breathe hard and to perspire.

I said, "We don't have to play."

He said, "She's . . ." But it would not come to him. Finally he said, "I don't know." There was defeat in his voice. He had lost the early confidence he had had when the game first began.

I said, "Let's try somebody else."

We turned a page or two. We found two women laughing, with their arms hooked together. One of them seemed to be inspecting the heel of her shoe. I said, "Are they sisters, maybe?"

Father was working hard. He wiped sweat off his upper lip and stared. At last he shook his head, very slow, side to side. He said, "I just don't know."

We tried other models, in other sections of the catalog. One man with a thumb hooked in his jacket pocket—he was looking back over one shoulder. There were men in hunting clothes and camouflage and raingear. Women in winter coats or in their underwear.

They seemed false. Nobody seemed alive. There was no geography to read from their faces, which were poses for a camera.

At one point my father said, "Your mom would look nice in a coat like this."

My father and I were incapable of inventing a world together. We were too much at peace in the one we already shared. The best we could do was to shop for clothes for the woman we loved.

My father seemed resigned but disappointed that the game was over. We sat back in our chairs. The kitchen was warm from the oven, where we had made cornbread. The dishes were still on the table, the food was beginning to congeal on the plates. Father closed the catalog.

And then, as an afterthought, he opened it again. He turned to Women's Clothing and found the picture of the woman standing in the wind and looking into the distance.

He said, "I think I'm beginning to see."

What might a man see, sitting at a table with his son? I wonder what I might say to my own sons if they were near me. I might say, "She is looking into the past to see what went wrong." Or maybe, "She sees pitfalls to avoid, opportunities to embrace."

At the time I only felt a vague fear, a tearing loose of something I had imagined to be permanent.

My father said, "She sees me."

It was in this moment that my father's imagination was born.

The rest of his days he spent in misery. He remembered the war. Though he had never spoken of it before, now he told funny stories about it, touching stories. Over time he changed the stories, embellished them, emphasized their comedy, their pathos, he added characters and details. He remembered a woman he had met in Florida at the circus. Later he said she worked in the circus as a sword swallower and fire-eater. Another time he claimed to have been in love with her and to have asked her to marry him. He could weep real tears over this loss.

He became secretive. He hid peppermint candy in his sock drawer. He carried his pistol in his car. He bought a black suit of clothes with the words *Rock 'n' Roll Music* spelled out in sequins on the back. He kept it hidden in the back of his closet and never wore it in public. He learned to dance at the American Legion Building and I am almost certain he had an affair with a woman who worked there. He watched television day and night. He thought about his childhood. The Sears and Roebuck catalog had ruined my father's life.

Even at the kitchen table I knew it was ruined.

I said, "This game is not true. This is Mother's game."

It didn't matter. The damage was already done. I looked at my father through the eyes of the model in the picture and saw what she saw: the face of a yellow corpse beneath our house and in that face an emptiness too vast ever to be filled up or given meaning. I looked away, in fear of what else I might see.

John Thomas Bird

Aunt Louise got Molly the date with J.T. It would do her good, her aunt said. And in the holiday sunshine of Gulfport, it didn't sound bad to Molly either.

But the minute she saw him she knew it was a mistake. He was beautiful. Spectacular, in fact. His skin was absolutely bronze and, still more astonishing, his body was bald. Not one hair that she could see on his arms or bare legs or the wide V of exposed chest. He was a magnificent golden statue of a man, blond and even blue-eyed, with strong limbs and a hard perfect waistline.

Molly wanted none of it. Or rather all, and so none. Handsome men scared Molly. Even ugly men were kind of scary if they were tall enough.

It was even worse to see him standing beside Aunt Louise waiting to be introduced. Together, in the cool breeze that swept off the Gulf and through the rattan blinds, Aunt Louise and the bronze young man looked like a Scotch advertisement in *The New Yorker*. Behind them, on a low table, stood a fishtank, large and bubbling, its translucent occupants as serene as sails.

Molly's aunt was forty years old, the image of all that

women diet to look like—tall and slim, her arms casually braceleted in thin gold rings. She wore tawny-gold bell-bottoms that she referred to only as "bells." A drawstring bunched up the waist so it almost but not quite covered the deep exposed navel beneath a silk halter, and her breasts were girlishly small. Molly folded her arms over her own large breasts to avoid a comparison.

"Molly," her aunt said sweetly, "this is John Thomas Bird—J.T." She was holding his hand and reaching out toward Molly to hold hers as well, smiling.

"Hi," Molly said, and allowed herself to be pulled closer than felt comfortable. She unfolded her arms unwillingly. Shit oh shit oh shit. Up close he looked even better. Why had she said Hi? Like a goddamn schoolgirl. "Hello," she corrected herself, grinning enormously for no reason that she could think of.

"Whatchasay there," J.T. said. The skin near his eyes twitched in what may have been a friendly way.

Aunt Louise was happy. She released Molly and put her arm around J.T.'s waist and pulled him along to a loveseat covered in a brocade of royal blue flowers. She told Molly, who trailed behind, that J.T. was second baseman for the Air Force Base Special Services team.

J.T. ground a silent fist into an imaginary mitt.

They met at the Officers' Club, Aunt Louise said, where Uncle Walter still had base privileges, though Walter was, of course, retired, whereas "our Mr. Lieutenant Bird," she said, and squeezed his hand, was just beginning his career.

Aunt Louise laughed gaily at this thought, and Molly

joined her, though as soon as she did she hated herself because J.T. did not laugh at all.

"We only danced the one time," Aunt Louise went on, "but I knew right that minute I would have to have him. For my little niece, of course. Who, by the way, isn't so little anymore." She laughed another silver laugh and Molly folded her arms again.

J.T. and Aunt Louise sat at almost the same instant on the loveseat. She snuggled comfortably in beside him and patted his naked knee in a confidential way. Even sitting so close on the little two-person seat, Aunt Louise could seem stretched out and luxurious. Molly took the seat nearest them, a Norwegian string chair. She had to remember to keep leaning back at all times to avoid having it snap shut on her like an oyster.

Having mastered the chair Molly suddenly realized it was her turn to speak. She had not been keeping up with the conversation, so she raced back to the information about the baseball team. "What position do you play?" she said. God-damnit, second base, you dumbass, you know what position he plays. Oh let me out of this.

Aunt Louise looked puzzled at the question, but pleasant, and across the glass table between them, offered Molly the sherry again. When Molly saw it she knew how far off the mark her baseball question had been.

"Second base," J.T. said.

"Ah," Molly said. She had practically forgotten the question.

Aunt Louise had been following their little question-and-answer exchange as though it were a tennis match. Molly's

"Ah," had gone into the net. Her aunt kept looking at her. Molly finally said, "What else do you do?"

J.T. said, "Stay in shape."

For a long ten seconds they sat in silence.

Standing abruptly, Aunt Louise said, "Now. You must please excuse me. I have stayed here too too long. You-all certainly don't need me, do you?" When there was no reply another wild silver-bells laugh leaped out. "So," she said. "You-all just talk and talk and talk without the likes of me around to . . ."

J.T. said, "Two of the most important things in life are a flat stomach and clear skin." He had apparently not noticed that Aunt Louise was speaking.

". . . interfere," Aunt Louise concluded, without much sound. For some reason she sank down onto the edge of the loveseat again.

I love you! Molly wanted to scream. Take me! Take me now, then kill me and my life will be complete. Forgive me for having big tits and a paunch, don't hate me for my freckles and my zits.

Instead, she said, "Does that include pregnancy and jock itch or just a fat gut and acne?" Why? she wanted to know. Why did she always say such things around men? Last year, when she was a senior in high school, a guy named Toby Blassingame found what he said was a sexual image in one of the assigned poems in English class. First thing after class she told him she masturbated. Why did she do things like that? Why did she make herself remember them? Toby Blassingame thought it was a joke. Everybody thought she

33

was a great joker. She wondered whether all the jokers of the world were doomed to be virgins. And J.T. was right, she knew that. She longed for clear skin and a flat stomach, like Aunt Louise's. How could she be that beautiful woman's niece?

". . . interfere," Aunt Louise said again, but produced only slightly more sound than before. She didn't try again. She rose from the loveseat and left the room, still wearing her smile, which looked now like a lightbulb slowly burning out. Her slender figure faded out of their sight into the cypress-paneled recesses of the house.

Molly envied Aunt Louise's grace, her sophistication. But right now she was too distraught over her jock itch remark to think of her aunt. Where are all the ugly boys in this world? she asked herself. There was not one ugly boy on the entire Gulf of Mexico. Anywhere else you would see one or two.

And why did she always have to fall in love? She waited for J.T. to leave in disgust—she hoped for it in a way, longed for him to leave so she could go down to the beach alone, as she always did, and smoke marijuana until her mind was gone and maybe forget who she was.

But J.T. didn't move. He said, "Fish helps." Molly did not know what J.T. meant by this, but the phrase seemed to be offered as a form of masculine generosity, so she felt a little better.

She still felt fat and freckled and her pores felt larger than usual, but when she tried to beg off the date—or rather to let J.T. out of it—he never seemed to understand. She let the subject drop. She loved him. Why was she always "like a sister" to the boys she loved? J.T. hadn't said that yet, but he would.

Aunt Louise came back to say that she had made reservations for lunch and to suggest that an afternoon excursion boat "might be just lovely for you-all." Molly was surprised at the relief she felt when her aunt declined their invitation to go along with them.

Looking across an expanse of white sand by the Gulf, in what Molly hoped might be seen as a sophisticated way, she dared the scallops meuniere and tomatoes florentine to give her hives, and they did not. She got diarrhea instead. Not bad, and not from the scallops and tomatoes, but as always from anxiety.

It was made worse by her unexpected confession of it to J.T. "Sorry I was so long in the john," she said. "I got a slight dose of the trots."

Would this ever be over? She hoped J.T. could stand it a little longer.

In response, J.T. said, "Digestion is related to metabolism." Though he was looking directly at her, Molly could have sworn he was reading from a book, perhaps slightly above his grade level. "The physical condition of the entire trunk of the body," he continued. This made no sense at all, but Molly was grateful for his strange kindness. He said, "Ted Williams swung a weighted baseball bat one hundred times a day."

"And never had diarrhea?" Molly asked with interest.

There was a pause. J.T. said, "I really wouldn't know."

There was another pause. Molly said, "Isn't Ted Williams a male model for Sears now?"

J.T. said, "I don't think so."

Molly said, "Hm." During this pause a thought came to Molly like a voice. You are bored, the voice said. Not fashionably bored. For real.

Impossible, Molly retorted, and the voice went away.

J.T. said, "Mickey Mantle sells Houn' Dawg dog food, though."

Molly said, "Now who is Mr. Coffee?"

Later, as they were leaving the restaurant, J.T. said, "Swimming is a healthful water sport which is gaining rapidly in popularity." He fielded a sharp invisible grounder in the parking lot and fired it to first base.

Molly did not allow herself to wonder where J.T. learned to talk like this. She said, "Really? I'm a pretty good swimmer myself." What on earth did she mean by that? She was not a good swimmer. She was an adequate swimmer. A Red Cross Life Saving drop-out.

J.T. said, "Wanta go swimming? I heard of a good lake."

"Sure," Molly said. "Great." Oh shit.

In the woods beside the lake J.T. astonished Molly by taking off every stitch of his clothing, right in front of her. She had already put on her swimsuit, a tight green atrocity with a skirt. After the restaurant they went back to Aunt Louise's to get it.

And now J.T. was naked. It wasn't sexual. Not even self-conscious. It was the only way he ever exercised, he said; he hoped she didn't mind. He always did warm-ups before he swam.

Did she mind, she said. No, no of course not, she didn't, not at all, go right ahead. Sure.

J.T. was the first man she had ever seen naked except in pictures. It is much better in the flesh, she decided. Entirely different. And much much better.

While Molly swatted mosquitoes under the moss-covered trees, J.T. counted knee-bends in the nude. His eyes became glassy, and three drops of sweat hung from his chin. His chest glistened like waxed oak, and hair stuck to his neck.

There was no other hair on his entire body. A living breathing Nair commercial—the thought was inescapable.

After fifty knee-bends J.T. stopped in the down position, his back perpendicular to the ground, his outstretched arms perfectly parallel with it. He was beautiful.

She wanted to tell him so. To say, "You are beautiful," or "I want you so much," anything to keep from saying "I love you." She almost took off her own clothes, just to make him notice her. She couldn't do it. He probably wouldn't notice anyway. Why had she been in such a rush to get her own suit on? She would look ridiculous taking it off now. It made no sense. Next time she would wear every article of clothing she owned so she could take it all off without embarrassment. Hell no, that was a lie and she knew it. Nothing on earth could make her expose those gargantuan jugs and freckled butt to J.T. or anybody else as beautiful as he.

J.T. said nothing and did not look her way. His gaze

remained firm as he held the position twenty seconds. Then he stood up and walked to a stump where he had laid out his swimsuit, jockstrap, and a clean white towel.

He dried each part of his body—carefully, thoroughly. Face, neck, arms, chest, legs. He used short rough strokes. Then he snapped the towel out to its full length and put it between his legs. He pulled it back and forth in a see-saw motion against his crotch.

It was too much for Molly. She could think of nothing to do with her hands, which suddenly felt fat. Nothing to talk about. She managed not to tell J.T. she loved him, so she didn't feel like a complete failure.

Then, without warning, she said, "I understand that masturbation promotes clear skin." Why in God's name had she said that? It was the worst thing she'd said all day. She might as well have told him she loved him. Her mind was gone.

And then she heard a voice say, "I've been masturbating for years and it hasn't helped a bit."

It was her own voice. My God, she thought. *I* said that. Why? I have now told two men, practically strangers, that I masturbate. One of them not even in a Lit class.

It didn't matter. J.T. seemed not to have heard. Placing the towel neatly on the stump, J.T. stepped into his jockstrap and red nylon swimsuit, bikini style, and if he noticed Molly there was no indication.

She followed him to the edge of the woods and sat beside him against a log. They looked at the water.

She said, "Seems kind of far across, doesn't it, Johnny?"

He may have nodded. She couldn't be sure.

The late-afternoon sunlight broke into a timid dappling around him and over his shoulders as it filtered through the long gray beards of Spanish moss in the trees above them.

If only she could leave now, get away and never see him again, it would have been a perfect afternoon and she could love him forever.

J.T. said, "John Thomas is a beautiful name."

Molly didn't know what to say, and nothing seemed required.

J.T. said, "It's such a strong name."

The head of a small turtle winked through the surface of the lake before them and stood still—so still that Molly thought for a moment she had imagined it, that it was a stick instead. The water blinked again and it was gone.

J.T. said, "Turtles are unusual." His tone and manner were serious. He sighed. Molly would have said a philosophical sigh. J.T. said, "Turtles are ashamed of their bodies."

There was nothing to say. Molly looked out at the lake and knew that no woman on earth, no matter who she was, could have thought of anything to say.

At last J.T. stood up and, without speaking, he walked out into the water. Molly watched him as if in a dream. She watched each step. The water seemed to sink beneath his foot like a pillow. And then the other foot, the same. A million speckles of rotted matter bubbled up around his legs in a brown fog.

Molly followed him into the water, and her legs became

suddenly warm, too warm. The lake bottom was not sandy but was soft with decay and then a little sticky when her foot had sunk as far as it would go.

With each step leaves and brown stringy things that looked like tiny root systems floated up from the bottom and brushed against her legs.

J.T. seemed already to be a mile ahead of her, still wading. She was trying to catch up when she saw him raise his arms and dive forward and become a long green submarine beneath the surface of the lake. She dived behind him and felt the water swallow her up warmly.

J.T. was a strong swimmer. He was outdistancing her rapidly.

Swimming behind him, with her face down in the water, she pulled two strokes and turned her face out to the side for a breath and pulled one, methodically establishing her rhythm. She felt her feet kick behind her. On each breath-stroke she watched her right arm rise streaming from the water as though it were lighter than air, and then her face was back down in the warmth, and she was plowing two deep furrows of tiny bubbles into the dark liquid beneath and around her.

Then, after a while—she couldn't say just how she knew—she felt that something was wrong. She stopped swimming and looked across the water at J.T. His movements in the water must have attracted her attention.

What the hell?—was he drowning? No, that wasn't exactly it, though it might be. He seemed not to have gone under but to be stunned, floating vertically in the water. She couldn't tell. "Johnny," she called. Near him she saw for an instant a flick of black, like the tail of a deformed fish. J.T.'s short hair undulated against his neck.

"Johnny!" she called, more frantic now. "J.T.—what the fuck is going on?" Green-black water lapped softly into his mouth and out again. He did not answer. *If this is a joke, you bastard . . . Probably it's just a joke.*

She approached him from behind, cautious. She called out his name several times, but there was no response. When she was close enough, she reached over J.T.'s right shoulder and took his chin firmly in her hand.

As soon as she did, he sank like a stone. He had fainted. Dead weight.

Molly went under with him, tightening her grip on his chin. Through the sudden boil of bubbles she thought she saw the strange fish again, but before she could think of it she struggled her way back up to the surface and air. She felt J.T. stir slightly, she felt him float, perhaps instinctively, even in semiconsciousness.

"J.T., she said. Her face was streaming with water. "Wake up." He was heavy and slick but not as hard to hold as he had first been or as she had imagined he would be. "You fainted," she said, and laughed, a little unexpectedly, hysterically, as she said it.

J.T. showed signs of waking up. Holding him became easier. With his chin still gripped in her hand, she used her forearm like a lever against his back. His legs floated up and he became easier to tow. She began her swim back to shore.

After a minute, she released his chin, careful not to drop

him, and slid her arm across his chest and under his left arm. With difficulty she scissored her way through the water. The cross-chest carry was the closest they had come to an embrace. She couldn't avoid regretting the reversal of her old lifeguard fantasy. She should be the one drowning, not stuck with a dangerous rescue that she would probably fuck up.

She swam on. She was surprised at her own strength and presence of mind. She was intrigued by the feel of J.T.'s body. Even in her growing exhaustion she felt a momentary impulse to reach down and stroke his prick. As long as he was mostly unconscious anyway. She didn't do it. She couldn't. For one thing she would probably drop him and he would drown. "Yes, officer," she heard herself say to the investigating policeman, "I was towing him in by his penis and drowned him." It was something to think about, especially for a person having as much difficulty as Molly was beginning to have as she became more tired.

She stayed calm and swam steadily, holding him in the cross-chest position. She stretched out her long legs so that sometimes she could see her feet beneath the water.

Then she saw something else. The deformed fish. More clearly than ever.

Goodbye, J.T., she thought in terror, you'll just have to drown. But she didn't let go. The fish seemed to be about three feet long, trailing behind as though it were following them. She breathed deeply and swam on.

It was a lamprey, an eel-like fish. She had seen them once before, with her father, when she was a child. Harmless, as far as she knew—she couldn't really remember.

Sometimes it was more clearly visible than other times, but it seemed to be swimming beneath her, or maybe between her and J.T. Or even, at times, between his legs.

Don't think about the eel, she thought, just don't think about it. Thank God she had not played with J.T.'s prick. She imagined herself reaching down for a feel and finding instead a three-foot living writhing monster with gills and pectoral fins. I will never go on another blind date. Not on any kind of date. Ever.

As she swam the eel swam too and seemed always to stay in about the same relationship to them. Once it lifted its spineless body into a strange loop so that its back showed for a moment above the surface of the lake like a sea monster, but in the air the lamprey was not so ugly. It was fawn-colored. It did not vary its path or change its position except slightly. Sometimes it floated closer to the surface, sometimes it seemed to have drifted a little to the right or left.

Very tired now, she looked at the shoreline to be certain she had not confused the time and distance. She had not.

Lampreys can attach themselves to other fish, she thought. That's what she had been trying to remember. It's how they eat. Couldn't they do it just as well to J.T.? Her father had showed her a trout with a half-dozen or so stuck to its sides, some no more than three inches long, trailing like banners. They slowly drained a fish's blood. Parasitic little sons-of-bitches. The sucker mouth draws the blood. She didn't know how long all this would take. Probably a long time. It could be hours, for all she knew. Days. It had to be, didn't it? She mustn't worry. J.T. must have seen the fish and stopped swimming, scared half to death probably. It could have attached itself if he were still for a second or two.

Then an even worse thought got in. Where it was attached. Could there be any doubt about it? It was on his prick, like an extension hose. The thought was staggering. How could a person stand it? How could J.T.? No, hell no, she thought. It couldn't be there. He had on the swimsuit. Thank you Jesus for swimsuits. Yet somehow even knowing this, that it was a physical impossibility for the eel to be on his genitals, she didn't feel comforted.

Swimming on, more and more slowly because of her fatigue, she wondered how long they had before there was a danger, before it could actually bore in and start sucking blood. She was almost too tired to care. There was probably more likelihood they would drown first anyhow. All she could do was swim. If only there were some safe way to shift J.T. to the other arm. She didn't try.

The shore was extremely close now. She could see the spot in the woods where they had sat. And, unexpectedly, she could see Aunt Louise waving at them, far down the shoreline. They had told Aunt Louise where they would be, when Molly went to the house to change into her swimsuit. Now here she was. It was like a dream. Molly swam on.

Whenever the lamprey touched her leg Molly's sidestroke became frantic and clumsy, though now it touched her and she hardly noticed. She was less and less afraid. She was exhausted. Aunt Louise was walking along a path, still some distance away. She was carrying a silver cocktail shaker and glasses.

When Molly thought the water might be shallow enough to stand in, she pulled four more hard strokes, her arms burning, and stopped swimming. Her feet sank beneath her into the mud and she held on to J.T. Her breathing was heavy and ragged.

She looked for the fish, but saw nothing. J.T. was standing, almost by himself but leaning heavily upon her.

The two of them stood for a long time without moving. At last Molly could breathe more normally. She surprised herself by reaching into the water and feeling around for the lamprey.

As she groped between J.T.'s legs she spoke soothingly to him. When she had checked his crotch and the fish was not there, as she knew it could not have been, she felt better.

She kept searching. She ran her hand along J.T.'s legs, she reached as deeply into the water as she could. Nothing. What would she do if she found it?

Then, as she drew her hand back toward the surface, it thumped against the lamprey's strange body.

Her insides leaped. It was higher up than she had expected. She could see nothing, but the long eel-like creature seemed to float horizontally at about waist level.

Reaching down, she found it again, and it moved at her touch. She put her hand around the fish and felt its body, muscular and firm. Though she could not hold it long before it squirmed from her grip, she was able to run her hand along its body, not even frightened now, until she found its head.

The sucker-disc mouth was stuck solidly to the skin of J.T.'s right side. For a few seconds she ran her fingers around the spot where J.T. and the lamprey were connected. She touched the little round lips, the size of a quarter, and she smoothed her hand along the body until the dorsal fin quivered beneath her touch.

J.T. was half-crying, paralyzed with fear.

"It's all right, John Thomas," she said. "You're fine. It's all right."

He was confused, distraught. She considered simply jerking the eel away from him if she could, but she hesitated. The spiny little teeth might already be boring in. She wanted to joke about it but could not.

"Snake," J.T. whispered, "snake . . ." J.T. was more awake now, he could stand by himself. His voice was a slow coarse whisper. "I've been bit by a snake."

"No, John Thomas, no," she said, like a mother. "It wasn't a snake. It was an eel—not even a real eel, a lamprey."

He didn't seem to hear.

With the lamprey trailing between them they walked a little toward shore into shallower water. J.T. stopped. "I can't go anymore," he said.

"Take it easy, John, take it easy. Lampreys are harmless. Sort of. As soon as we get out of the water, we can pry it off, maybe. Or—or we can take you to a . . ." Who could help them?

His face became a death's head as she watched it. His eyes grew wide and vacant, his lips curled back. He had not known the fish was on him.

He ran for shore. He was not crying, not even screaming. He vomited sound.

Molly chased after him, she called out his name. She heard Aunt Louise cry out, for now she too had seen the fish. Molly saw only the frightened boy and the eel. Even in shallow water the eel hung on, and it still hung on when J.T. left the water altogether and ran aimlessly upon the lakebank. Finally his movements were a comic and terrible turning and half-turning as he stood in one spot. The lamprey clung to him, swinging this way and that, like the untied sash of a little girl's dress.

As Molly caught up with him she grabbed the lamprey and yanked. The mouth popped away from J.T.'s body with a swack. There was no blood.

J.T. sank to the ground with his face hidden between his knees. Molly stood and watched him and did not know what to say.

She carried the lamprey back to the water. For a moment the lamprey lay in the shallows above Molly's hand, then swam away.

Molly walked up the bank, more tired than she had ever been. Aunt Louise was sitting near J.T. in the foreground of the ash-colored trees. She seemed uncertain, and was neither with J.T. nor away from him. Molly felt love for her aunt, and for the first time she felt sorry for her.

Molly wanted to help her, to make her know what had been going on, except that Molly was not sure herself. So much of what she had just done seemed unconnected with herself.

She walked over to the spot where she had left her shirt.

Her arms and legs still ached from the swim, and now suddenly she was very sleepy.

The swimsuit was too much for her. She pulled down first the straps, then the whole top portion of the suit, so that her large breasts swung out free. She put on the shirt and buttoned it carefully. The bra portion of her suit flapped in front of her like an apron.

Molly lay down in the grass and felt the Gulf breeze push the grass against her skin.

Molly wondered whether anything ever really changes.

J.T. was crying softly and Molly loved him and hoped she had not embarrassed him by saving him. Aunt Louise moved close to Molly and took her hand into her own.

The Sin Eater

Later, when the child would go over these events in
his mind, he would imagine the old woman, Mrs. Tremble,
as she would have appeared a moment before she heard the
sound of the ambulance. The peacocks, living wild in the
cottonwoods, descendants of birds that once strutted tame
across this property, would have heard the siren first. Their
shrieks and shrill comedy might have alerted her, their thun-
derous bustle and flutter across pastures and into the deeper
woods. The slave-built house, with its spacious porch and
gently sagging roofline, visible from the child's bedroom if he
had thought to look a hundred yards across the goat pasture,
would have sat bright and unchanged in the late-morning
sun. Inside the house would have sat Mrs. Tremble, by a
small fire in her living room. Her high windows would be
closed, as would the drapes, against the first chill of the Mississippi autumn. A floor lamp, with a brass base and a tasseled shade, would be her only light. When the sound of the
siren reached her, she would remove her glasses from their
place on her nose and lay aside the needlepoint motto on
which she had been working. "What on earth can it be?" she
might have said, in her ridiculous, grandmotherly way. "I

49

swan." She would have put aside the pipe that she was smoking.

The child who would imagine her was ten years old, named Robert McIntyre. In his bedroom, in this more modest house, he saw the green bottle, which he had filled with kerosene. He saw it touch the lips of his baby brother. Like a kiss, he thought, even as the oily fluid flowed over the lips and off the infant's chin. Even as the little head jolted backwards. The eyes rolled up and became white and senseless. The baby had drunk the kerosene Robert was hiding. The kerosene he had thought even a parent could not find.

But Robert did not move, not yet. He could not. His brother, already unconscious but not yet fallen, weaved drunkenly, like a comic actor on a television screen. Who was that actor, Robert thought. The child fell, and the bottle clattered against the floor. The kerosene darkened the wood, and Robert saw the future. He knew his brother would not live. As soon as he knew that, he screamed.

He lifted his brother's head. With his too-short fingers he reached into the narrow throat to call back the kerosene and cause the accident not to have happened. An oily froth covered Robert's fingers, warmly. The pupil-less eyes were still open. Then, in revulsion, he jerked away. He stood above his brother and scrubbed his fingers against his pants.

He saw the objects of his house, and the sounds and persons, as if they were old, recognizable photographs. There was his mother on the telephone. There was the empty bottle, the stain on the floor. There was a voice, the color of indigo, his mother's voice, and there were his own words, like mice, scuttering and scurrying and contemptible. A white ambulance was in the driveway, surrounded by the peacock's cries, and, immediately, his father's car also. Robert noticed two patches of rust on the roof of the car and found that he hated his father for them.

His father's voice seemed to be the color of grapes. It said, "Robbie, listen. Go to Mrs. Tremble's. Tell Mrs. Tremble what happened. I'll call from the hospital." When his mother came back into the room, Robert realized he had been seeing her all these years only in miniature, as if he looked at a dense concentration of the woman and not, perhaps, as everyone else had already seen her. She seemed now to be a tree, one of the ancient sycamores in the back pasture, silver-blue and enormous. A red-tailed hawk swooped near but did not light, balancing upon the wind.

When the ambulance was gone, Robert was alone. He stared at the bottle, which was no longer there, because his father had taken it in the ambulance, but which he could still see. The bottle he had filled and hid. The kerosene he planned to use for—he didn't know what. Games, on the lakebank. Little fires.

Before the sound of the words reached him, or any sound, he knew Mrs. Tremble was in the room. Kindly fat rich ancient shaky-hands old Mrs. Tremble, with the white hair and wild peacocks and the gaseous aroma of pipe tobacco and face powder. Her breath preceded her like a messenger of lightning and thunder. "Robert," said her voice. "What on earth has happened, child? I saw the ambulance." Robert turned to face her, since doing so was unavoidable. Because of her concern, perhaps, she had become even more of what she had always been, old and quiet and kind and repulsive and grandmotherly, and somehow frightening now as well. She had thin, pale lips, which seemed always to be chapped. In them were tiny vertical lines that looked painful, and her breath, which could travel long distances without diminution of effect, stank like a pipesmoker's. Though she was never actually known to smoke a pipe, it was never doubted by any child who drew within her considerable range that she did so and that the pipe, should it ever be discovered, would be of briar and grotesque of shape and deadly poison. "Whatever in the world has happened, child?"

In Mrs. Tremble's living room, Robert became very small. By magic, he had shrunk, as soon as he walked through the front door. He sat as far forward as possible in a blue brocaded chair, but still his feet would not touch the floor. His elbows, no matter how hard he strained, would not rest comfortably on the chair arms. He had been in this room many times, but it had never shrunk him before. The colors had never been so bright, nor the ceilings so high. Long-necked golden birds shrieked at him from the Chinese carpets. There was a tiny fire in the fireplace, though it was only October and not really cold yet, and there was a smell, sulfurous and sickening, which Robert believed must be the moist, solid residue of Mrs. Tremble's breath, growing and reproducing in the rugs and drapes and upholstered chairs.

Mrs. Tremble fussed around the room, out again and back again, monstrously cheerful. Everything would be fine, she said, just fine. Her breath streaked around the room like a laser, rebounding from the walls and floors and ceiling. Robert watched it and stayed out of its path. What Robert must do, she said, must *promise* her right this minute he would do, was not worry. Worry was by far the worst thing in the world he could do right now. His little brother was going to be fine, yes siree, just you wait and see. Robert was afraid she might hug him, but she stayed her distance. Her breath idled between them like an engine.

There was to be a choice: lemonade, or hot chocolate, or spiced tea. Now which would it be? she wanted to know. Which do you choose? He could have a cinnamon stick with the tea, she promised. For a moment a strange feeling passed through his body. He believed he might be a character in a book that somebody else was reading. He looked at Mrs. Tremble, and at her breath. It was the spiced tea that made him wonder. He tried to see Mrs. Tremble as he had seen his mother, the larger tree in which her miniature was contained. But nothing changed. He could see nothing differently. "No, thank you, Mrs. Tremble," he said. "Nothing for me, thanks."

So he waited. He moved from the brocaded chair to the fire and looked into the little wreckage of coals. Even the fire had an odd smell, a little too sweet, as if she might be burning applewood. The firescreen was black and large, with tiny brass handles at either side. The poker and shovel and tongs were also heavy and black. When he tried to think of his brother's dying, he found that he could not. He remembered Jack and the Beanstalk, disobedient child of a grieving mother. The harp and hen and golden eggs. The race downward through vegetation, the ax, the collapse and fall and death of the giant. The green breath streaked suddenly over his right shoulder and made the fire blaze up. Sparks crackled and shot up the chimney. "Do you like the fire, Robert?" said the words that came trailing in the wake.

He struggled not to flinch. He thought of Hansel in the wooden cage. He saw Gretel stare deep into the oven. He braced himself but could not force himself to turn and meet her unbelievable, cheery eyes, or risk breathing her fumes. "Yes ma'am," he said, into the fire. Did he like the fire? What might such a question mean? "Yes, it's nice," he said. "A nice little fire."

There had been a grass fire once, set accidentally by his father in the back pasture. Robert helped fight it with rakes and wet rugs. The smoke burned his chest when he breathed it, but Robert had not minded. When it spread to the edge of the woods, tractors plowed lanes around the flames. His father, riding one of the tractors, was the handsomest man in the world that day. His eyes had streamed with tears in the smoke. There was a gasoline fire too, another day, set by a child Robert's age. It caught the child's clothes and burned his jeans and boots into the flesh. Robert had not seen it; only, later, the grafted skin. He had seen it in his dreams, though. He had smelled the flesh and rubber in his dreams. There was a house too that burned, a shack. He remembered the pathetic few pieces of furniture someone had saved. They sat beside the smoking ashes and standing chimney, a chair, a wooden table, a dark wardrobe. They sat in the weather, long after the ashes had cooled and washed away. They whitened and rotted and finally were gone. There would have been his own little fires, on the lakebank. The kerosene. Burning ships, forts surrounded by Indians, volcanoes, human sacrifice. He wondered if kerosene felt like fire in the baby's throat. He wondered how people died.

Once, in a museum, he had thought of dying. He saw a stiff brown hunk of contorted clay in a glass case, and he learned it was a mummified child. This was the first time he ever thought he might die. He had seen his father kill wild dogs, the packs that sometimes came out of the woods and took down a goat, or larger stock. Brass shell casings would leap from the rifle, and the animals would scatter and drop. Sometimes they were only wounded, and his father would close their clear eyes at closer range.

He went outside the house. A noisy, noxious rocket of pipesmoker's breath streaked past his ear and struck a fence-post deep in the pasture. It crumbled and collapsed into ashes, and the six-gauge barbed wire fell slack in that section. The voice said, "Robert. Oh, Robert dear. Won't you need a coat, child?" Beds of fire ants crackled and burned and lay silent and gray and motionless. "Please don't go far. Promise you won't, Robert. If anything happened to you, I'd . . ." What would she do? he thought. Would she die? He tried not to wish that she would die. He tried not to wish that he would die. "I'm sorry," he prayed.

He was deep in the back pasture now. A she-goat was stuck by her horns, like small scimitars, in the squares of fence wire, where she had tried to reach a sweeter clump of grass. He walked to the crying animal and released the horns. He crossed the fence and walked toward the lake and woods.

It was afternoon now, and the air had more chill than he had thought. He could not go back for his jacket. What kind of person would call a boy "Robert dear" or "child"? What kind of person would have pipesmoker's breath and shaky hands and be named Mrs. Tremble?

The trees had begun some subtle change. The black-green lushness of September had become a lighter, friendlier green. The persimmons were ripe on the trees, and sullen wasps staggered fat and gorged in the pink-gold sweetness of the fallen fruit. Here and there he noticed hardwoods in which some of the leaves were already brown, but most were still green and, every so often, in a spreading oak or maple, a bouquet of red and yellow leaves appeared like decorations. The squirrels were busy; acorns were thick underfoot.

To his left, from a thicker brake of trees and cane, emerged first the movement and then the head and then the entirety of a large dog. A fear rippled through him and caused him to forget the afternoon chill. He did as his father had taught him. He kept an eye on the wild dog and, at the same time, scanned the woods to see whether there was a pack. He started a slow movement backwards, trying to put distance, a tree or two, if possible a fence, between them. He kept looking. He could not find a pack, not another dog, no movement in the woods or cane. The dog before him was long-legged and black and thin. The long muscles seemed almost to show through the matted hair.

He backed away. The dog had not yet really looked at

him, not directly. It sniffed the ground and raised its chin to the breeze. It did not look, but it was aware of him. Robert looked hard at the dog and thought he saw something, something like himself and other than himself. He was distracted by a noise that, at first, he thought belonged to the wind.

"Robert, oh Robert dear." Pipesmoker's breath blazed through the trees and pasture, killing leaves and grass, setting fire to old bird nests. The surface of the lake was choppy and uneven. The wind increased and raised chillbumps on his bare arms. He remembered the years he had been the only child in his family. He remembered the fear and the envy he felt when his father came to his room. "Robbie," he had said, "son. You're going to be a big brother. Can you believe it? Mama's going to have a baby." He remembered the loathing. He looked at the two of them, mother and father, and imagined the cloying sexuality, vague and terrible, the dominance of his father upon his mother's nakedness. "It's the gift of life," his father had said. Afterwards, Robert held the child and began to love it. He gave it its bottle and was thankful his mother had not breast-fed. He brought friends home from school and showed them the baby. He taught them to hold its head. He learned to forget the baby and, in that way, to love it more. He went to fourth grade and learned to play two songs on a plastic recorder; he kissed Melissa Townley outside the skating rink. He helped his father bale alfalfa for the goats; he took pictures with his father's reflex camera and learned to read a light meter. "Oh, Robert dear. Telephone."

He turned from the dog and walked through the pasture, deliberately not running, but walking fast and, twice, almost falling. He looked back. The dog had lain down and was licking a paw. The goats bleated and fanned away. "Here I am, Mrs. Tremble," he said. "I'm coming."

The telephone was on the wall, a boxy, old-fashioned instrument that only Mrs. Tremble would have owned. The earpiece was shaped like a bell and was separate from the mouthpiece, which was part of the wooden box.

His father had not meant to tell him on the phone, but Robert asked the question directly and made him answer. The answer was no surprise: the child, Robert's brother, was dead. Robert had known. All through himself, inside as well as outside, Robert felt a pain, like that that seemed so constant in Mrs. Tremble's split chapped lips. Then the silence was over. "These will be lonely, bad days, son," the voice said, his father. It was impossible to imagine a voice so kind or so tired. "But it's no one's fault."

"I love you, Daddy."

"I love you."

"Tell Mama . . ."

When he had hung up, Robert remembered a movie he had seen on television, a western, filmed in Utah and full of wide desert and red buttes. A faint cold fear thrilled through him. He thought of graves and of museums with large bottles filled with fetuses, two-headed sheep, and piglets with human faces. He felt responsible for each one. No warmth, he thought. No breath. He tried to pray for museums. He asked forgiveness for Siamese twins and freak shows. No tears came to him, and he was dry all through.

A meteor of Mrs. Tremble's breath struck the gold-colored drapes on the west windows and exploded into light like the sun. "It will be better with them open," she might have said. She pulled the tasseled cord hanging beside the windows and made the light from the floor lamp unnecessary. Robert watched her carefully, knowing that she knew. But she did not try to hug him or kiss him. She moved slowly through the room and seemed older than ever. Robert didn't know what to do. "He's dead," he told her, having nothing else to say.

Without answering him, Mrs. Tremble moved to a table that sat in the sunlight near the windows. It was a large table, round and topped with creamy rose-veined marble. She opened one of its several shallow drawers and removed a pipe and a pouch of tobacco.

The pipe was not at all what he imagined. Its bowl should have been black and shaped like the head of a wild horse or an African woman with tight kinky hair and swollen lips and a gold nose-ring, or it should have been chalk white, the face of a madman or a coolie, or it should have had no shape at all, formless and chaotic. It was not a large pipe, very ordinary-looking, a light reddish brown in color. When she had sat in her chair before the little fire, she filled the pipe with tobacco from the pouch and lighted it with a kitchen match. It smelled like chocolate, cooking on a stove. Robert sat in the upholstered chair with blue brocade and did not notice whether he felt large or small. Grief was everywhere, but it was hard to form a mental picture of the dead child. He remembered skinning a catfish with his father. With the fish still alive they cut a circle around the head and pulled off the skin, strip by strip, with a pair of pliers. He prayed forgiveness, or tried, and did not feel forgiven. He wanted to be alone. He didn't want to be here with Mrs. Tremble. But if he went back home, across the pasture to his own house, he would be too much alone. He was afraid of what he might do, or become. Mrs. Tremble was talking. He tried not to listen, but it was impossible.

She stopped and puffed at the pipe and struck a new match to goad it to life again. "That was a long time ago," she said. "I was younger then than you are now. That year—one of those years— a man came, an old man, and camped out, right in the middle of town, not so far from my family's house. We called them hoboes back then. There were more of them then, it seems to me. He put up a tepeelike affair, made from—oh, you know—one thing and another. Packing crates, scraps of lumber, an old door from no-telling-where. Right beneath the old railroad trestle." Mrs. Tremble's voice was odd. There was something in it, like pain, but that was only a part. There was old-lady nostalgia, and obsession, and senility, and yet none of these exactly. Robert believed that later she might not even remember saying these words, telling this tale. Now and then he saw the green bottle, the stain on the floor. He wondered how he could continue to live, knowing he had killed his brother. He wondered what his father must be feeling. For the first time he thought of suicide.

"Everyone talked about the hobo," Mrs. Tremble went on. "Children sometimes slid down the clay embankment to his tepee and sat with him. I did so myself. He was kindly, and he stank, of course. I think now he must have stolen food to stay alive. I'm not really sure. People might have given him things. He called himself a 'Sin Eater.' No one knew what he meant, or cared, I suppose. There were so many odd ones . . ." She blew a long stream of smoke through the firescreen, and the hot coals flamed up and danced.

"Someone died not long after, a few weeks after we first noticed him. It was a woman, some old woman. I don't even remember her name, I only remember it was the first funeral I ever went to.

"It was held in the old lady's home. That was the way then, the corpse laid out—'decently,' was the expression— for viewing. People came and brought things. There were covered dishes of food, and a bottle of bourbon in the linen closet. The men drank from it—discreetly they must have imagined. Afternoon changed to dusk, and dusk to night, and most of us were still there.

"There was a knock at the kitchen door. It was not a thing you would expect. Persons either come to a wake or they don't, you know. No one comes so late, or to the back door. When someone finally heard and went to answer it, it was the hobo, the man who called himself the Sin Eater. His face was yellow-looking, probably from jaundice; so many of the old-time ones were sick, or alcoholic. He was wearing a dark coat of some kind, and probably nothing else. His legs and feet were bare. He stank terribly, an odious, leathery old man. But something about him—something about the out-rage of his coming to that house, at such a time— caused my father and the rest not to send him away just then. They opened the screened door and he came in."

Mrs. Tremble let out a small, mirthless laugh, bewildered almost, and bewildering. Robert was careful not to be struck by her breath. "The house grew quiet," she went on. "He came farther in, and the crowd parted to let him pass. Food was spread along a makeshift counter in the kitchen, put together out of boards and saw horses. Butterbeans and crowder peas and fried squash, all the rest, a typical wake in a little Southern town. Somebody had brought a ham.

"The Sin Eater looked at the food. He had a quiet, ordi-nary voice. We had not expected that, somehow, even those of us who had talked with him. 'Put some in a bowl, please'm,' he said, almost shy, 'a wood bowl if you have it.' One of my aunts, a large-breasted woman with her slip always showing, did as he said. She put a little of each food, one thing right on top of another, in a big maple salad bowl. I thought he was just begging. Everybody thought so, prob-ably. We were all terribly embarrassed, even outraged, I sup-pose. All we wanted was for him to be gone and for this to be over. But you couldn't help feeling sorry for him.

"The food, all the juices, mingled together in the bowl. My aunt tried to hand it to him, but he turned and wouldn't take it. He walked through the house, big as Ike and twice as natural, and went in the living room, where the old woman lay her coffin. It was no more than a pine box, with the lid not yet nailed down. 'I'd be proud to receive it now,' he said, meaning the bowl of food. He wanted it handed across the corpse. I'll never forget his quaint, countrified way of speaking. He'd be 'proud to receive it.' Some of us children giggled behind our hands.

"He took the bowl from my aunt and held it over the corpse, just for a moment. He placed the bowl upon the dead woman's breast. Why on earth he was allowed to do such a thing, I will never understand. Old men like him were never really welcome in town, certainly not in our homes. Why didn't someone say, 'Well, now, wait just one minute here'? Some red-faced man, maybe, like my father. No one said anything, though. Not a word. Then, with no utensil except his filthy hands, he ate the food, every morsel, right over the woman's corpse. Can you believe such a thing? When he had finished, he burned the bowl in the fireplace with fat pine. We just stood there, men, women, and children. It was all we could do, just stand there looking like fools. All of a sudden he was speaking again. It was still the same countrified, untutored voice but different now, not affected at all but slightly more distant, more formal and yet more filled with passion. 'I am the Sin Eater,' he said. 'I am the propitiation for your sins. I have taken unto my flesh all the sin and guilt of these here assembled, and especially those of the woman who lies dead before me. I am unclean with them. I feel them. They burn inside me. Despise me, and beware of me. Touch nothing of me, neither of my body nor of my clothing. Azezial rages inside me. I am the Sin Eater, and I am doomed.'

"By now, of course, the outrage could not be ignored. Several men—probably most of them had drunk an extra share at the linen closet by now—ushered him roughly out the back door and warned him not to show his face around here again. Maybe he had better get moving, get on out of town, they told him. The next day he was not in the tepee, the little hovel he had set up beneath the trestle. When he still failed to show up that night, the tepee was dismantled and burned."

Mrs. Tremble lighted the pipe again and blew out the match with smoke. A sickening cloud of her effluvium seemed to have formed in the air of the room. It was not the pipesmoke itself; that smelled good, like candy. It was something from inside herself, a malodorous, personal stench, that stank up whatever space she occupied. She puffed deeply on the pipe, again and again. Skyrockets of her fetid breath detonated about his head, fulminated in the air. The paint on the walls blistered and cracked and fell away. Plaster crumbled to dust and sifted down into his hair. He was determined to think of his dead brother. The death-pale face, the rolled-up eyes. This beastly old woman! Her boring spew of boring childhood!

Suddenly, he was taken off guard. He had not been looking at her, and while his attention was away, she had moved from her chair and was standing directly above him. Her breath, her filthy, stinking breath, covered him like a sour, damp blanket. He was sick; he began to retch. "I just want you to know how sorry I am, child," she said. "I swan." She bent over and took him in her arms and kissed him with her split, chapped lips. "I'm just so sorry, child."

"Get away from me!" he screamed. He struggled and

kicked and flung his arms. He dug his nails into the brocade of the chair and squirmed free, squirting from her bewildered grasp and almost knocking her over. "I hate you!" he screamed. "I hate you! I hate you!" He ran from the room and burst out the back door into the yard. When he had crossed the fence into the pasture, he stopped and looked back. She was at the back door, looking as if she had aged a hundred years in the last sixty seconds. "You stink!" he screamed. "Your breath stinks, and I hate you!"

He turned and ran toward the lake. Goats parted, bleating, fanning out before him. There was a stitch in his side when he stopped, and his breathing was raw and painful. He fell to his knees and gasped for breath. He got up again and ran again until he fell, this time near the lake. He cried, so loud and so strenuous, he wished he could see himself in a mirror. He had never heard such crying. He hated that damned old stinking woman. He hated her.

Later, when he was finished crying, he could not remember having stopped. He may have slept. He was very tired, and he wished his father would come home. He felt the back pocket of his jeans for a handkerchief, but did not have one. He blew his nose with his fingers and wiped his hand on his pants.

He was embarrassed at what he had said to Mrs. Tremble, but he was not sorry. He did hate her. He wondered why he had put up with her for so many years, and why his mother and father had forced her on him. Later, he would apologize, just to keep everyone happy. But he wouldn't mean it, and she would know he didn't.

As he was trying to decide whether to go on and get that part of it over, or whether to sneak across the pasture to his own house, he noticed something in a patch of cane to his right. It was the partly eaten carcass of a baby goat and, just before it sank into the woods out of sight, a glimpse of the black dog he had seen earlier. He was not afraid, exactly, since he knew the dog had eaten; there would be no reason for it to attack. But he did not feel safe enough to stay alone any longer either. He walked up the pasture toward Mrs. Tremble's house.

It was odd, he thought, feeling the cockleburs and beggars' lice collecting in his socks. It was odd that nothing was changed. It was not like in stories, where people always seem to change. He felt different, of course, emptier, because he had cried; but nothing had really changed. He had learned nothing that would make him, overnight, grow into a man, the way people did in stories. He was not better, or wiser. A brother was dead: that was true. But not even that loss, that diamond of pain and emptiness, could be transformed to abstraction, to innocence, or its loss. The marvel was, in fact, that everything could be so much the same, that what his father said could be true: no blame, no guilt. Life was not a dream, he thought, or a story; the persons you meet are not fabulous, or enchanted. Mrs. Tremble was no witch. The wonder, whether you liked it or not, was the choppy surfaces of lakes and the mounds of fire ants and the wild peacocks in the trees. The miracle was the hunger of wild dogs and the availability and vulnerability of goats.

Wild Dog

When the first dog appeared out of the cane, the farmer was dozing with his back to a tree. The dog stretched its neck and put its nose into the wind, which was in the farmer's favor. The farmer shifted the rifle and released the safety.

Another dog stepped from the brake and stood with its fur riffling in the wind. Then others came out, younger dogs some of them, frisky and nervous. They prowled and pranced on the edge of the pasture.

The moon was high and white. The dogs grew calmer and began to bunch up. They scratched at fleas, licked a paw.

The rifle began. Brass casings leaped from it and brushed the farmer's cheek as he fired. Two dogs did not get up. The others scrambled, frantic, soundless, trying to become invisible in the moonlight, not even howling, not even those the bullets hit. He had to aim at each target.

Four were dead. Two others lay wounded, with their clear eyes open. He put the rifle to each head in its turn and closed the eyes. About a quarter of the pack. Not bad. Not bad shooting.

His shoes were bloody, and his hands, from dragging the

dogs to a ravine. To keep Sally from seeing, he didn't turn on the water at the spigot. He dropped the bucket to the bottom of the cistern and drew it back, brimming, on the pulley. The water was ice cold on his hands and feet.

With her hands Sally smoothed flat the invisible wrinkles of a comforter and turned back the covers of the bed.

The ribbon at the throat of her gown was untied. She said, It's not just me, is it? I mean, I wish you would tell me if it is.

He said, No, I'm no farmer. It was a mistake. We've said this.

Still, she said, I feel, you know, guilty.

He said, We both tried. It just couldn't be done.

Later, in bed, she was silent. He thought she was asleep. Then she said, Did you do it?

Do what?

You know.

I got six of them.

That was all for a while. This time he was almost asleep.

She said, I know they are dangerous. I know that.

All right.

Maybe rabies.

Yes, it's necessary.

She said, I love you.

He said, I love you.

She said, I'm still afraid you hold this against me. You worked so hard.

He said, No, of course not. It's necessary. We have to move back.

She said, In a way we are lucky.

He said, That's true. We're lucky.

Her voice was growing sleepy-sounding, and he knew it was almost over, for today anyway.

She said, Did they die right away? I mean, did they suffer?

He said, It was very quick. Don't think about it.

Do you ever think they are beautiful?

Don't think about this, Sally, if it upsets you.

*A*gain the next night he was asleep in the pasture with the rifle across his lap. He dreamed an old man and woman in a car stopped beside him and asked directions.

The farmer woke. He could smell chimney smoke from the house. There were no dogs tonight. He heard a goat bleat, a doe that had gotten its horns stuck in a square of fence wire, where it had tried to reach a clump of grass on the other side. He walked to it and released it and watched it bound away from him, the little tail writing curlicues in the moonlight.

Above him, on the mill road toward his house, clear as day, he saw a dog, a single. He could almost wonder whether this were another dream, an apparition, it seemed so strange to him. He did not reach for the rifle, which he had leaned against the fence. He watched the dog.

It moved as if through liquid, flowing along the road above him, following the narrow road through the moonlight like a magic thing, and then it was gone

The farmer knew already, though. It was a bitch, slender and long-legged and big in the belly. He knew where it was going.

He took the rifle and ran, clumsy and stumbling. He crossed the fence so he could see past the little orchard, but he didn't see her.

The white smoke from his chimney was visible, and the night was bright—but she was gone. She had found the house already, was already under it. He knew she would have her pups there. Wild dogs beneath his house.

☀️nto his plate, beside the sausage and bread, Sally spooned brown applesauce. He ate without speaking.

She said, Will you kill it?

He said, Yes.

He remembered their first year here, four years ago. Sally had bought a quilt at a roadside stand. An old-fashioned design was stitched into it for decoration, a double muscadine. At the time it had not seemed a self-conscious thing to do. The quilt had seemed a necessary purchase for a proper farmer and his wife.

He said, Remember that quilt you bought? He almost said that quilt you made. The one with the grapes. Could we sleep under that quilt tonight?

She said, Remember?—it's already packed. You said maybe we could hang it on the empty wall near the staircase.

He didn't answer.

The apartment, she said. In the city. Then she said, I could get it out. I think I know which box.

☀️t was colder tonight, he thought. The new owners would have to take care of the apples when they were ready. The young goats would have to be cared for—the billys would have to be castrated.

Sally found the right quilt and put it on the bed, but when they got under it they were too warm and had to push it back. They propped up on their pillows in the dark and let their legs touch down their whole length.

She said, Can the new owners take care of it?

He knew what she meant. The wild dog. He said, It's no trouble. I'll do it in the morning.

Some time passed. He wasn't so sure he would do it in the morning. Something changed when he admitted he was not a farmer.

She said, Do you enjoy killing them?

It was her neutral tone. He would remain neutral as well.

He said, Farmers kill wild dogs. It's just the way it is.

She said, You said yourself you're no farmer.

Now they were close to the brink, so they stopped.

Later she pulled up her nightgown and he entered her. He felt her arms tighten around him and she felt his breath on her neck and ear. Soon it was over and both of them wanted sleep.

She said, I love you.

He said, I love you.

She was snoring lightly, and he was still awake. From beneath the house he heard a quiet yip-yip-yip from the bitch, and then that was over. He slept knowing the wild dog was already licking the wet dark eyeless shapes to life and form.

· · ·

Before Sally woke up he left the house with the rifle and squatted at the trapdoor in the foundation of the house. He got on his hands and knees and then flat on his belly and began to pull himself along beneath the floorboards of the house and the network of water pipes that lined them. He dragged himself forward a few inches at a time, then reached back for the rifle and pulled it to his side and started again. His legs cramped, and his neck and back.

The underside of the house was dark, but he found the dog. Despite the danger, he moved very close. The dog's breath was warm on his face, and it smelled of afterbirth. He wondered what strangeness the dog might smell in him.

He had not known he was going to do this. He touched the dog on its side, though he could scarcely see it and did not know whether his touch might provoke an attack. He knew this must be the first time the dog had ever been touched by a human hand. The fur was matted with beggars' lice and cockleburs. She did not flinch. He found her lean front leg and shoulder, and then he found the first pup at her side.

One, he counted aloud.

He removed each pup from its sucking, and allowed each to return.

There were seven.

His hand returned to the rifle. The dog's head was still raised and the calm breath still on the farmer's face. He held the rifle to the dog's head and did not release the safety. He would tell Sally there were seven.

The days passed and grew colder. More red and yellow dyed the skins of the apples. Slow rain changed the leaves to a dark shade of green. There were good crisp days of sunshine, and acorns beneath his feet.

The farmer split a fifty-pound sack of dog food and placed it by the trapdoor of the house. Mornings some of the food would be gone, so he knew the she-dog was eating, though he never saw her eat.

Nights, by the pond, he sat with his back to the big cottonwood and watched for wild dogs. The nights were clear, and he loved the solitude of the fields and the constellations above him.

A few times he got a shot at a single or a pair, but the pack was gone, had moved on. Seven miles away, near the river, a man lost a colt, so the dogs were heading west.

The she-dog stayed away from the house and nursed the pups at a safe distance in the pasture. The bag of dog food continued to diminish, so the farmer knew she was eating at night.

Preparations for the move back into the city continued. The rugs were rolled up, the curtains were taken to the cleaners.

In the kitchen one day he looked at the boxes and the clutter and the handful of dishes they were still using and he said, I should have killed the bitch and the pups. I'm so mixed up.

She said, I tried to love it here.

He said, It's not your fault. It's nobody's fault.

The pups were everywhere now, all over the yard and porch and pastures. They were big-footed and clear-eyed, clumsy and domesticated-acting. Each had a name now, and each had a collar and a tiny white flea collar. Each wore a silvery vaccination tag.

The she-dog did not come near the house, except once each night to eat in secret. She fed the pups their meal of milk far out by the pond.

It was the farmer who first brought one of the pups into the house.

She said, Do you think we should?

He said, I guess not.

She said, We really don't know what will happen—I mean, what we'll do with them . . .

He agreed that she was right, but he brought them in anyway. One at a time, evenings. He watched them play on the rug. He held them in his lap and scratched their ears with his finger. The she-dog moved closer to the house when the pups were inside, but still she kept her distance.

Sally wouldn't touch the pups. She wouldn't sit in the same room with them when they were in the house.

She said, It doesn't seem right.

He said, Why are you so cold?

She said, I'm not cold. Stop accusing me of being cold.

He said, You are cold.

She said, What are you going to do about these dogs? That's what we're fighting about.

The farmer said, We're not fighting about the dogs.

She said, It's horrible, it's perverse.

She was crying now.

He held her and tried to make her stop.

He said, It's nobody's fault. I'm no farmer.

She said, Let's go today. Let's leave everything behind and just go away this minute.

He said, I don't think I can start over again. We've started over so many times.

She said, I love you. She said, Maybe I don't love you. Maybe I just say that so you'll say you love me.

He was still holding her, with his face in her hair. He said, I'll take care of the dogs. I won't bring them inside again.

She said, I hate this goddamn farm.

He released her and walked away from her. He said, Stop punishing me, will you. Will you just stop? I know you hate the goddamn farm, so just stop saying it, all right? Jesus.

She said, I love you. She said, Maybe I don't. I don't know. Jesus, oh Jesus.

He didn't bring the dogs back in the house, but he didn't shoot them either. He stopped feeding them. When the last of the dog food was gone, he did not buy a new bag. He thought they would go away, try to find the pack again. The she-dog would have the instinct, he thought. When she got hungry enough, she would take the pups and locate the pack. That's what he hoped.

When the food was gone, the pups were frisky and confused for a day. In two more days they still had not eaten.

They were frantic. They had been weaned but they tried to suck at the she-dog. She snapped at them and kept them away from her. When one of the pups insisted, she took its face in her mouth and shook it and blinded the pup in one eye. She would not let them touch her.

In a week they were more frantic. In another week they were mad with hunger. They howled with pain. They scratched at the doors, back and front. The farmer and his wife felt like prisoners. The dogs' ribs stuck out. They were gaunt and horrible and did not resemble the dogs they had been.

The she-dog had been hungry before. She didn't care. She liked hunger as much as she liked food. Her eyes were crazy and resigned and looked like shattered glass, there was so much pain in them. Her fur fell out and her legs became stiff and painful to walk upon. She could have gone and hunted, but she didn't want to. She was arrogant, she was a judgment on the farmer and his wife.

They watched the dogs from their kitchen window. The pups were wretched and terrible. They lay in the pasture and ate grass. They wandered through the fields and scratched at the clay on the ditchbank and ate bark from the trees. They put their muzzles into ant beds and lapped up their own urine. They had no instinct for survival.

The farmer and his wife closed the shades against the sight of the miserable dogs. The farmer and his wife stood in their kitchen and sometimes they held each other and asked each other what to do.

The farmer said, They are wild dogs. Why don't they chase rabbits, or mice? Why don't they attack one of the goats?

The farmer's wife said, Shoot them. Get the rifle and kill them. I can't stand this.

At night the farmer and his wife slept, or tried to sleep. They decided to make love and then they changed their minds and did not. They lay naked without touching and listened to the pups whining at the doors. This happened many nights.

The pups changed more and more in appearance. Some of them were almost hairless now. Their bottom teeth showed above the gums, and the gums were discolored and gray.

The farmer's wife said, I'm going to feed them.

The farmer said, Yes, all right, let's do it, let's feed them.

They did nothing. They didn't kill them and they didn't help them live. Somehow the dogs' lives had gotten out of control, out of their hands.

So the farmer and his wife did nothing. They cleaned the oven and mended a board in the floor and swept cobwebs from the ceiling. They wrapped the last of the china in newspaper and packed it into boxes.

They tried not to listen to the voices of the starving dogs. And then they noticed that the dogs were not making noise any longer. The pups became old-looking and resigned and sickly. They lay in the yard and made no movement to look for food. There were other farmers, not a mile away, other houses, but the dogs did not try to find them. They did not search through the garbage. They became silent and almost sweet in their contentment with starvation. Their faces changed shape. Their hipbones were prominent. They lost their identities and could not be recognized by sight, and the names they had been given became pointless and irrelevant.

In the goat shed the alfalfa was as sweet as apples. The floor was fragrant with sawdust.

The she-dog was quietest of all. The farmer and his wife watched her and feared her. They were not sure why.

At first they said it was because they were afraid she would attack them. She's wild, they said. A few months ago she was part of a vicious pack. She was killing livestock. She could kill us.

The farmer's wife said, Let's not take a chance. Kill her first. She's dangerous.

The farmer said, I know I should.

The farmer's wife said, Do it then. Why don't you do it?

The farmer said, I will. I really will.

One of the pups died of starvation.

It helped. It was a release of sorts.

The farmer took the rifle from the closet and loaded the magazine and walked into the pasture and killed five of the others.

They were easy to find, and killing them was easy to do. The farmer wondered why he had allowed the punishment to go on so long.

The seventh pup he could not find. He looked in the goat shed and under the house and in the woods and cane. The seventh dog was missing.

He said to his wife, I can't find it.

She said, Did you bury the others?

He said, I threw them into the ravine.

She said, I wish you could find it.

The moving company would come in one week exactly and they would move away from the farm forever.

The farmer said, I'll look for it tomorrow.

Sally said, Have you noticed the smell?—you can smell the she-dog all the way out in pasture.

The farmer said, I'll do her tomorrow too. Not today. I can't do her today.

The farmer and his wife were naked in bed. They did not allow their bodies to touch.

She said, Tomorrow, then.

He said, Yes, tomorrow.

She said, I love you.

He said, I love you.

She said, Why can't we stop saying this?

He said, I don't know.

She said, I never pictured myself as this person I've become.

They lay side by side for a long time.

He surprised his wife when he touched her, but she responded to his touch. She rolled over toward him and allowed him to hold her.

He wondered if she would say I love you again, and she did.

She said, Today I couldn't find the broom. I didn't really need it, I just didn't know where it was, and it was all I could think about.

The farmer thought of the seventh pup and of the smelly old starving she-dog out in the darkness.

The bed the farmer and his wife lay in together felt as cool as the moist earth.

One-Man Band

The preacher told his daddy he would see him again next week if he could get into town. He had a wake to go to today, Rhema Fritz was dead. The old man could not speak at all since his stroke, so the preacher expected no answer and received none.

His mother was there too. She got off her Exercycle and noted the miles on the speedometer. At the door, the preacher asked if she would like to drive out to Line Creek with him. She declined, as she did all invitations to go out, even to funerals. Before he drove off she said, "A wake is a lonely place for a preacher, son."

The wasps were droning in the persimmon trees. The preacher—his name was Jewel Pilkington—parked his pickup and told his birddog June to stay in the bed, he didn't know how long he would be.

He spoke to the family of the dead woman. Nell was there, from Jackson, with a new permanent and frost. Myrtis was there, wearing pointy-framed bifocals. Lawrence and Gloria and others were there too, members of Brother Pilkington's Line Creek congregation. Lela came out of the kitchen drying her hands and scratching her nose with her forearm. She asked Brother Pilkington had he had a chance to speak to Hot. "He's out back somewhere," she said, "deviling the children. Old as dirt and rich enough to burn a wet bull and all he can think to do is devil a bunch of children." Marcus was there too, from Louisiana. Gresham hadn't been able to get away from his mission work in Mexico, but somebody said he called awhile ago and sounded real good.

"In the midst of life," the preacher said, "we are in death. As for a man, his days are as the grass. But the mercy of the Lord is from everlasting to everlasting, and his righteousness unto his children's children, A-men."

He offered a prayer of thanks for Aunt Rhema's long life and fruitful issue, for her faith and strength and beauty. He was grateful, he said, for the grace of the Lord and the hope of glory and the promise of the life everlasting. This phrase caused him to remember, for some reason, a flying rooster his father had kept in their yard when Jewel was a boy, nearly forty years ago.

He had entered Aunt Rhema's house through a side door and made his way through the bedroom and the kitchen and a sleeping porch, speaking to family. In the living room, Leda Jane Fritz sat alone, weeping. She was a fashionable young woman, home from college in New York. The living room was rarely used, and the couch where she sat was protected by a clear plastic "dust cover." The preacher remembered Leda Jane as a child in his choir. He thought better of speaking to her just now. It is a rare occurrence he reflected, unable to keep the rhythm of his preacherly voice out of even his silent thoughts, that a college girl wearing velour slacks, no brassiere, two gold chains around her neck, and yellow sunbursts on the ankles of her boots is given benefit from a Southern preacher's voice.

He moved silently through the room. He picked up a couple of doodads from the mantle and looked at them. One was a china cup with no handle and a deep saucer. On the white background of the cup and saucer was painted a country scene in a dark, eerie color of red. It was unlike any other the preacher had ever seen. There were tall, foreign-looking houses, all in red, with dark, red-shingled roofs. There were spires and cupolas and prominent window seats. There were odd red trees growing along a red river, and around the borders of the scene were irrelevant red baskets of red roses. The scene gave him a queer feeling, unearthly. He looked at Leda Jane and saw that she was scarcely aware of his presence.

He looked at the scene again. He tried to imagine living in one of the red houses and dropping a hook into the red river, catching the unearthly fish that swam beneath its surface. He looked into the yards in the scene to see whether there were red people in red clothes. There were none. Then, as if it had not been there before, he saw a small red chicken. He looked twice to be sure it was really there. He searched the other yards but could find no other chickens. He set the saucer back on the mantle and picked up the cup, which was painted with the same design. There was no chicken in the yard on the cup. The painter had forgotten to put a chicken there. It was like seeing into another world. He took up the saucer again and stared deeply into the yard. There it was,

83

the red chicken in the red yard: there and nowhere else in the world. He looked at Leda Jane and knew he had been in the room a long time without speaking, or without her speaking to him. He tried to catch her eye, but she would not look. He looked again at the saucer and remembered two things.

One was the flying rooster from his childhood. On the ground the bird seemed gray in color, but in flight an eccentric and vivid cast of red shone in all its feathers.

The other memory was of his father. Not the silent, faded ghost in the apartment, but the quiet man of Jewel Pilkington's childhood. Even then he rarely spoke, as if he were preparing for the enforced silence of his old age. Even then he shied away from telephones; he never wrote a letter. When he wanted a second helping of food, he would stop eating and stare at the dish until someone noticed and passed it to him. "The butterbeans, Daddy?" Jewel's brother Sam might say. "The okra?" Their mother would be lifting this bowl and that, hoping to hit upon the right one. "The cornbread?"

Leda Jane was still crying, noiseless. He was able to catch her eye for a moment. When he did, she picked up a magazine and started thumbing through it. He took the saucer with him from the mantle and sat beside her on the couch. She shifted her body and turned so that they would not have to speak.

He gazed back into the red scene on the saucer. He imagined he was looking into the world of his childhood. It was September, late afternoon and hot. Jewel was frightened of the rooster. He stood outside the chickenyard fence beside an open spigot and considered a drink of water. He watched his father's car pull into the drive, a green Dodge with racks on top and two paint-stained ladders lashed to the racks. Just then the rooster took flight.

In the western light of the Mississippi afternoon, the bird rose from the ground—this was the first time he had seen it fly—no longer gray, but suddenly the color of blood. There was nothing graceful about the rooster, there was a monstrous absurdity, frightening and comic, a pinwheel of activity, like a cartoon of a fistfight, a whirl, blur, fists, and elbows and kneecaps sticking out in all directions, a hand at a throat, both cartoon and a creature of nature, soaring, large as a turkey and ungainly as an Irish setter and, in flight, resembling both. It flew not just with wings but with all its parts, feet and head and neck and tail and parts no man ever saw on a chicken, arms and sails and pogo sticks, paddlewheels and steam whistles and circus tents with banners whipping in the breeze, the work of God gone mad, freakshow in sunset, stasis, confusion, and locomotion in a single beast. It covered a distance of twenty feet and stopped outside the chickenyard. His father turned and went into the house without speaking.

Brother Pilkington placed the saucer on an end table and decided something had to be done about Leda Jane. He placed his hand on her shoulder. He had not noticed before what a country-boy hand it was, the big fingers and hard nails. The hand made his voice sound monstrous. "Job said, 'Naked came I out of my mother's womb and naked shall I return, the Lord gave and the Lord hath taken away, blessed be the name of the Lord.'" She looked at him directly for the first time.

"We're all just so gamestuck, though," she said, through her earnest tears. "Not you, or Aunt Rhema, and all. Just everybody, though. Just so completely gamestuck."

The tempo of the wake was picking up now. A good deal of food had been brought in—a custom left over from a time when Mississippians would not cook in a house where a corpse lay—and a great many people had come. There was the usual amount of low talk and hugs and expressions of sympathy. The food was spread along counters and tables in the kitchen, and on the stove top and oven door. There were plates of chicken and ham. There were dishes of vegetables, a mess of greens and a skillet of cornbread, many desserts.

Miss Hunter was there, who had taught Jewel Pilkington third grade, old as ever and a little blinder. Allie Jean Jackson was there, calling herself Lucinda now. Allie Jean and Jewel had started first grade together, and he could still remember her book number. "Do, Allie Jean," he said, right to her. She didn't look at him. He was no good with names.

Kimble Gregg shook the preacher's hand and thanked him for being with Aunt Rhema's people in their time of need. "I could have used you myself a time back," he said, "but I was out of state then. I guess you heard." Kimble explained that his older son, Talmedge, was killed in a plane wreck in northern Florida. Brother Pilkington said he was sorry he hadn't heard. "We're beginning to pull through," Kimble told him.

The preacher said, "He will make us strong in the hour of adversity."

"Aw, yeah," Kimble said. He put his hands into the pockets of his suit coat. After a while, he said, "Talmedge was hauling six tons of marijuana from the Keys when his plane went down. Treasury asked a bunch of questions, but they didn't make no arrests."

The house continued to fill, the talk became louder and less restrained. Brother Pilkington wondered whether now weren't maybe the time to slip out.

He eased through the living room, then stepped into a corner bedroom to get away for a minute or two. A breeze had come up and was blowing the gauzy curtains out like balloons. He gathered one side of the curtain in his hand and looked out at his truck. He knew when he parked there he was going to get blocked in. Over to one side, among the parked cars, a half-dozen men were having a nip from a bottle they were passing around. He also noticed that the bird-dog was not in the back of the pickup. A wake is just the place for an old dog to get run over, too, he thought. Then, Brother Pilkington heard crying. Most of the crying should have been over by now.

He stepped out of the bedroom into the living room to see who it might be. The minute he was out the door, the sound was gone. He looked at the people holding plates on their laps. No one seemed to have been crying recently. He stepped back into the bedroom.

There it was again, the sound of crying. It had a desperate sound, and it worried him. Then he understood. Someone was in the pantry, just on the other side of the closet wall. He made his way through the house and found the pantry door.

He stepped inside and eased the door shut behind him. It was Woodrow Fritz, a child of sixteen, too old to be out playing with the other children, the youngest of the adults. Woodrow's daddy had talked to the preacher about him before. "He's big as a walrus," the man had said, "you can see that yourself, and real morbid for his age." Woodrow was a big boy, there was no denying that, but not big like a walrus. He was big like a man of thirty. At least six inches taller than the preacher, six foot four probably, with long, dark hair on his forearms. He was weeping uncontrollably over the death of Aunt Rhema. The light had not been on, so the preacher reached up and felt for the string.

The light startled the boy. "Don't you come in here with that damn sanctimonious voice of yours, preacher," he said. "Ain't nothing going to keep old man Morocco from pickling Aunt Rhema, so just keep that goddamn self-righteous voice of yours to yourself. Ain't nothing going to keep me from being mad about it."

Brother Pilkington would have liked to oblige, but it was the only voice that would come to him. "Anger is no sin," he said, "it is a cleansing. Even our Lord and King felt anger."

It infuriated the boy. He strained his neck muscles, tears flowed from his eyes. Worse, he was pacing around the room, slamming his fist into his hand. He wanted something to hit.

The bulb and cord swayed back and forth. The light caused strange shadows to fall around the little room. Mason jars wavered in the light, sliced pears in syrup, glistening red plums. Light caught and released the bottles: clingstone peaches, with their blood red centers and orange meat, pickled okras, animal-like in the vinegar and dill, cucumbers and green tomatoes, row after row of Blue Lake green beans, dewberry preserves and whole figs. They moved with the bulb and cord. The boy's grief threatened to turn to violence.

Brother Pilkington thought of Aunt Rhema as the boy might be remembering her, solitary old woman picking fruit along a ditchbank, beneath the Petticocowa bridge, or by the cow pond, wondering as she picked whether the winter would be cold enough to kill the duckweed on the water. He imagined her, as he had seen her, with a bandana tied around her neck, her unlaced brogans flopping on her feet beneath a fig tree. She reached up and felt the ooze of fig milk on her rough fingers. He imagined those same fingers rubbed over the smooth-skinned plums, the lean, wiry old woman, whose death this child grieved without understanding grief. She stood with uplifted arms among the fruit trees, as if she were a tree herself, growing up out of the Johnson grass and lespedeza, arms upstretched like branches.

"I'll tell you what," the boy said, with decision in his voice, "I'll tell you. I'm going to break every goddamn jar in this pantry."

Woodrow grabbed one of the jars of green beans and turned as if he might actually hit the preacher with it. It was not a thing he was incapable of. When his mother lost a child a year ago, a premature birth that lived only seven hours, Woodrow brooded and wept and, finally, threw a double-bladed ax through the window of his father's pickup. Only luck prevented someone's being in the truck at the time.

"Woody, for God's sake, man," the preacher said.

"I'll bust your goddamn face."

"Woodrow, the time is at hand. Seize it." Brother Pilkington was not sure what he meant by this, but it affected the boy. It seemed right, psalmic and magical and wise, in his preacherly voice.

"I can just see her, though," Woodrow said. He held the quart jar behind his head, and the preacher knew he might still throw it, but his voice had already begun to lose the anger, to take a tone of despair and pleading. "I can just see her, out by the chicken house, and it getting dark and the air so cool and no sound except the cluck-cluck-cluck and her going 'Chick, oh chick-chick,' in her little old-woman voice, like nobody's listening, not even the chickens, just talking to herself and scattering shelled corn, you know, and maybe an owl just starting to hoot or that sound the big plums make when they fall off the tree and hit the grass out by the fence, and all the shadows, and when it's over, putting her old skinny hand back on her neck where it's aching and then knocking the dishpan against her leg to shake out the corn dust."

So, it was over. Woodrow put the jar of green beans back on the shelf and took the handkerchief the preacher handed him. It was the same one Leda Jane had used, but he didn't notice. He looked like a giant, and his great arms hung down.

"Woodrow," the preacher said, when some time had passed. "Son, do you know what is going to happen to you the next time you speak either directly or indirectly of the sanctimony you say you find in my speaking voice?"

The huge boy said, "Yessir."

"I'm going to whip your ass like you got caught stealing chickens, ain't I?"

"Yessir," he said.

The sun was a good deal declined and had lost its ardent interest in the pastures and fields and ponds and sheds. The shadows of the house and trees fell across one side of the yard and made a pleasant shade.

Funeral guests had been leaving for a while now, and others were starting up their pickups and station wagons and cars. Breeze from the back pastures, where Brother Pilkington could still hear children playing, brought a fresh smell of hay and manure and fishy pond water to his nostrils. He was tired.

The men were finished drinking whiskey. They sat around the backyard, a few on the porch steps, others in chairs they had brought out. A cow with a bell walked toward the shed.

Brother Pilkington stepped out onto the porch and found an empty spot on the steps. He hiked up his pants legs above his socks and sat slowly. Yellow and pink were already smeared through the clouds in the south and west. June, the preacher's dog, with cockleburs in her ears, eased into the company of men and took her place beside the preacher. "Old liver-spot," he said.

In a little while, the men were talking in quiet voices, telling stories. The women were mostly inside, talking about Lord knew what. Everybody was gone now except family and a few close neighbors. One man asked did they remember back when Line Creek used to flood. "Back before they built the levees on the Yazoo and Tallahatchie," he said. "The water used to come up past the road and get in the hen houses. If you weren't careful, it would drown the chickens and the eggs would float off and rot. Children would paddle out in wood boats and gather rotten eggs to throw at one another. Miss Bartlin had a cow drown one time. There was cholera somewhere or other, not right around Line Creek, out in Carroll County, maybe, or down to Morgan City. All the dead livestock had to be burned, didn't matter what they died of, even drowning. She burned that cow for a month, seem like, before it would ever burn up. Just keep on throwing stove wood and coal oil on it. And stunk, godamighty. Just keep on burning it, night and day, and the colored folks all down Line Creek keeping an eye out, trying to see can they pick up sight of a cross in the middle of all that burning. And then even them able to forget about it. Truckers and travelers—I used to think about this all the time when I was a boy—folks driving out on Highway 49, seven eight miles away, could see the smoke, that old greasy black smoke, and they'd say, 'There's the Line Creek community, Miss Bartlin still burning that cow,' and Miss Bartlin real mad at Lonnie Weber, used to be town marshal—he's the one made her burn it, said he was under orders from the Public Health, and her not saying nothing except how she's just a poor woman and can't afford to burn no cow. Law," he said. He slowed down the pace of his tale to signal the end. "Law, them was funny times, long time ago. Funny times."

For a while nothing was said. Then the man who had been talking said, "Which, I don't know if you know it, is where that expression come from, when you say a man is rich enough to burn a wet bull. And stunk, godamighty."

The colors in the sky were more vivid now against the clouds. The cow whose bell the preacher had heard had made its way up the pasture to the feed trough and was switching horseflies with its tail. A couple of egrets, solemn birds far from their homes in the cypress trees on Roebuck Lake, stood around the feed lot looking at the cows.

The preacher stood up and stretched. It was late, he said. About time for him and old June to be moving toward home. He still had his horse yet to feed. The other men began to stand up too and agree that it was late. They shook the preacher's hand. Somebody kicked the cat off the porch to stretch his legs.

Inside, he said his goodbyes to the women. Some shook his hand, others gave him a hug and thanked him. Woodrow Fritz avoided his eye, but Leda Jane followed him out to his truck and told him she would be heading back to New York soon after the funeral. If she didn't get to talk to him later, she just, well, wanted to say goodbye. Brother Pilkington was too tired to figure out what she was trying to tell him.

He helped June into the bed of the pickup and noticed that she was more feeble this year than last. He slammed the door and said, "Now don't you forget us up there in the big city, Miss Leda." He started the engine and began backing out of the drive. He could hear Uncle Hot, herding up the children with promises of sweet things to eat.

He had started to tell the men in the backyard about his father, the story of the flying rooster. He could have made them laugh. Or he could have been serious. He could have told them the rooster was an emblem of Aunt Rhema's soul's ascension, released at last from the clay, speeding heavenward, monstrous and swift and absurd, without grace or beauty but confident and purposeful, hightailing it for a neighbor's chickenyard or the streets of gold. He might have told them he worried about his father and mother, and wondered that their lives could have come to so little. He might have said that when he tried to understand, he could remember only the rooster. When he sees, in his memory, the rooster in flight, he sees also a world of bright skies and pungent catalpa beans and honey in the comb, he sees planets and suns and galaxies infinitely deep and beautiful, and he hears music. He believes every image and every song come from his sad mother and father, a tale of growth and death and resurrection, of irrevocable loss and unexpected joy in the hope of renewal.

It was just as well he had not told them. He switched on the headlights and headed out the gravel road toward the parsonage.

By the time he pulled his pickup around behind the

house, the sky was dark. There was a moon, though. He fed his horse and stood beside it in the dark for a while as it ate, then he opened the shed door for it to go in.

The porchlight was not on, but he could see. He stamped his feet on the board floor of the porch and went into the house by the kitchen door. He had not known just how tired he was. He struck a match and lit the oven to take the chill out of the room.

He sat heavily in a chair at the kitchen table and stretched out his legs and closed his eyes. He wondered how much longer they could keep his daddy at home. For a while he thought nothing else, he just sat. He may have slept for a minute.

When he opened his eyes, he felt better, less tired. Still, he didn't get up yet. The table where he sat was made of wood, with a square of oilcloth to cover it. He drummed his fingers against the tabletop, slowly at first, and the rhythm pleased him. He stopped and let his hand rest, palm down, on the oilcloth. He started again, drumming his fingers and listening to the sound.

He drummed harder, and a little faster, and he kept on drumming. He wondered where the rhythm was coming from, what part of his mind had invented the rhythm his fingers made. He listened inside his head, and he drummed what he heard. He kept on drumming. For emphasis he struck the table extra hard with his index finger, and sometimes with his thumb; for a different sound he angled his fingers so that his nails hit first and then the blunt tips of flesh and bone. He listened in his head and he kept on drumming, imitating the sounds that he heard. He loved the sound, he had heard it somewhere before. Now he used the heel of his hand sometimes, and sometimes he would slap the table with his palm, a-rat-a-tat-tat and a boom slap crack, and the drumming went on, hard fingers and hard nails and a country-boy hand going bang-bang-bump. And he bumped and he banged and he listened to the Psalms and he looked down from heaven on the children of men, and he wished he had married and fathered a son, and he missed his brother Sam who lived on the Gulf, and he thought about his mama and he grunted and he whistled and he clicked with his tongue, Hambone. Hambone, Hambone, have you heard, Papa's gonna buy me a mockingbird. He sang out loud to the yellow walls, he breathed the heated air from the open oven door, he wanted Leda Jane, he wanted her in his bed, Hambone. He slapped with his hand from his leg to his chest, from his chest to his leg, and he made a loud pop on his open-oh mouth, and he ached for his daddy and the rooster and for death, and he sang to his mama of a one-man band, oh he sang of a one-man band.

Rat Song

Missy first approaches us about the rats. They are just the most darling things, she says, and may she bring them home for the weekend, *all* the kids are getting to take care of them over the weekend, and they can't just be left in the classroom to *starve* till Monday, can they, so can't I, please?

Rats? I say. You mean hamsters? or gerbils?

Well, sort of, she says. They're in a hamster cage, and one of the kids in the split section of her learning pod (which I take to mean the sixth grade) donated them, you know, when her father was transferred back to California or somewhere, and now Miss Cheshire, our unit leader (which I understand to mean teacher) is lining up volunteers to keep them on weekends, so can I, please?

Rats? her mother says. You mean mice?

White mice? I say, encouraged.

Well, no, Missy says, not exactly white, but can she?

Oh, I love gerbils, her mother says. They're so educational, and so natural.

Well, I don't know, I say. The fish were one thing—and I have to admit, I say, you're doing a fine job with the fish, feeding them and so on—but white mice, I'm not so sure.

I love the rats, Daddy, she assures me. I love them more than anyone else in the pod, more than the unit leader even, so can't I, Daddy, please? She will take full responsibility, she swears. Really.

Have you fed the fish today? I say impotently, vanquished with the word *daddy*, the first time she's called me that since her mother decided Roy and Meredith sounded more mature than daddy and mommy.

Missy brings the rats home, two of them. They sit on the top shelf of their yellow plastic hamster cage, motionless. They are rats all right, and not white.

Aren't they beautiful! Missy says.

None of us can disagree with that, her mother says enthusiastically. Their fur, she says, is so thick and glossy, their eyes so—so vulnerable!

I am horrified by them. Everyone looks at me for a statement of approval, so I manage to say, Very attractive pets, but I don't think . . .

Their names are Harriet Tubman and Diphtheria Jean Johnson, Missy tells us, two historical figures her pod has been studying. (*Exploring* is actually the word she uses.)

Hm, kind of super names for gerbils, her mother says seriously.

My God, I think. My idea of boldness in education and child rearing is letting Missy watch the black mollies give birth in the aquarium.

Oh, this is nothing, her mother assures me in private, as I gulp J&B. You should have been in town last year when

Missy's pod went on a field trip to the large animal clinic and helped foal a mare. Bloody hands and all, she assures me.

*W*ell, all right, I think. The rats are in the house for the weekend; there is nothing I can do about that. And in any case, the beasts are caged, and besides that, I tell myself, it's an old prejudice anyway. What if hamsters had been responsible for the plague? Or featured on *60 Minutes* as a commentary on inner-city living? What if gerbils lived in barns and sewers and cut chickens' throats and carried rabies? Wouldn't we probably keep rats as pets and buy poison for the others? Yes, but it's the other way around, I reply logically and without feeling much comfort. (It has taken me most of several months to get used to the fish.)

But now the fish, I remind myself, are another matter—I was certainly wrong about the fish. I have indeed grown accustomed to them and have even come to enjoy them, to think them beautiful. Some of them anyway. And it was I who suggested buying the larger tank. Seventy gallons. The same might be true this weekend of the rats. I might become their champion. Well, no, not that, but it will work out, I tell myself, or at least it will be over soon enough and the rats will be back in the schoolroom where they belong. I look into the fish tank and tap lightly on the side of a yellow tin of fish food and watch the flakes drift down through the crystal water like snow. The algae-eater, a rock-colored fish I mistakenly contributed to the collection in a moment of familial zeal, has grown in a relatively short time from the size of a finger joint to a great menacing beast of five or six inches, thick as a cigar. I watch him now, swimming his buzzardly way among the angels and mollies and tetras. He eats not only algae, he has eaten one of the snails, torpedoed it against the glass wall until it released its grip and fell to the bottom of the tank, then ripped away the sticky flesh from its underside and sucked it out. That was months ago. The thought comes back now as the hideous creature settles behind an electronically operated sea chest which pops open every ten seconds and reveals a grinning skeleton.

The rats are placed in their cage on the second tier of a wood-inlaid table near the aquarium. They can be friends with the fish, Missy tells us, and introduces them by name. Oddly enough, the rats do seem interested in the fish. Look, my wife says cheerily, I think they notice each other.

The rats sit on their shelf behind the yellow plastic, glaring at the fish and slowly grinding hunks of wilted lettuce between their teeth.

Maybe they want to go for a swim with their new friends, my wife jokes prettily.

Maybe they want to tear out their gills and drink their cold blood, I try to joke back, but no one laughs. I would gladly give them the algae-eating snail murderer.

Yet, despite my prejudice against the beasts, the rest of the afternoon and evening go fine. Friday. The rats do no more than stare at the fish and eat lettuce. Missy changes the paper in their cage once, very handily and with genuine affection for the creatures inside. She strokes their necks and ears and calls them Harriet and Diphtheria, and sometimes Hattie and Dippy, and the rats respond gently to her touch, not stupidly like gerbils but more like house cats, turning their little heads to direct the passage of her finger over their bodies, then nuzzling their faces into her hand and into each other's neck. Missy accepts their gentle behavior with delight.

You must admit . . . her mother says, looking meaningfully at me and without finishing her sentence.

I admit that, yes, yes indeed . . . with no thought of finishing my sentence either, and head for the liquor cabinet.

And in truth the whole business would be not simply, in my wife's words, an educational experience; it would be tender and touching and sweet, if the creatures were anything less repellent to me than the filthy monsters behind that yellow plastic. Not that they actually appear filthy, or monstrous; they are quite domestic in appearance, their fur does have a healthy look, a sheen. They scratch and lick themselves frequently. Nevertheless, I lie awake listening for them to move. I hear nothing. I prop against my pillows and examine my aversion to rats, bring to memory every rat I have ever encountered.

The memories are few enough and unspectacular: one monster caught in the barn by a large collie on a farm I visited as a child. But that is a good memory for the most part, and at the time I didn't really get a good look at the rat. Another, more recently, peered out of the metal door of a Dempster Dumpster at the liquor store—momentarily frightening, no more than that. Still another rat, also in my childhood, ate fig preserves in my grandmother's pantry. This memory brings me straight up in bed. The rat cracked the paraffin seal of the jar and dipped out whole figs with its front feet and slipped them dripping with syrup into its mouth. I turn on the light and listen for a rustling sound. Jesus, I say aloud, but hear nothing more than my own cantering auricles and ventricles and my wife's regular breathing beside me. Daumier's barrister above the bedroom mantel threatens to gavel out my brains, so I turn off the light again and lie awake. And in fact the gavel brings back another childhood memory. Once in an early June my father was getting the croquet equipment out of the summerhouse in Old Saybrook when a mouse scuttled across the floor. In a single wonderful motion, as though the mallet were part of his graceful arm, he swung in a wide arc and came down directly on the mouse. It splattered everywhere. But that was a mouse, I remind myself, not a rat. I listen again and hear nothing. I turn on the light and pick up a book.

My wife turns halfway over in her sleep and with her creamed face argues for a face-lift, the promise of one if she should ever need it. She'll never need it. I stay up alone all night.

Saturday goes much the same. More lettuce, more cage cleaning and stroking. When Missy is not handling them, the rats snuggle contentedly together in the top shelf area and stare at the fish. After lunch Missy takes them onto the patio and out of the cage. Settled into the hammock with her head on the pillow, she allows the rats to crawl over her An Ounce Of Kif Makes You Feel Like A Camel T-shirt, which reveals her newly formed and embarrassingly untrained breasts. It is more education than I can take, except that all three of them, Missy, Dippy, and Hattie, look so contented and relaxed. The rats' movements across her little hillocks are slow and at times comically clumsy, but at the same time alert and domestic-looking. Harriet scratches behind one ear with her hind foot, Diphtheria picks a flea out of her fur with an agile hairless little monkey hand. That afternoon I buy two Sergeant's Sentry IV flea collars and ask Missy please to put them on the rats and wash her hands. My wife tells me how thoughtful I'm getting to be. Missy calls me daddy a hundred times a day. I get the impression she is counting how many, but it makes me feel good anyway.

Don't the gerbils look cute in their teensie flea collars, my wife wants to know. We should get little tinkle bells for their necks, she believes. Suddenly I feel the way I felt last vacation when I agreed to wear a Have A Happy Day button.

I advise against investing too much money in the rats, since we only have them for the weekend.

How much could two tinkle bells cost? she laughs with a scolding music, and I have to agree that they needn't be silver, need they? and try to laugh a little myself.

Oh, can they be silver, Daddydaddydaddy? Missy says, Oh, please, can they?

Goddamnit.

:Ö:n Sunday I take the call from Miss Cheshire, Missy's teacher. She sounds drunk. Listen to me, she says with authority, I've been thinking about this rat business all weekend, have been up nights and have looked at the problem from, so to speak, every angle, so understand that this is not just something I thought up today, so anyway, this is the thing, don't bring those rats back to school. I don't want them, and if Missy shows up with them I'm going to send her back home, I'm not going to let her in the schoolroom, so don't try it.

Well, now, wait just one minute, I say, but with no luck, since Miss Cheshire does not stop talking and does not hear me. She is through with the rats, she says, she made a mistake in ever accepting them in the first place, Missy is the only child who's ever been allowed to bring them into her house, none of the other parents would hear of it, and listen to me, sir, she says, I have had the full responsibility for those goddamn rats ever since they showed up. I've had them every weekend and have lied to the pupils that other pupils were taking them home with them, so don't bring them back to school. I am a young woman, youngish, and have plenty of problems without rats, and you might as well know this too, I'm not wealthy like you, no, and never have been, I live well enough, I'm not complaining, but it's not much and it's sure as hell not enough to support two rats as well as myself in this rattrap garden apartment I live in, but the money is not really the issue; it's the rats themselves, I don't like rats, I hate them, not that they've ever done anything to me, in fact these two, Hattie and Dippy, are wonderful with the children, so there's nothing personal, but no more, I can't have them in the room another minute longer.

I think, This woman is insane, and I know also that she will beat me, that I will end up with the rats, but still I like her, I feel close to her, I suspect modern education might be improving. I tell her the story of the fig preserves and of the splattered mouse. Over the line I hear ice click in a glass and a deep gulp, a fit of coughing that ends in several sneezes. When Miss Cheshire comes back on the line she is even more forceful than before.

Don't bring them back, she begins, with renewed vigor, flush them down the toilet, whatever you want, but I won't take them, and don't try to impress me with your summer-house croquet-mallet bullshit because I've got rat stories that will float ice cubes in your blood and which I could proba-bly sell to *Reader's Digest* for a great deal of money as true first-person accounts if I chose to do so, which I do not, and not one of them involves a croquet mallet.

A new thought almost staggers me with surprise: I'm falling in love. She is from Mississippi, she says, she has spent her entire life getting out of Mississippi, where, she says, the first rat in the history of the world drew breath, and now she is out, not far out maybe, a Connecticut suburb is not far out but it's out enough, and she saw plenty of rats when she was in Mississippi, she says, and she isn't going to see another one, not even to kill it, though when she accepted them into the classroom, she says, she thought, well maybe, maybe I can do it, but I can't, I know that now, it's like your childhood religion, she says. You never get over it but you don't have to stare it in the face every day, so now it's over, you've got the goddamn things, you keep them.

Then she tells a story that almost does freeze my blood. Her father, she says, was a tall, fat, ironic man who drank heavily, talked through his nose, and carried a loaded gun in his pants, whose given name on his birth certificate was Big

Boy, named, she says, for a tomato vine that grew outside his mother's window when he was born, which his father (her grandfather) chopped down with a sharpened broad-blade cotton hoe because he (the grandfather, a short man, practically a dwarf, she says) swore he'd never again as long as he lived harvest tomatoes on a stepladder, and sometimes I wish, she says, he'd chopped off my daddy's vine too, because when I was just a little girl, about like your own child, like Missy, she says, my daddy took me with him to a roadhouse called Upchurch's Gas and Gro., which had not one gallon of gas nor one loaf of bread nor anything else except some sorry old booths covered with checkered oilcloth and plenty of sorry whiskey and a low ceiling, and he tapped me on the shoulder when we'd been there awhile and said, Hun, lookee hyere, just like that, and showed me directly up above us, not one ass kiss from his head, a rat tail as long as a foot ruler hanging out of a crack in the ceiling boards.

Whispering coarsely, I astonish myself: I think I love you, I suddenly say, but she never hears me, never breaks the headlong progress of her story, talking on, the accent and rhythm and image and idiom of Mississippi slipping more and more into control of her voice, the most beautiful thing I've ever heard, great rivers thudding against barge hulls, lynchings and banjos, sheer music.

He reached up over his head, she says, and looped that rat tail once around his index finger and held on, the rat squealing and squalling and running in place, scuttling and scurrying, scrambling, scratching, spinning his wheels, and going nowhere except in a circle with my tall, fat, ironic horse-ass daddy hanging on for all he's worth and laughing until his shoes were full and took, she says, that damn pistol out of his pants, a big nickeled .44 pistol with *Big'un* spelled out in the handlegrip in twenty-four carat gold letters, which meant my mama's mama had to be buried in a cardboard coffin because that's all we could afford, and held that chunk of nickel up to the scrambling rat and blew him into so many pieces, not to mention the board ceiling of the store, that we never again saw two hunks of meat or hanks of hair bigger than the snippet of tail that broke loose and stayed in my daddy's hand when the rest of the rat went through the roof and a trained bluetick hound out the back door, so keep your goddamn rats and your fig preserve rat stories and shove them up your summerhouse ass, but don't send the rats back to me, I don't want them and I'm not taking them. You can keep the cage, free-gratis.

I love you, I say to the dead phone. She has hung up.

We can keep the rats, I tell Missy. I've already discussed it with your teach—ah, your unit leader, and it's all right with her.

My wife tells me how sort of family-oriented I'm proving to be after all and how proud of me she is. Missy burbles to overflowing with daddydaddys. She has special collars made for them and attaches them with sterling silver tinkle bells. The Sergeant's flea collars stay in place but seem to do no good. The rats continue to pick at their breast fur and scratch behind their ears.

I ask my wife if she thinks the scratching means anything.

Like what? she wonders through Cointreau in a manner

that assures me of what I already suspect, that I don't know what I'm talking about.

Like, well, I don't know, some disease or something, diphtheria maybe, or, hell, I don't know, bubonic plague, what do I know about rats?

She says I'm overreacting but that I'm a sweet sort of silly thing to think of it and why don't I take the pets to a veterinarian if I'm worried, have him give them a complete checkup. That's the only *sensible* thing to do, she reasons.

Missy takes them in while I sit in the car. They come out with little tags to go on the hooks with their bells, and documents declaring them free of disease and immune from distemper. I doubt they were checked for plague but say nothing.

The rats grow to incredible size, barn rats if there ever were two, as big as house cats, still crouched onto the tiny shelf of the yellow plastic hamster cage, their fibrous ropy tails hanging to the bottom floor of the cage. Their bells don't tinkle. They watch the fish.

The fish start to die, the silver-tipped tetras. Maybe it really is the plague, I think, or the evil eye. Or maybe I'm just going crazy. In any case, I certainly don't seem very sensible. At first I can't know for certain the fish are dying, I can only guess. None but the five tetras seem affected.

Daddy, look, Missy says, feeding them from the fish-food can. The tetras all have their mouths open, aren't they silly?

Oh, Jesus. It's true, all five are swimming around the tank with their mouths locked open. I squat and look at them in horror. They can't live like that, I almost tell her. They can't live with their mouths locked open. But I say nothing.

The fish are dying, I tell my wife later. The tetras.

Oh, well, she says, tetras never last long. We can get more.

No, I say, I mean I think the rats killed them. (This comes as a rather large surprise to me as well as to her, but the moment I say it I almost believe it.)

Whaaaaat? she says, exaggeratedly suspicious. How?

By looking at them, I almost say, by giving them fleas. Instead I say, I'm not sure, they're just doing it. I'm worried.

They don't look dead to me, she says, looking at them. You haven't mentioned this to Missy . . . ?

Certainly not. I drop the subject for now.

The next day the fish are ravenously hungry, and the algae-eater is subdued into hiding behind the grinning skeleton. The tetras are eating every morsel of food in sight, swimming to the top of the tank, diving, feeding, skimming along the surface of the water with their mouths wide open sucking in food. It is obscene. The rats pick at invisible fleas.

Don't feed the fish anymore, I tell Missy. They're sick.

But Missy feeds them more. The other fish will starve, Roy, she says. The greedy old tetras are eating just everything.

Which they are, scooping up every flake into their gaping mouths, no matter how much is poured in. Missy feeds on.

Then the strange movements begin. Without warning the tetras suddenly plummet to the bottom of the tank, then as rapidly flash upward and leap from the water. After skimming the surface again for a few minutes they drop again with incredible vertical speed to the bottom. Then up again, down, all five of them, day and night, day in and day out for a week, scooping up gargantuan amounts of food from the surface with their locked-open mouths. I become a nervous wreck trying to watch them.

I call Miss Cheshire and tell her who I am. Can rats carry plague? I say into the phone. I mean this to be a joke, but suddenly it isn't. There is no answer. I notice that I sound a little frantic. Can rats, I inquire in a bizarre parody of self-control, transmit bubonic plague to fish? (The idea seems ridiculous even to me, but I fear it nonetheless.) There is a long pause on the telephone as I wait for her answer.

Finally she speaks: I really wouldn't know, she says, and hangs up.

The tetras die, all of them. I am the only one who seems to recognize the possibility of a connection with the rats. I devote myself to a proof of the connection. I scan a decade of old newspapers in the city library, I live with the *Reader's Guide* and the *Encyclopaedia Britannica*. At night in bed I say to my wife, I think the rats have fleas of the type that carry bubonic plague. (The notion is extreme, as I recognize even as I say it, but I want so badly to be right about something, anything, that I can believe it.) I've looked it up, and I'm pretty sure of it. I think the fish died of the plague, some form of it. I don't know how.

I hope you haven't told Missy that! she says, startled. And because I haven't even thought of telling her I believe for an instant I am less of a fool than I am—that I am sensible and winning.

No, I say, I haven't. I think we can just get rid of the rats quietly, and that will be that. We can get another pet for her.

What! says my wife, astonished.

Maybe the state health office should be the ones to handle this, I say, feeling more sensible than ever, and well loved. And Missy should have a complete physical checkup, of course. We all should.

Are you mad? my wife says. When I said I hoped you hadn't told Missy, she says, I meant I hoped you hadn't jeopardized your credibility with her, because I honestly believe if you can just sort of cool it with a low, and I mean looooow, profile . . .

Look, I say, unable even to wonder that credibility and profiles had got mixed into a conversation about plague and yet pretending to be much calmer than I am in order to preserve whatever insane credibility I might have left, see this newspaper clipping? There were three recorded cases of bubonic plague in Utah last year. Do you realize what that means?

I certainly do, she says, it means Utah is just as unenlightened and filthy as everyone has always known it was and has caverns full of bats and God knows what else; besides the gerbils have been checked by the vet.

They are not gerbils, I say evenly, they are rats. I leave the bedroom. And they've got the goddamn plague! I shout back over my shoulder, trembling. And it's New Mexico that has all the bats, not Utah! A geographical victory, I think, seems better than none at all. Besides, the plague theory is becoming enormously important to defend.

In my anger I dial Miss Cheshire. Miss Cheshire, I say, you are, in a primitive way, quite lovely, I suspect, certainly plain-spoken in your crudely attractive way, and probably a good teacher, but despite all that, madam, you are a hick, one who—very like my wife, in fact—is self-serving in the extreme, a bully, and profoundly rude. My rats have bubonic plague, and your telephone manners are quite coarse. Good-bye. I slam the receiver.

I wake up Missy. Missy, honey, I say, Harriet Tubman and Diphtheria Jean Johnson have bubonic plague. We've got to get rid of them right away.

Oh, please no, Daddy, she weeps, seeming to come awake immediately, please no, get them shots for it.

Get up.

She pops out of bed in her blue-and-white nighty saying, Please don't kill my friends, don't kill Hattie and Dippy, please. Her devastating loveliness and disarming selfishness remind me of her mother when we met. I press on.

Where did you say that child's father was transferred back to? I say, imagining a rhetorical premise: California is in the West, Utah is in the West, there is plague in Utah . . .

What child? she says.

The kid who gave the school the rats; where was it they lived before coming here?

I don't remember, she says. Utah, I think, or New Mexico, somewhere out West.

Utah, for Christ's sake! I screech, forgetting my premise. It was not Utah; it was California! Wasn't it?

Utah or California, someplace like that, she says.

112

Missy, listen to me, how in God's name can you confuse Utah and California, honey, which was it?

I don't know, she moans, crying now.

Her mother gets out of bed. What on earth! she says, what are you doing to her?

Trying to save her from bubonic plague, I say, and teach her some geography. (Why, I wonder, has elementary geography assumed such a central importance in this household?) Honey, I say again to Missy, were you dreaming about Utah? Did you hear me talking about Utah in your sleep?

She bawls and won't answer.

Why don't I shut up? I wonder.

Leave her alone! her mother demands.

Look at those goddamn rats, I demand right back, clearing my head of the Golden West and not even bothering to point out that the algae-eater is devouring one of the tetras—there is plenty of other evidence. Harriet Tubman is staggering around in the floor section of the hamster cage, her jaw locked open and her pink tongue lolling out of her mouth. She pants for breath. Diphtheria Jean is on the top shelf doing nothing but looking at the algae-eater.

Well, clearly, I say with justification, the tetras are dead as hell. I dip out the four-and-a-half remaining ones from the tank in a little net and hold them as I speak, droplets of water darkening the maroon sparrow in the rug. And, I continue, can anyone deny that Harriet Tubman is seriously ill? (No one can.) That she is unusually clumsy and her jaw is locked open? (The same.)

Animals die of a thousand things, says my wife sensibly.

Is lockjaw part of the bubonic plague? Missy says.

No, not that I know of, I admit, probably not.

Can fleas bite fish?

No, I say. No, of course not.

Well, there you are, her mother concludes, squashing me with the unspoken remainder of a syllogism.

Still, I notice both Missy and my wife are impressed, pale and stunned by the specter of the sick rat. The four-and-a-half fish.

No logic in the world, I conclude, will save that dying rat. I fling the fish aside and sleep in a guest bedroom.

Harriet Tubman dies the next day with her gaping mouth rested across her right foreleg and a slab of lettuce beneath her belly. Her eyes are wide open as a fish's. Missy and her mother are silenced by the death. I can scarcely feel good for seeing them so humbled. I think they might respect me.

Then contagion becomes a problem. Diphtheria Jean stumbles as she comes down from the top shelf. Her breathing seems strained. Missy, I say, come look at this. She comes down the stairway holding the rosewood bannister and limping slightly. My heart leaps. I'm afraid to mention the limp, afraid my words will intensify the disease as surely as they have conceived and already begun to spread it. The thought is inescapable: through my skillful argument my daughter has contracted black death. Jesus. Is that possible?

What is it, Roy? Missy asks.

Look, I say at last. Look at Dippy. See how clumsy? That's how it starts. See how hard it is for her to walk?

Missy is haggard, puffy about the eyes. Missy, are you all right? She seems feverish and distracted.

Honey, sit over here, no here, on the couch, lie down. I want to look at you. Where is your mommy, I say, probing deeply into her groin for the telltale swellings of the lymph glands.

She's in bed, Missy says, she doesn't feel well, and, Daddy, I'm so sleepy.

I carry her to bed.

The next day Diphtheria Jean dies. No one cares. My wife has a temperature of 102 degrees, Missy is flushed and too listless to get up. I take them to the hospital emergency room, where a doctor sees the two of them.

A virus, he thinks. If your wife's fever goes higher, the doctor says, please do call me. Otherwise I see no reason for alarm. I've treated dozens of similar cases recently. It comes on suddenly, but it doesn't last long, he assures me.

When I mention bubonic plague and tell him about the rats and fish, he laughs. Check with the vet, he says. Or the pet shop. Plague isn't a virus anyway, he says. It's bacteria. It would have shown up in the white-cell count. He laughs a great deal and shakes his head. Plague, I think I hear him say, blowing his nose vigorously into a handkerchief, bubonic plague. When I ask what other patients he has treated, what schools the children are in, he ignores me.

He refuses to hospitalize Missy. She's probably coming down with the same thing as her mother, he says. It's never as severe in children.

I consider changing doctors but do not. I take both of them home and put them to bed beneath down comforters.

I go to the kitchen for aspirin and lemonade, thankful I've not given them a dread disease after all. If it's true I haven't. No argument, even between a man and a woman who are no longer in love, should end in black death. Both are already asleep when I reach their rooms with the lemonade.

The phone rings. It is Miss Cheshire, speaking with an ice cube in her mouth, apologizing, as I finally understand, for her earlier manners.

Take that ice cube out of your mouth so I can understand you, I say, though I am touched by her call. It is, as far as I can remember, the first time anyone has ever apologized to me. A woman anyway. Not removing the ice cube, or even apparently hearing me, she wonders if I might come over for a while this afternoon. Her apartment is on Maple, she explains, serving me the address over ice. One of the garden apartments, she says. It's really nice.

I decide I rather like the ice cube after all.

She wants to discuss a compromise of some kind, she says. About the rats. She feels guilty, she says, for her irresponsibility in this matter. And especially, she says, about my rudeness to you. And in a delicious ice-warm whisper into my earpiece tells me I am a generous and very forceful man, and please do call her Fanny. She hopes I don't hold any of this against her, she's been a little desperate these past weeks, she sighs. It's a lonely, lonely place, the East, for a country girl.

I don't tell her the rats are dead. Not yet. I don't even tell her I love her, though I do again. No, I think, maybe I don't. No, of course I don't. Not exactly.

I hang up and wonder whether I should take a little gift, a peace offering, some type of counterapology. Something for the classroom maybe, an ant farm. I knot a fresh tie and stand at the hall mirror to catch the three-quarter frontal pose. One hand on a hip, the other hooked carelessly by the thumb in my jacket pocket. Not exactly what I'd hoped: a parody of the Jack Nicklaus men's casuals advertisement. A little ridiculous, but not bad. Not at all. In fact, I look pretty damn good. I unbutton the jacket and quick-flash the red lining at the mirror. Or maybe she would like an amusing little wine, I think. Perhaps a single flower.

Welcome to the
Arrow-Catcher Fair

The usual long banner with red lettering had been strung from tree to tree on the pasture's edge: WELCOME TO THE ARROW-CATCHER FAIR. The Indian was shooting arrows, first from a small straight bow of hardwood, then from stronger, surer bows, and the Arrow Catcher was catching them. A crowd of spectators had gathered, but not so large a crowd as would congregate later.

Miss Golden Rondelle, the Arrow Catcher's sister, cursed softly the two of them. "You low-lifed fugitive from the Indian Removal Bill, Redboy, if you shoot one more arrow at that sweet child, gotdoggit, I'll . . ." And, still softly, "Arrow Catcher, I swear before the tomb of Tishomingo I wish I'd never paid for your shock therapy, you dried-up little schizophrenic fart, you . . ." There were a few snickers from the nearest spectators, but not many. Her voice was soft, and this was a familiar curse, one that had lasted three years longer than three-quarters of a century, a curse spanning all those years since, in a wooded glen of wild pecan and tupelo and sweet gum, a five-year-old child at the turning of the century caught his first arrow and became the Arrow Catcher. Of the three the Arrow Catcher was youngest, the baby: he was eighty-three.

The fairgrounds covered a five-acre tract of flat but various ground, the well-mown bank of Roebuck Lake. Chickasaws in dugouts once floated upon these cypress-darkened waters past the single white-man's cabin and, pointing, named the spot in their own tongue, *biccauhgli*, a word that once meant perhaps "home in the woods" and later became the name of the town standing upon this site, Big Ugly, Mississippi.

There were camp tables and card tables and sawhorses laid with clean boards and covered with white tablecloths. Women set out hot casseroles and bowls of steaming vegetables and platters of sliced meats and fruit. There were Methodist folding chairs and Baptist coffee urns; there were plastic dispensers of iced tea and Kool Aid; there were stacks of paper plates and boxes of plastic forks. There was a bluegrass band from Memphis, and the community's Bicentennial flag was flying. Charles Kuralt was rumored to be in town.

There were bows and arrows everywhere, straight bows, recurved bows, hardwoods, fiberglass, laminations, longbows of yew, flat bows of lemonwood, steel bows with metal sights, stabilized bows, twins, monos, balls, and outriggers. There were all manner of archers, young and old, blind and sighted, crippled and crazy, those in uniforms and those near naked, Robin Hoods and college girls, snapshooters and practitioners of Zen, wheelchair archers and power archers, all of them in teams of two, an archer and a catcher, and in each team at least one who was willing to kill for the right to enter this competition and at least one willing to be killed for that right.

Or so most of them probably told themselves, though it was not true. Competition in the Arrow-Catcher Fair required rubber-tipped blunts, and while an arrow from a strong bow could knock a man down, injuries were rare. Most "misses" never touched the catcher, since a proper catch required at least a partial turning of the body, and arrow burns on the palms and fingers were the most common injury. Resin helped prevent blisters. The Arrow-Catcher Fair was, all agreed, no threat to the health of Mississippians; the true threat, according to local wags, was the annual Snuff-Dipping Convention in Grenada.

The first elimination trials were over. Last year's champion had been put away early, an arrow catcher of about sixty-five and his archer grandson. A youthful team from Montana made the first and second cuts and was as impressive as the rumors that preceded it here. There were other hopefuls as well, including a number of local teams.

The crowds grew larger, most of their number only spectators. Couples and families gathered on the grounds, a sweet hint of marijuana smoke hung in the air. Here a young mother dangled a careless foot in the cool lake's edge; there clustered a family beneath a spreading cottonwood. The women's competition was already finished; mixed team competition was in its last round. Charles Kuralt's CBS van had been spotted for certain, and—so another rumor had it—the governor of the state was on the grounds again this year.

The Montana team continued to practice, the archer standing at some forty yards' distance from his catcher. The archer drew and the arrow was gone. The catcher did not watch the arrow because he could not, he watched only a furrow in the atmosphere where he knew it flew. He did not feel his body turn left at thirty degrees because now the turning was reflexive, he did not know how he knew to make his sudden move toward the colored density that was the arrow because that too was reflex, he did not know how he plucked the arrow from the air and held it vibrating in his astonished hand. There was a small, desultory round of applause from the group that happened to be standing nearby. The Montana catcher tossed the arrow aside and waited for the next.

The scene was repeated many times throughout the little fairgrounds, archers and catchers performing for each other. But it was not these moments of practice or even the more tense moments of competition that were the true center of the day. The center was the blood and flesh of the three ancients who were the originals of this celebration, Redboy, Arrow Catcher, and Miss Golden, launching and catching and cursing, the first three human hearts to have quickened when the first wobbly arrow flew, a sharpened stick merely, almost fourscore years before from the Indian's homemade bow.

Golden's brother lost his real name at the age of five when

121

he became the Arrow Catcher, and though Golden remembered her brother's birth that summer long ago on the mosquito-loud sleeping porch of their home, where her schizophrenic helpless mother lay upon a mattress stuffed with the down of fowls killed and plucked by Golden herself and beneath a clean comforter stitched with muscadines by Golden's grandmother during the Mexican War, she was not certain she remembered her brother's name. It might have been Gilbert. He had been the Arrow Catcher too long to remember.

She remembered her father as a quiet, gentle ghost who long ago slipped away from her mother's bedside and madness and was forgotten, who left before Arrow Catcher was born, and she remembered her mother only in bed, usually crying. Her memories survived from a time when the railroad came to Big Ugly. Her mother, beautiful and schizophrenic for many years before Mississippi even had a name for the problem, lay abed and wept and believed from the year 1894 until the day of her death that she herself was the train for which tracks were being laid near their home. "Chuffa-chuffa," that sick woman called during hard labor. "Chooooo choooooo," she had cried in childbirth. She believed also that in the large old drafty house in which she lay there were narrow-gauge rails on which in time of emergency she might fit her wheels and escape calamity, fire for example, or flood, both of which she expected almost daily. As a girl Golden sought and sought the tracks that her mother supposed lay upon their floors and never found them. For this folly she hated her mother. "Clickety-clack, clickety-clack," the poor woman said, considering her escape. Golden hid in a cedar wardrobe and wished she understood. "Clickety-clack, clickety-clack."

Golden hated the railroad, the real one, the felling of the trees, and the raising of great blackened timbers from which bark had been hacked for depot shingles, the timbers that would become the columns for the trestle across Roebuck, the iron and the hammers that made and laid the rails, the section gangs of bare-chested men, white and black, the oak that became the crossties and the rock that became the ballast, where, in the clash and clatter and clutter and enormity of its building, her mother's mind would steal quietly out of town and never be heard from again and in which her brother would catch his first arrow and become the Arrow Catcher.

It was in one of the years of the railroad's construction that Golden would first curse the Indian. "Listen to me, you no-count redskin," the child-woman would say, cursing above the trundle and thunder of construction, the clink of steel upon steel chiming in her brain as the rails went down, the first arrow from the first little willow bow already in flight as she spoke, and yet hardly an arrow at all, a sharpened branch of wild pecan in wobbly career toward the little white boy's bare frail breast, "if one of those pecan arrows hits my little brother, son," she would say on that morning of a leafy-warm mid-June when the Mississippi Delta air was already dense and heavy and sweet with humidity and honeysuckle, "you won't be able to trade your greasy scalp and nappy ass together for a handful of strung beads, so got-doggit, Redboy, just be careful."

The five-year-old boy, her brother, already at so early an age beginning to withdraw like his mother into a strange quiet netherworld into which no one else, except perhaps the Indian, successfully entered, picked the arrow from the air like a bursting-ripe wild plum from a laden tree, and became in that moment the Arrow Catcher.

The red boy, older than the others but no one knew how old except that he was old enough to smell worse than the white children and most of the black ones, fitted another crude barreled shaft of pecan onto his bowstring and loosed a second shot.

Golden Rondelle cursed him again. "You useless low-class wild Indian savage bastard," she cried, "shame on your shameful red ass shooting sticks at that sweet little child, you are shameful and useless as tits on a boar hog shooting arrows at that child."

The quiet small hand of the Arrow Catcher collected the second speeding shaft from the air as easily as he might a fat late-summer firefly lazy with August.

The Indian child, handing his bow and a little clutch of arrows to Golden Rondelle, unhitched and took down his tattered filthy breeches to urinate into the lespedeza. "Hold my quiver, Goldie," he said. "I got to dreen my lizard."

Redboy no longer stank, and his clothes were neither tattered nor dirty. Today at the Arrow-Catcher Fair he was a quiet ancient little man, almost black and no more than five feet four inches tall, the tight mahogany of his skin rendering his face almost invisible in contrast to the brilliance of his false teeth. He wore a carefully tailored sport jacket of a fashionable cut, deep burgundy in color. The lenses of his sunglasses were also shaded burgundy. In his hands he held his best bow, a recurved composite with an ebony grip and a fifty-five-pound draw weight. A leather ground quiver of new arrows was stuck by its spike into the earth nearby.

"Arrow Catcher," said Golden Rondelle, trying again to remember whether they had named the child Gilbert and remembering only the down mattress and the unbleached muslin sheets and the comforter and remembering also the perfect little child, her brother, who had issued from her mother's body as Golden brought forth sweet artesian water drawn up from the cistern in a zinc bucket, remembering also the midwife, whom Golden called the granny-woman, the near-blind black woman who made the delivery, and remembering the clean glass jar of afterbirth and the placenta, which frightened her because she did not know what it was, and the strong white thread that cut the fleshy cord from her brother's body, "that renegade is going to shoot a hole through you one of these days big enough for a hen turkey to jump through and where please tell me will you be then? Dead is where, so don't bother to make reply. I don't want to know."

"Hush up now, Miss Sister," the Arrow Catcher said, or might have said if he still spoke, as he had not for sixty-five years, but saying as much to Golden in his unspeaking as other men said with a million words, speaking perhaps through his beatific smile. "Hush now, Miss Sister, it's all right."

"Gotdoggit, Arrow Catcher," she said, "you were blessed from birth with the lowest blood pressure on the planet Earth and not enough sense to crap in a hole."

"Step back, Goldie," the Indian said, polite as always. "You don't want to give the boy reservations."

"Don't you get ironical with me, Redboy," she said, "because I have no reservations whatsoever about turning your hide into a Chickasaw hook rug and selling it in Oklahoma. And don't shoot another arrow at that white boy until I say so, do you understand me, or I'll make you think the Trail of Tears was the Amtrak Special to Miami. Gotdog. I can't stand an aboriginal."

The Indian chose an arrow from the ground quiver and inspected its fletching. Real feathers, four of them, and thick enough to slow the arrow drastically upon its leaving the bow. He liked to give the Arrow Catcher a few of these first, once he had started using the heavy bow. The sleek shafts with three narrow strips of plastic fletching would come later. Then he would alternate a few, some slow arrows among the swiftest. Therein lay the Arrow Catcher's true genius and mastery of time and space and the bodily organs. There was the reason the competition halted when the Arrow Catcher began work, and there was the reason the Arrow Catcher and the Indian were never a part of the competition and were never expected to be. Therein lay the artistry to which young men whose aspirations lay in the field of arrow catching aspired. He held the shaft lovingly in his hand, turning it. The blade—and this also was a difference between the Arrow Catcher and the rest—the blade that the

Indian held and that the Arrow Catcher would catch was a bodkin, a triple-edged hunter's blade, solid sharp steel.

"Don't you do it, Redboy, don't you even think about it. Don't lay one more arrow on that string."

"Aw Goldie, come on now, hell," the Indian said, "give the boy time to think."

"Move back, Miss Sister," the Arrow Catcher might have said, though there was no sound, "move back, please'm."

"If you shoot that arrow, Redboy . . ."

The arrow was already gone. The bow from whose string the arrow flew was a precision instrument, a slender core of cedar laminated with fiberglass, and the arrow was not hardwood but a twenty-eight-inch tube of aluminum, a flu-flu arrow with three red fat turkey feathers and a yellow cock feather, an ariel hunting shaft, slow but with this bow faster than anything he had yet shot today. The arrow was in flight as the curse organized itself in Golden Rondelle's brain and upon her lips.

". . . I'll fix you so . . ."

In near-invisible flight the arrow traveled the thirty brief yards that it would travel between its anchor point at the Indian's chin and its destination in the Arrow Catcher's hand or heart, the thick fletching bustling and ruffling against the air like a small covey of quail rising from sorghum . . .

". . . your scalp won't sell for low-grade dog food . . ."

. . . not even quite visible, the shaft of aluminum, merely a disturbance of the atmosphere, not only to Golden Rondelle but to her brother the Arrow Catcher, who both saw and did not see, heard and did not hear the flurry and bustle and rush and flutter of tumultuous gossiping feathers, and yet not invisible quite, something there in the sun, metallic and swift and formless, a thickening . . .

". . . I'll sell your scalp to a chiropractor with Ohio license plates . . ."

. . . and the Arrow Catcher, now as she watched him, seeing and not seeing, hearing for the first time distinctly the shaft bearing, preening down upon him, turned, only slightly, to his left, dropping his shoulder, the left shoulder, ever so slightly, and grasped in a perfect marriage of firmness and gentleness, as one lifts a warm speckled egg from beneath an old hen, in the smallest portion of a dangerous second, the hurtling aluminum streak. It was no longer the whispering whistling lustering mystery it had been one second earlier in the air. It was a quick momentary hum and drone upon his hand's flesh and in his ear and then nothing, a shaft of aluminum, a bodkin, four bright feathers. He tossed the arrow aside.

Golden was finished. Not all of the curse that passed through her mind was ever actually formed upon her tongue; there had been no time. The curse faltered and sputtered to a halt, stopped. Her little brother was safe.

"Let's go grab us a bite of that chicken and potato salad," said the Indian.

"I'm not eating fried chicken with an aboriginal, I can guarantee you that, Little Beaver," said Golden Rondelle.

They stopped now and ate without speaking. The crowd around them began to disperse. On the public address there was an announcement for qualifiers in the late rounds and then another announcement concerning novelty events.

The Arrow Catcher and the Indian sat facing different directions, eating little, and taking no coffee or tea, no stimulants. They rested and said nothing. Miss Golden sat apart from them, as she always did when the Indian was near, but in a position to see them both. She ate two helpings of bean salad with red onions.

The final arrows of the competition were shot and caught, the young Montana team progressing through the final round but losing, as expected, to an experienced pair of brothers from Bellafontaine. The bluegrass group was better than last year's, an energetic combination of banjos and harmonicas and guitars and a very tall young man with a washboard of elaborate design. *Bisquick* was the name printed on the drums.

Later the lieutenant governor was introduced from the bandstand and was helped up to the microphone. He was received with polite applause, and when the microphone and speakers stopped squealing he began his annual address, "Welcome, friends, welcome to the Arrow-Catcher Fair." As it became clear to the audience that the band was taking a break, there was a good deal of milling around and moving away from the platform to other parts of the grounds.

Still, some remained, and there was something about the speech that caught the ear of Miss Golden Rondelle. At first she could not hear well, so she turned and stood up, moving away from the Indian and the Arrow Catcher toward the speaker. She dropped the rest of the bean salad into the trash barrel. A few others had begun to listen as well, more than a few, a great many, though they had not intended to listen. The crowd moved back to the places where they had stood or sat for Bisquick and could not believe what they were seeing and hearing. The lieutenant governor was drunk and, whatever his subject, he was warming to it quickly. Charles Kuralt and CBS were filming and taping.

The lieutenant governor pointed across the fairgrounds at the raised flag of the Bicentennial. He spoke of the people of this great and solemn state—sovereign state, he had meant to say, correcting himself, then reneging on the correction and saying solemn again and again.

Miss Golden was at last close enough to hear, and now the noises of the crowd were quieting rapidly. The lieutenant governor had found his proper distance from the microphone and his voice rocked the Arrow-Catcher Fair like a calliope. Many were listening now, and others were on their way. The speech continued, wildly, the lieutenant governor borrowing freely from the Sermon on the Mount and Lincoln's Gettysburg Address and anything else that came to mind. "Hernando by-God de Soto," she heard him say. "Hernando buggering de Soto," he was saying, "great spic founder of this solemn state . . ." This was not the first time the lieutenant governor had embarrassed the state, but it was the first time on national television, and, as everyone must correctly have supposed, it would be the last time he would embarrass anyone ever again, for could there be any doubt that the governor would have him executed?

". . . led a band of eccentric white men through this stinking buckshot and gumbo shithole that tries to pass for the real world and began," he said, "by mating with the abominable Chickasaw and Choctaw to people our solemn shores with lunatics, made these alluvial fields and pastures and piney woods and swamps and bearcats and all our abominations of geography America's first and last rich stronghold of lunacy and feeblemindedness and dwarfism in a proud and unhappy land . . ."

The crowd was dumbstruck. They were both moved to laughter and unable to laugh. They were silent and horrified; they were mass silence masking hysteria. Every man and woman among them was scandalized and stood in dread of some unnamed impending doom about to fall like acid rain upon the state and this pasture. Those who liked the lieutenant governor and those who despised him were equally scandalized and horrified, those who voted for him and those who had threatened him with homicide. It was a dark day for the Arrow-Catcher Fair.

". . . proud of our individualism in Mississippi," he was saying, "individually, man for man, woman for woman, child for child, the most individually obscene and corrupt populace and geography, save only Los Angeles and Gary, Indiana, in an entire obscene civilization . . ."

To all who watched and listened, it was finally clear: this was no ordinary drunken scene at a fair. This was no ordinary exhibition of a failed man and a ruined rummy politician. This was the ugly deliberate song of a mortally wounded political swan, a deliberate humiliation of the governor and of the entire state. "This is Charles Kuralt" was the phrase that in this crowd every mind's ear heard upon every mind's evening news, "on the road. Welcome to the Arrow-Catcher Fair." Someone rushed from the crowd to find out whether the governor had yet left the fairgrounds. A large red-haired, red-faced man stood reduced to tears, begging Charles Kuralt please to stop the cameras.

". . . proud," the lieutenant governor was saying, "of our individualism, proud of our pain, we are proud of our neurotic romanticism and our feelings of inferiority, proud of our pathetic apologies and of our pathetic failures to apologize, proud of the bloody stains of our guilt, we are proud of our psychotic rage never to question or wonder and always to justify and create . . ."

A shout came from the crowd. The governor was on his way, someone cried. Make way for the governor. There was a sudden release of the silent storm inside the crowd, a partial release anyway, a flurry of whispers and uncertain movement and coughing. "Come on down, Lee," an older man at the foot of the platform said to the speaker, "come on down, man, that's enough, godamighty." But the lieutenant governor did not stop.

". . . proud," he said again, pointing again irrationally at the flag and again no less careless of historical accuracy, "to have become inhabitants of this blessed land of perversity, founded by an insane Spaniard in his insane and successful discovery of that mightiest of insane rivers, insane father of insane waters, potent puissant pregnant pointless pissant stream! That very snakish flood in which God's own unholy self of the Holy Ghost resides, yea verily I say unto you, even unto this day in the form of an alligator gar, molded from the Mississippi clay by God's own mighty hand upon Christ's eternal wheel in prescient anticipation of our present governor's mind and soul and face, I have a dream, brothers and sisters, I have a dream . . ."

Two state troopers in uniform mounted the bandstand and tried to lead him gently away. He would not be led. Both troopers, trying not to face the whirring cameras, were embarrassed literally to tears. They tugged at him and he would not move. There was a scuffle, a brief struggle, which the lieutenant governor won because the troopers were unsure what to do, how much force to use. "Turn off the camera, Mr. Kuralt, please Jesus just turn it off," one of the troopers begged, directly into the microphone, but the film kept rolling.

Unnoticed, across the pasture, the Indian and the Arrow Catcher had begun work again, shooting arrows and catching them. Golden Rondelle, in these first stirrings of a recognition of the futility of her own bitterness, had forgotten to watch out for her brother. She was not there to curse them.

". . . I have a dream," said the lieutenant governor, kicking at those who would restrain him, "of the scaly, snouted gar-God and life-giver and life-destroyer of all Mississippians submerged in the bloody rivers of our lands and hearts . . ." He held the microphone in a passionate triumphant death-grip, the state troopers tugging hopelessly at his shirt. The governor of the state, a handsome man in a white Prince Albert suit, mounted the platform, grappling with the lieutenant governor for the microphone, but in the confusion could not wrest it from him. One of the troopers, suddenly feeling sorry for the lieutenant governor, began to fight on his side. Fists flew, none of them yet touching the lieutenant governor.

". . . eternal sustainer of our inherited alluvial madness and more green-headed mallard drakes in the rice brakes than you can shake a shitty stick at, hand me up that Co-Cola bottle, sonny, I got to dreench my weasle . . ."

His words were becoming incoherent now and crazy and something in them and behind them—it was the distant but very real sound of a diesel freight that Golden did not know yet that she heard—made her remember what she had forgotten, the Indian and her little brother.

Frantic, she looked behind her, far across the astonished flood of faces, and saw the two of them. "Arrow Catcher!" she screamed, already pushing through the crowd. "Redboy!" People stepped aside for her, she bumped against them roughly, making her way. "Redboy, don't do it! Arrow Catcher! This is the hour of your death!"

On the bandstand there was a second, more violent struggle, and this time the speaker was subdued. He fell to the platform, kicking and biting and cursing. The microphone crashed to the earth, the amplifier screaming, the lieutenant governor grabbing for it and pulling it to him where he lay. Several men fell on top of the downed lieutenant governor, the two troopers and the governor among them, scuffling and scratching and punching. "Goddamn this very Delta earth beneath our feet," boomed the calliope voice of the amplifiers, "goddamn these spreading trees, goddamn these matchless Mississippi blue skies." These were the last words audible in the struggle.

The train was approaching the trestle, Golden's only thought was of death; she could not say why.

"It is the hour of your death, dear Lincoln," she cried to her brother. "Don't release the arrow, Redboy, or Lincoln will die!" So that was the child-man's name, she thought, her brother's name. Lincoln, not Gilbert. She had remembered. It seemed impossible that she should ever have forgotten.

She shoved and jostled and bumped and pushed. The crowd opened for her but slowly. Lincoln had caught two arrows since she started making her way toward him. At last she broke through the unsteady crust of the crowd's edge and began running, as fast as she could, old woman with the yellow hoot and rumble of the diesel in her ears, across the pasture, straight for her brother. She was still screaming. Lincoln had caught another arrow.

There was time somehow to wonder at the coincidence of the lieutenant governor's insane speech and the approach of the train to the trestle. She wondered whether it was really a coincidence at all that these two things should happen just as she remembered her brother's name. She believed rather that on this instant she had suddenly become old enough and wise enough and bitter enough to swim beyond her lost childhood and bitterness and to take all the earth's available phenomena, natural, mechanical, and political, and shape them into meaning. The speech from the platform had made her old enough; the approach of the freight translated the lieutenant governor's voice to the voice of memory. She ran toward her brother, screaming. She reached him, calling his name, Lincoln Lincoln Lincoln. She touched him.

As she did, as her hand felt the soft fabric of his shirt and felt through the fabric the tense little muscles of her brother's shoulder, she thought, Uh-oh. She thought, I shouldn't have done this. Redboy has not seen me, he sees nothing but his target. He hears nothing. An arrow will be leaving his bow soon, and my hand on this little shoulder may distract, may prevent my brother from catching it. She wondered if the arrow would hit her brother, or if it would hit herself. It could scarcely be hoped to miss both of them. Or could it? He had never missed before, not once in decades. But he had never been touched upon the shoulder while trying. Oh dear, oh shit.

Too late the Indian saw Golden Rondelle move into the tunnel of his pinpoint-focused vision, the narrow squinty line of sight that was the concentrated entirety of his attention. Too late he saw that the bowstring was no longer in his fingertips, that the arrow was already inexorably launched.

The arrow carried a broadhead, a razor-sharp hunting blade of triangular shape, and the fletching was sleek swift plastic. She thought, though there was no time for thought, that the sound of the train, both the remembered steam engine in her mind and the yellow diesel not forty yards away on the trestle, was the sound of her mother's voice: "Chuffa-chuffa," during labor. "Chooooooo choooooooo," during birth. "Clickety-clack," in her imagined escape from fire and flood and probably from everything else that this handkerchief-sized spot of earth had meant to her.

As the train approached the trestle, Golden thought that not far from here where we stand waiting upon death or salvation there are children waiting. If children were today the same as they had been so many years ago, they were hiding in the great ditch bordering the tracks, waiting in lespedeza and Johnson grass and wild chinaberries, children black and white and even red, boys and girls, waiting for the train to slow almost to stopping before it crossed the Roebuck trestle. There were children, she thought, at this moment waiting until the last possible second to rush from their hiding to grab the cold ladder of a boxcar, to pull themselves shrieking and squealing and swinging aboard. These children would, as Golden and Redboy and Lincoln had done, ride the train across the trestle triumphant and then, like the lieutenant governor, jump suicidal to safety before the train took speed again on the other side.

The voice of the train was the voice of her mother naming rivers, as sometimes for hours she would do, the rivers and tributaries of Mississippi, most of them with Chickasaw and Choctaw names, the rivers she would cross when all the trestles were built and she would be allowed to roll free at last from the bed of her affliction and confusion and from the geography that had confused her. "Coldwater," the woman-train would begin, slowly, "Yazoo," still slowly, "Yazoo, Yocona," heaving, straining for even the smallest increase of speed, "Yocona, Skuna, Bogue, Hickahala," faster now, faster and faster, sobbing deeply and more deeply, "Hickahala, Hickahala, Yalobusha Yalobusha Tallahatchie Tallahatchie whoooooo whooooooo!" faster and faster, into the final register, crossing at full tilt the mighty river at Greenville, not even bothering to slow down for the trestle, "Tallahatchie Tallahatchie Mississippi Mississippi Mississippi, whooooo whooooooo!" headed west, westward westward forever and away.

And if there are children there today, she thought, waiting in their secret ditch for the train, this yellow diesel, was there not also in the reeds among them a little girl, as once she had been, whose mother was too sick ever to tell her she was pretty? Was there in the reedy ditch or on the boxcar's rusty ladder one who, like Golden Rondelle, reared her mother and was not reared by her? who reared her brother and forgot her father and forgot her brother's name? and before that a child who watched, still holding the zinc bucket so heavy with sweet water that it cut into her little palm, her brother's painful emergence like that of a train from a tunnel unimaginably deep and dangerous? a child whom first she would protect as a man-child and then, as he joined his mother, and somehow also the Indian, in a netherworld in which he might escape his original emergence, protect him as a childman? Was there a child in the blackberry vines this moment as the arrow flew who found for so many years no source from which to draw either strength or sweetness and so drew it from within herself, from the deep cistern of heart behind the sweet face which no mother ever told her was beautiful, though then it was and even as the arrow continued in its flight remained so, drawing from this deep but finite source, unreplenished and unreplenishable, until she became almost as crazy as her mother and brother? And yet a child who, after so long, did love her brother and loved, at least in this insane moment, the strange memory of her strange sick mother and felt, painfully, an emotion for the Indian that she had carried inside her for so long and which even now in its sweetness she found impossible to give a name, knowing, however, something of that emotion because for so many years she had seen it shared between Lincoln and the Indian in their dangerous necessary game of habitual love made possible by death's terrible, sweet omnipresence.

Golden watched, though there was no time to watch, and saw, though even the slow arrows were invisible, the loosed arrow as it left its place upon the bow and string, this fastest and most dangerous of arrows. It seemed to bend upon the bow, first right then left, then to straighten itself in flight. Oh, this swift arrow was a deadly arrow and, as it slammed shut the distance between the archer and the catcher and as her fingers' grip tightened upon her brother's shoulder, she remembered that the Indian's name was Gilbert. So, she thought, that was why she had been mixed up. So Gilbert is the Indian's name, she thought. Hmm. Well, it's not a bad name, not at all. It's a nice name. But it's a damn strange name for an Indian.

Part II

The Attendant

Winston pulled the stick and turned his wheelchair and motored out of the living room and negotiated the corners of the apartment and finally stopped in the bedroom near the bed. Harris followed close behind him. Harris was sixteen, and this was his first day on the job.

Harris pushed the hydraulic lift close to the wheelchair and fitted it in tight. He slipped a canvas strap beneath Winston's legs and another strap behind his shoulders and then he attached the straps by their metal hooks to the chains on the lift.

He pushed at the long handle on the lift until Winston began to rise up in the air. When Winston was a foot or two above the chair, dangling in the straps at the end of the chains and high enough to clear the bed, Harris heard him say, "At euf." It meant, "That's enough," and was the way Winston was forced to talk when he was bunched up into this odd bundle.

It was the first time Harris had seen Winston on the lift and he thought that Winston looked like a sack of grain, and this made his stomach feel a little queasy.

He concentrated on looking only at Winston's face, but

this was not very pleasant either. Winston's eyes bulged and protruded from the pressure of hanging by the straps. Now Winston looked a little like a side of beef. The job was temporary, just until a permanent attendant could be found. Maybe it wouldn't take long to find somebody.

Harris positioned Winston above the bed and twisted the release valve slowly. The chains clanked and creaked and Winston was lowered, inch by inch, onto the sheepskin, first his butt and then slowly backwards. Harris put his hand behind Winston's head and neck as he would a baby and aimed Winston at the pillow. Finally Winston was stretched out full length on the bed.

Harris removed the straps and chains and pushed the lift into a corner. All right, that wasn't so bad.

Harris began to undress Winston for bed. First the shoes, then his socks and trousers and the support hose that kept Winston's feet from turning blue, and then the shirt and the corset.

Naked, Winston looked like a corpse. He was soft and white and his arms and legs were atrophied and small. Harris suddenly believed they would never find a permanent attendant to replace him.

Harris removed the leg-bag and pinched shut the opening in the tube so the urine would not leak out. He held his breath so that he did not smell the urine. He attached the catheter to a tube that ran into a gallon milk jug beside the bed. It would drain into the jug during the night and he would empty it in the morning.

Taking care that he did not accidentally dump Winston

off the bed, Harris rolled him onto his right side and propped him there with pillows behind his back. This would be Winston's sleeping position.

Winston's rear end was flat as a squashed hat, from being sat on all day. Harris could not even think about Winston's you-know-what—his penis—which was the only normal-looking part of him and so somehow the most abnormal part of all. He flexed Winston's legs and separated his knees with a pillow to prevent pressure sores. He put another pillow between Winston's feet.

Now the worst part. After this it would be over. With a large syringe, Harris drew irrigation fluid from a glass bottle and forced the fluid, with slow pressure on the plunger, through the catheter and into the stoma. He had looked at everything but the stoma, and now he was having to look at it. It was a strawberry-colored hole in Winston's lower belly, where the catheter was permanently implanted, a place where the bladder had been pulled forward and turned back and surgically sewn onto the stomach. The fluid was dark yellow and thick and some of it bubbled up out of the hole in Winston's belly and had to be sopped up with gauze.

And so then that was that. The day was over. His first day on the job. He hated it and he hoped Winston would find a replacement for him right away and that he would never have to look at another sick or crippled person for the rest of his life, but the good part of it was that the day was over.

One of Winston's nightly medications was a sleeping pill, a strong sedative, so when Winston had swallowed that, it was not long before he was asleep.

Harris was tired. He went into his room, the room he would sleep in.

He undressed to his jockey shorts and lay back on the bed. It was stuffy in the room, but he was too tired to try to open the window. He picked up a paperback novel he had brought with him and tried to read but he couldn't stay with it. He put the book aside.

He may have dozed for a while. When he looked at the clock, it was past midnight.

Harris was homesick. He thought of his mother putting up pints of dewberries at the kitchen sink, and of his father listening to old-fashioned music on the phonograph. He thought of his upstairs room—the only room he had ever had since he was a baby—with its deep angles in the ceiling and the luminous decals of stars and planets stuck to a portion of the ceiling over his bed.

He wished he knew someone to call. He realized for the first time how few friends he had. Even if it had not been past midnight he would not have known anyone to call.

He dialed a number for the time of day and listened to the friendly voice of the recording, a man, who spoke to him through the receiver. Next he called the weather and a recording of someone named Debbie started to talk to him.

Just then Harris heard Winston calling out from the other bedroom. Winston's voice was thick with the sleeping pill.

Harris hung up and went into Winston's room. Winston said, "Did we remember the suppositories?"

Harris could tell what a great effort it took for Winston to come awake from the drugs and to deal with responsible matters.

Harris said, "Suppositories?—no, I don't think I knew about them."

Winston said, "And the chuck."

Now Harris remembered. Winston was supposed to have a bowel movement tonight. He had one once a week, and it just happened to fall on Harris's first day on the job. Harris knew of the procedure, he had just forgotten. Harris longed for his own bed and the tiny worlds on the ceiling above it.

Harris found the box of "chucks" in the supply closet— things that looked like huge paper diapers to be spread under Winston's hip to protect the sheepskin. And then the suppositories, three of them. Harris felt a surge of panic overtake him for an instant, and then it subsided. He was not at all sure he could do this.

He held the three suppositories in his hand for a minute as if they were bullets. He stripped off the silver-colored foil and held them longer, looking at them in the half-light of the room. He opened the jar of Vaseline and greased them good, all three, and then, without any hope that he could look up a man's asshole and not be changed forever, he found the darkness at the center of Winston's flattened-out rear end and stuffed in one suppository and then the second and then the final one and withdrew his hand, his index finger, and wondered who on earth was this stranger occupying the same space as himself.

He washed his hands at the bathroom sink and floated—

seemed to float!—to his bed and lay back on the sheets, mindless and strangely happy, and did not even notice when he went to sleep.

*A*t first Harris did not know what had waked him. He looked at his clock and saw that more than three hours had passed.

He was groggy and confused. For a moment he believed he was at home—his parents' home—and that something was wrong, that someone was sick or in danger. Then he remembered that he was living with Winston.

Still he was not sure why he was awake. He considered this for a long time, two minutes maybe. As his head cleared, he understood that he had been wakened by a smell.

Harris struggled from his bed and bumped against a table and knocked something heavy onto the floor. It was the small suitcase he had brought with him. It contained all his clothes and his good shoes and a cap he never wore but that his mother had thrown in.

He groped his way over to the window and tried to open it and found that he didn't know how. He had lived in a house all his life, he didn't know how to open these dinky little apartment windows.

He had had no idea the smell was going to be so bad. He had not allowed himself to think of it at all. When he had greased and inserted the suppositories, he had allowed himself no fantasy of the results they might effect.

He wanted to hold on to something that he owned. He felt around in the dark for the suitcase. He picked it up and set it, at first, on the little table where it had been, and then on second thought put it on the bed where he had been sleeping. He felt along the wall for the light switch.

When the light was on he felt better. But the smell! The smell was like nothing else he had ever smelled before. No dog, no cat box, no baby's diaper, no open outhouse—nothing had ever smelled so bad as this.

He opened the door of his room. The smell buckled his knees. It was much worse in the hallway. His stomach heaved, but he forced it into submission.

He shut the door and turned off his light and hid in his dark room. He went back to his bed and lay down beside the suitcase. He held the suitcase to him like a lover, if he had ever held a lover. He broke into a sweat. His eyes were stinging. The smell was forever. It was as permanent as gravity, unavoidable.

He wanted to run away. It was not possible, he could not run.

He swung his legs off the bed. There was something new in him—like madness, and like prayer. He found the light switch, he opened his door again.

The smell was there, as fierce as an alligator, as fierce as grief.

He stepped into the hallway. He reeled around and bumped into the walls, he staggered and almost fell. It would get no worse than this.

And yet when he opened the door to Winston's room, it was much worse. A tomahawk of shit-smell struck him from ambush. Poisoned darts of shit-smell flew up his nose. He collapsed backwards and caught himself in the doorframe.

This was a turning point, when he did not fall down and die. Suddenly he knew that he was invincible, he was superhuman. No power in heaven or on earth could fell him now. There was no such thing as unbearable sorrow, no pain that could not be borne. The world was a golden place, filled up with good souls and a loving God.

Harris turned on the light and saw that Winston was still sound asleep. The smell had not awakened him. The instinct to survive could wake a man from strong narcotics to ask for a laxative, but the smell of mere shit could not. It put life into perspective, it encouraged Harris and gave him hope for the future of man.

He looked down at the covers on Winston's bed, the massive corpselike lump beneath them. The sheet and light blanket and spread would have to be pulled back.

He kept standing there. He didn't want to do it.

He remembered that he should have plugged in Winston's chair before he went to bed, to recharge the battery. He would do that now, before he forgot again. He picked up the heavy cord and the plug and stuck the large end into the wall socket and the small yellow tips into the chair receptacle. He turned the dial on the charger to five hours. He took as long as he could, doing this, but then he had to face the covers again.

It had to be done. Harris walked around to the far side of the bed, behind Winston's back. He took the covers in his hand, making certain he had them all, sheet, blanket, spread. He hoped the chuck was secure.

He pulled the covers back and exposed Winston's rear end. No smell could harm him now.

No smell—but the sight of it sent him reeling backwards again. No cow in the pastures could have made a plop so large as the one Harris was looking at. In fact, it looked exactly like cow plop. Same size, same shape.

Harris's surging stomach settled back into place. He tried to remember the fresh clean fragrance of the pastures nearby, a smell of large slow animals and of hay and red clover and fresh water and salt licks on the posts. He could not make the cow-smell come to him.

Winston woke up. His voice was thick with the sleeping pill. He grunted something that Harris could not understand. Harris was amazed that he could feel miserable and joyous at the same time. Harris said, "Time for a little cleanup." He would have described his own voice as chirpy.

Winston said, "That's the, ah, that's just what . . ." He was too sleepy to finish.

Harris took the nearer side of the chuck between his fingers and gave a slow even tug, just an inch or two, to see what would happen. The chuck was backed with blue plastic, which slipped evenly along the sheepskin and brought the pile with it.

Harris stopped. That's the way it worked, then. He would pull it out, very carefully. He would make sure he kept the sheepskin clean. He might have to get some toilet paper. Then he would roll up the whole package and get rid of it.

That's what he did. It took a little while, but it was no problem.

When he was done, he put on his jeans and walked out

the door with the rolled-up chuck and went to the Dempster Dumpster in the parking lot and tossed it in.

The night air was clean and lovely. The clouds were rolling, and sometimes the moon showed itself from behind them. The streets were wet beneath his bare feet, and the streetlights were reflected in pools of water left by a light rain. Harris felt wonderful and awake and alive.

He went back inside the apartment, which did not smell so bad as before. Opening the doors had seemed to help. Harris's stomach was still jumpy, but he was not sick. He got a basin and filled it with warm water. He took a washcloth from the bathroom.

Winston was awake enough to say, in a sleepy voice, "All done?"

Harris said, "Just about got her whipped." Nothing chirpy about that voice, nothing phony.

He squeezed warm water through the cloth and began to bathe Winston's rear end. He dried Winston with a fresh towel and pulled the covers up so that Winston would not become chilled.

Harris turned and looked at the window in Winston's room and saw that it opened to the side. He flipped a small latch and moved the glass to the left. It slid easily and let in the smell of summer rain and new greenery.

"Okay, then," Harris said, with confidence. "We'll get a few more hours' sleep."

Winston said, "Uh, better, ah, get a few . . ." He was asleep before he could finish.

Harris walked to the bathroom. So this was the way it was

going to be. That was all right. He emptied the water from the basin into the bathroom sink and washed his hands. He went into his own room and opened the window easily. The slow soaking rain, which had started again, made its small sound in the parking lot.

Harris lay in his bed and listened. He breathed deeply and thought he could smell the cows, dry and dusty in their barns somewhere across the fields beyond the road, and he was certain he could smell wet clover and hay bales and melting salt licks and wooden troughs filled with rainwater.

Harris made coffee the next morning, and soon Winston was awake. From the kitchen window Harris could see the slow movement of tree limbs and telephone wires in the breeze, and he saw the ungraceful flight of a flock of black-birds.

Harris gave Winston his morning bath, there in the bed. He used the same basin as he had used the night before. Harris could look at every part of Winston's body without fear, even at Winston's normal-looking penis, which was erect this morning and stayed erect during much of the bath. Even it did not seem grotesque. Harris powdered Winston's feet and pulled on the support hose and hitched up the corset that corrected Winston's spinal curvature. He fitted the leg-bag onto Winston's thigh and attached the bag to the catheter. Next his trousers and shirt, and next the clumsy ride on the hydraulic lift and into the wheelchair. Harris brushed Winston's teeth and shaved him with an electric razor and combed his hair.

He went to the living room and put music on the phonograph and heard the hum of Winston's chair as it motored through the house toward the kitchen table.

Harris knew nothing about the music Winston listened to. He looked at the album covers and saw a picture of Louis Armstrong as a young man. Louis Armstrong was the only face he recognized among the photographs on the albums. There was a band called King-something and another called Kid-something else.

Harris said, "There was a red place on your balls this morning, when I bathed you."

Winston said, "Hm."

Harris said, "It was like a stripe. A bright red stripe."

Winston said, "Remember you set me up straight in the chair yesterday, when I had slumped down? It must have pulled my pants up around my scrotum. It could have caused a lesion."

Harris knew this was dangerous. He was disappointed in himself.

Winston said, "No harm done. It happens sometimes."

Harris said, "I'll do better. I'll be more careful."

Harris poured coffee. The music was still playing. It was not Louis Armstrong, it was somebody else. He didn't know how to listen to the music.

Harris put a long plastic tube into Winston's coffee cup and guided the other end to Winston's mouth. He watched Winston drinking the coffee—his high forehead, his wiry black hair, his big handsome face. Harris squatted and unzipped the zipper on Winston's trouser leg and checked

154

the bag and found that it was filling properly. He gave Winston his medication—this pill for muscle spasms, this capsule for something else, this for something else again.

He walked behind Winston to the refrigerator and saw the back of Winston's head. There at the crown was a bald spot. It was a large piece of scar tissue left over from an operation, or maybe many operations.

He asked Winston about the scar and Winston only said, "I had two holes drilled in my head."

Harris sat at the table across from Winston and said, "I like this music, I think."

Winston kept drinking his coffee through the tube and said nothing at all. This seemed very right to Harris. It was a quiet grown-up life, Harris thought.

Mornings Harris bathed and dressed Winston. He cooked the coffee and scrambled the eggs and spooned them into Winston's mouth. He took Winston to the office where Winston worked as a counselor.

And then Harris was alone at the apartment. It was early summer, so there was no school. Sometimes Harris's mother called to see if Harris was all right, to ask if he was eating any vegetables, and he was always happy to hear her voice.

Once he went over to his parents' home for a visit and found no one at home. He let himself in with a key his mother kept in the bird-feeder and went up to his old room. He saw the blue nylon satchel he kept his soccer equipment in and for some reason he laughed, a little sadly, when he saw it.

He took the family dog for a walk through the woods of a

park near the house and he felt for the first time in his life that he had a past.

Back at the apartment he listened to music on Winston's phonograph. He tried a record by someone called Sidney Bechet and found that he could pick out the saxophone from the other instruments and was happy to learn from the album jacket that this was Bechet himself. He listened and thought he could pick out a couple of other instruments as well, but he was not sure.

He read on the dust cover of the album that Bechet's "vibrato" was particularly strong, and he felt stupid that he did not know the meaning of the word.

Grab your coat and get your hat . . . , the horns told him. Somehow the words of the song were in his head, though he could not remember ever having heard the song before. *Leave your worries on the doorstep* . . . Every note seemed to apply directly to himself. *Just direct your feet* . . . A saxophone solo came on. Now he understood vibrato. A trumpet took over the melody, pure against the throaty voice of the saxophone. And then a trombone. How did he recognize it? He had never heard a record so clearly before. This was what it meant to be grown-up.

He turned off the phonograph and sat in the fullness of the silence around him.

There was one more thing that happened.

It was near the end of summer. Harris had held the job nearly three months now. School would be starting soon, his senior year.

Harris's replacement had been found, the permanent attendant. He was a middle-aged man, very short, a midget almost. He wore a dapper moustache that, along with his rolled-down white socks and run-down shoes and polyester shirts, made him look all the more foolish. Dallas Armstrong was the new man's name.

He had no experience, Dallas Armstrong admitted, but he needed this job, he said, he really did, and he sure was willing to learn, he could learn almost anything if he was given half a chance.

Harris was secretly pleased at the pathetic figure Dallas Armstrong cut.

And Dallas was very clumsy, it turned out. His hands trembled as Harris showed him how to irrigate the catheter. He averted his eyes at the sight of the stoma. With Dallas Armstrong at the controls of the hydraulic lift, Winston looked like a daring trapeze act in the circus. The first erection Dallas saw on Winston sent him into a spasm of hysterical giggling. He forgot to plug the chair into the battery charger and Winston had to creep around at the slowest speed all the next day.

In private Winston asked Harris to stay and help train Dallas Armstrong. Winston said, "I'm not so sure about this guy."

Harris said, "He's all right. Give him some time. He'll be fine, just fine."

Harris agreed to stay a few days, a week maybe. Dallas could have the bedroom, Harris didn't mind sleeping on the sofa, no problem.

It was late August. The summer heat rose from the asphalt outside in the parking lot. Winston kept the air conditioning on high, to prevent excessive sweating and irritation. In the pastures cattle stood knee-deep in the black ponds.

The day came when it was time for the suppositories.

Harris had not mentioned the procedure to Dallas until now. He said, "The Vaseline is there, on the bedside table." He held out his hand and showed Dallas the little bullet-shaped devices in his open palm. He felt cruel and powerful and complete.

Dallas's moustache twitched, his eyes stared straight ahead. Written on his face was the question, How badly do I need this job?

Dallas Armstrong extended his hand and took the suppositories from Harris. He held them there and stared at them. He said, as if to explain something to someone, maybe to himself, "I am a bachelor."

Harris had never tortured anyone before. There are so few persons vulnerable to torture. And yet that was not the reason. The reason was that he had been a child until now. Torture was an act of adulthood, the same as love. What he had shared with Winston was love. It was marriage. The incredible intimacy, the physicality and shared need. And now this, whatever it was, this power.

Dallas Armstrong had broken into a smelly sweat.

Harris said, "Just put them in."

Dallas uncapped the jar of Vaseline. He dug in his index finger and brought out a glob of grease.

For a moment Harris was disappointed. He thought Dallas had fully recovered himself. Dallas's hand did not tremble. In his own prissy clumsy way Dallas Armstrong seemed to be taking care of business.

Then Harris noticed that Dallas was greasing the suppositories without having removed the foil wrappers.

Harris feigned gentleness and took the suppositories from Dallas and removed the foil and showed him the correct procedure.

Winston was already drugged and lay snoring in the bed.

Harris pulled back the sheet and exposed Winston's rear end. "Right there," Harris said, pointing.

Harris watched Dallas Armstrong move into position and find the dark little puckered opening into Winston's squashed-hat ass, and then he watched the little bullets disappear, one two three, and he heard Dallas Armstrong release a long sigh and withdraw his finger.

Waking on time was second nature to Harris now. He came awake on the sofa where he had slept these five days. There was a streetlight in the parking lot outside, the objects in the room seemed silvery and familiar.

He looked at the clock, and saw that a few hours had passed. He sat up and rubbed his face in his hands.

It was odd that he didn't smell anything. Was Winston slow tonight?

He walked to Winston's room and opened the door, and still there was no smell.

When he pulled back the covers there was nothing on the chuck.

He looked at the clock again. It should have happened by now.

He went back to the living room and lay on the sofa again and propped his head on his pillow and he thought, "I won't be able to go back to sleep," but the next thing he knew he was dreaming about trying to dial a telephone number and not being able to get it right.

He woke up and looked at the clock and saw that another hour had passed. When he pulled back Winston's covers he saw that there was still nothing to clean up.

In a couple more hours it would be daylight. This had never happened before.

Winston was awake now. He said, "What's going on?" in a voice not so sleepy as Harris might have expected.

Harris said, "Nothing's happening."

Winston said, "I thought so."

Harris said, "How did you know?"

Winston said, "My face. The tingling in my face is so fierce, it's like somebody jangling bells."

Harris said, "We'll try again later."

Winston said, "It has to be done now."

Harris said, "What has to be done?"

At this moment Dallas Armstrong came into the room, tiny and sleepy and confused. Dallas said, "Is everything all right?" He looked like one of the seven dwarves in his long sleepshirt and cracked leather bedroom slippers.

Winston's voice was strong, even above the drugs. He said, "There's a bit of a dangerous situation. Harris has it under control."

Harris said, "Danger?"
Winston said, "It will have to be dug out."
Harris said, "Dug out?"
Winston said, "With your fingers."

Many years later Harris would remember this failure of his nerve and would wonder what it had to do with the course of his life, his failures and his new starts and his letting go of regret.

That night there was no question: Harris could not do what had to be done.

Harris wondered whether Dallas Armstrong saw this night through the same unhappy silvery haze that he himself watched through.

He saw Dallas Armstrong move into position behind Winston. He saw Dallas's hand disappear inside of Winston.

And when he saw Dallas draw forth the first of the nine or ten nuggets that he would produce from this strange familiar mine of a body, this physical warmth to which Harris had felt married and which he now believed he had betrayed, he watched Dallas Armstrong hold out his hand with the first hard brown walnut-sized object in it.

What did Dallas mean, holding it there? It was not triumph, not worship, not fear.

Dallas said nothing. Harris said nothing.

For an instant Harris believed Dallas was handing the nugget to him, and for the briefest second he considered taking it.

Instead Dallas placed it on the chuck and again reached

his hand inside Winston's body and brought out a second one like the first and laid it on the chuck also and went back again and again and again until it was finished.

Harris watched him and expected him to change miraculously, to become a confident swaggering pirate, at least to grow taller. Nothing of the kind happened.

It surprised Harris when Dallas spoke. Dallas said, "My mother stays up half the night watching programs."

Harris said, "I'll be moving back with my parents in the morning."

Dallas carefully wadded up the chuck and laid it aside and covered Winston's rear end.

Harris said, "Sometimes I listen to Winston's music."

Dallas said, "It happens over and over. There are too many new lifetimes to count."

Wheelchair

Winston Krepps had been abandoned by his attendant, and the door was shut tight.

Winston pressed the control lever of his chair. The battery was low, so the motor sounded strained. The chair turned in a slow circular motion; the rubber tires squeaked on the linoleum floor of the kitchen.

For a moment, as the chair turned, Winston saw two teen-aged boys on a bridge. Winston released the control lever, and the chair stopped. The boys were naked and laughing, and the Arkansas sky was bright blue. Winston recognized himself as one of the two boys. He pushed the hallucination away from his eyes. It was the day real life had ended, he thought.

The clock above the refrigerator said four—that would be Thursday. Jesse, his attendant, must have left on Monday.

Winston turned his chair again and faced the living room. He saw a boy lying on his back on a white table. Winston turned his head and tried not to see. Doctors and nurses moved through the room. The prettiest of the nurses stood by the table and chatted with the boy. The boy—it was Winston, he could not prevent recognizing himself—was embar-

163

rassed at his nakedness, but he could not move to cover himself. An X-ray machine was rolled into place. The pretty nurse said, "Don't breathe now." The boy thought he might ask her out when he was better, if she wasn't too old for him. He had not understood yet that this was the day sex ended. Winston looked away and pressed the lever of the chair.

The motor hummed and he rolled toward the bedroom. The tires squeaked on the linoleum, then were silent on the carpet. The motor strained to get through the carpet, but it did not stop. Monday, then, was the last day he was medicated.

Winston negotiated the little S-curve in the hallway. He could see into the bathroom. The extra leg-bag was draped over the edge of the tub, the detergents and irrigation fluids and medications were lined up on the cabinet. Winston saw his mother in the bathroom, but as if she were still young and was standing in the kitchen of her home. He saw himself near her, still a boy, strapped into his first wheelchair.

He closed his eyes, but he could still see. His mother was washing dewberries in the sink. There were clean pint Mason jars on the cabinet and a large blue enamel cooker on the stove. His mother said, "The stains! I don't know if dewberries are worth the trouble." Winston watched, against his will, the deliberateness of her cheer, the artificiality of it.

He stopped his chair in the bedroom. There was the table Jesse had built, the attendant who had abandoned him. Jesse had been like a child the night he finished the table, he was so proud of himself. He even skipped that night at the country-western disco, where he spent most of his time, just to sit home with Winston and have the two of them admire it together. Winston resented the table now, and the feelings he had had, briefly, for Jesse. How could a person build you a table and sit with you that night and look at it, and then leave you alone. It was easy to hate Jesse.

He looked at the articles that made up the contents of the room—his typewriter, his lamp, and books and papers, a poem he had been trying to write, still in the typewriter. His typing stick was on the floor, where he had dropped it by accident on Monday.

Then Jesse stepped into the line of Winston's vision. Winston had not realized you could hallucinate forward as well as back, but he was not surprised. It was the same worthless Jesse. "I'm a boogie person, man," Jesse seemed to explain. He was wearing tight jeans and no shirt, his feet were bare. He was tall and slender and straight. "I'm into boogie, it's into me." Winston said, "But you built me a table, Jesse." Then he said nothing at all.

Winston's hunger had stopped some time ago, he couldn't remember just when. He knew his face was flushed from lack of medication. His leg-bag had been full for a couple of days, so urine seeped out of the stoma for a while. It had stopped now that he was dehydrated.

Winston heard cars passing on the paved road outside his window. He had cried out until his voice was gone. He imagined bright Arkansas skies and a sweet-rank fragrance of alfalfa hay and manure and red clover on the wind from the pastures outside town. He thought of telephone wires singing in the heat.

Winston looked back at the floor again, at his typing

stick. The stick made him remember Monday, the day Jesse left, and before Winston knew he was abandoned.

He had been in his chair at the kitchen table with his plastic drinking straw in his mouth. He was sipping at the last of a pitcher of water. The time alone had been pleasant for him—none of Jesse's music playing, none of his TV game shows or ridiculous friends and their conversation about cowboy disco and girls and the rest. Winston sipped on the water and felt the top of the plastic tube with his tongue.

He pressed his tongue over the hole in the tube and felt the circle it made there. He thought he could have counted all the tastebuds enclosed within the circle if he tried. He thought of his father holding a duck call to his lips to show Winston how to hold his tongue when he was a child, before the accident. Winston remembered taking the call from his father's hand, and he wondered if that touching were not the last touch of love he had felt—the last in the real world anyway, and so the last. The touching of the tube to his tongue brought his father back to him, the smell of alligator grass in the winter swamp, a fragrance of fresh tobacco and wool and shaving lotion and rubber hip-waders, and more that he had forgotten from that world.

He had gone to his typewriter, and had meant to write what he remembered. He had almost been able to believe it would restore him, undo what was done.

He had rolled up to the table, as close as the chair would take him. The stick with the rubber tips was lying on the table with four or five inches sticking out over the edge. Winston used his single remaining shoulder muscle to push his left hand forward onto the table. His fingers had long ago stiffened into a permanent curl. He maneuvered the hand until the typing stick was between his second and third fingers.

At last he dragged it close enough to his face. He clenched one end of the stick between his teeth and tasted the familiar rubber grip. He steadied himself and aimed the stick at the *on* button of his typewriter. The machine buzzed and clacked and demanded attention. For an instant, as he always did when he heard this sound, he felt genuinely alive, an inhabitant of a real world, a real life. And not just life—it was power he felt, almost that. Writing—just for a moment, but always for that moment—was real. It was dancing. It was getting the girl and the money and kicking sand in the face of the bully. He began, letter by letter, to type with the stick in his mouth.

When he had finished, what he had written was not good. The words he saw on the page were not what he had meant. What he had felt seemed trivial now, and hackneyed. He said, "Shit." He touched the *off* button and shut the typewriter down.

He tried to drop the stick from his mouth onto the table again, but the effort of writing had exhausted him. The stick hit the table, but it had been dropped hastily, impatiently, and it did not fall where Winston had intended. It rolled onto his lap, across his right leg, where he could not reach it. Finally it rolled off his leg and onto the floor.

That was on Monday. He could have used the stick now to dial the telephone.

167

There was a series of three muscle spasms. The first one was mild. Winston's left leg began to rise up toward his face. The spasm continued upward through his body and into his shoulders. For a moment he could not breathe, but then the contraction ended and it was over. His foot settled back into place. He caught his breath again.

When the second spasm began he saw the center of hell. A great bird, encased in ice, flapped its enormous wings and set off storms throughout all its icy regions. In the storms and in the ice was a chant, and the words of the chant were *Ice ice up to the neck.*

Winston's legs, both of them this time, rose up toward his face and hung there for an eternity of seconds. He watched the ice-imprisoned bird and listened to the chant. His legs flailed right and left in the chair. Now they settled down. They jerked out and kicked and crossed one another and flailed sidewise again. Winston's feet did not touch the footrests and his legs were askew. His shoulders rose up to his ears and caused him to scrunch up the features of his face and to hold his breath against his will.

Then it ended. He could breathe again. It was easy to hate his useless legs and his useless arms and his useless genitals and his insides over which he had no control. He was tilted in his chair, listing twenty degrees to the right.

Winston felt an odd peacefulness settle upon him. He saw a swimming pool and a pavilion in summertime. The bathhouse was green-painted, and the roof was corrugated aluminum. He saw himself at sixteen, almost seventeen. For the first time he did not avert his eyes. A radio was playing, there was a screech of young children on a slide. The boy he watched stood at the pool's edge, a countryboy at a town pool, as happy as if he had just begun to live his life inside a technicolor movie.

There was a girl too, a city girl. She told him she was from Memphis, her name was Twilah. There was a blaze of chlorine and Arkansas sun in her hair and eyes. No one could have been more beautiful. Her hair was flaming orange, and a billion freckles covered her face and shoulders and breasts, even her lips and ears. The radio played and the sun shone and the younger children screeched on the slide.

Outside his window, where he could not see it, a bird made a sound—a noise, really—an odd two-noted song, and the song caused the memory to grow more vivid, more heartbreaking. He wanted to see all the places Twilah might hide her freckles. He wanted to count them, to see her armpits and beneath her fingernails and under her clothing. He wanted to examine her tongue and her nipples and forbidden places he could scarcely imagine. It was easy to fall in love when you were sixteen, almost seventeen and a lifeguard was blowing a steel whistle at a swimmer trespassing beneath a diving board.

The third spasm was a large one. It seemed to originate somewhere deep in his body, near the core. The tingle in his face that signaled it was like a jangle of frantic bells rung in warning.

He imagined great flocks of seabirds darkening the air above an island. He saw wildlife scurrying for shelter.

Motion had begun in his body now. His legs were rising as if they were lighter than air. Then, suddenly, and for no reason—it may have been merely the nearness of death—Winston did not care what his legs did. He watched them in bemusement. For the first time since the accident, they were not monstrous to him, they were not dwarfish, or grotesque. They were his legs, only that. For the first time in seventeen years, he could not discover—or even think to seek—the measure of himself, or of the universe, in his limbs. He was in the grips of a spasm more violent than anything he had ever imagined, in which for a full minute he could not breathe at all, could not draw breath, and yet he felt as refreshed as if he were breathing sea air a thousand miles from any coast.

He began to see as he had never seen before. He saw as if his seeing were accompanied by an eternal music, as if the past were being presented to him through the vision of an immortal eye. He was not dead—there was no question of that. He was alive, for a little longer anyway, and he was seeing in the knowledge that there is greater doom in not looking than in looking. He fixed his eye—this magical, immortal eye—on a swamp-lake in eastern Arkansas.

In the swamp he saw a cove, and in the cove an ancient tangle of briars and cypress knees and gum stumps. He saw water that was pure but blacker than slate, made mirrorlike by the tannic acid from the cypress trees, and he saw the trees and skies and clouds reflected in its surface.

The eye penetrated the reflecting surface and saw beneath the water. He saw a swamp floor of mud and silt. He saw a billion strings of vegetation and tiny root systems. He saw fish—bright bluegills and silvery crappie, long-snouted gar, and lead-bellied cat with ropy whiskers. He saw turtles and mussels and the earth of plantations sifted there from other states, another age, through a million ditches and on the feet of turkey vultures and blue herons and kingfishers. He saw schools of minnows and a trace of slave-death from a century before. He saw baptizings and drownings. He saw the transparent wings of snake-doctors, he saw lost fish stringers and submerged logs and the ghosts of lovers.

He saw the boat.

The boat was beneath the surface with the rest, old and colorless and waterlogged. It was not on the bottom, only half-sunk, two feet beneath the surface of the swamp.

The boat was tangled in vegetation, in brambles and briars and the submerged tops of fallen tupelo gums and willows. It was tangled in trotlines and rusted hooks and a faded Lucky 13 and the bale of a minnow bucket and the shreds of a shirt some child took off on a hot day and didn't get home with.

The world that Winston looked into seemed affected by the spasm that he continued to suffer and entertain. Brine flowed into freshets, ditches gurgled with strange water. The willows moved, the trotlines swayed, the crappie did not bite a hook. Limbs of fallen trees shivered under the water, muscadine vines, the sleeve of a boy's shirt waved as if to say goodbye. The gar felt the movement with its long snout, the cat with its ropy whiskers, the baptized child felt it, and the drowned man. The invisible movement of the water stirred the silt and put grit in the mussel's shell. The lost bass plug raised up a single hook as if in question.

And the spasm touched the half-sunken boat.

Winston was breathing again, with difficulty. He was askew in his chair, scarcely sitting at all. He thought his right leg had been broken in the thrashing, but he couldn't tell. He wasn't really interested. He knew he would see what he had been denied—what he had denied himself.

He watched the boat beneath the surface. The boat trembled in the slow, small movement of the waters. The trembling was so slight that it could be seen only by magic, with an eye that could watch for years in the space of this second. Winston watched all the years go past, and all their seasons. Winter summer spring fall. The boat trembled, a briar broke. Oxidation and sedimentation and chance and drought and rain, a crumbling somewhere, a falling away of matter from matter. In the slowness the boat broke free of its constraints.

It rose up closer to the surface and floated twelve inches beneath the tannic mirror of the lake.

The boat could move freely now. Winston was slouched in his chair, crazed with fever but still alive. He knew what he was watching, and he would watch it to the end.

Jesse said, "I didn't know you would *die*, man. I never knew boogie could kill anybody." It was tempting to watch Jesse, to taunt him for his ignorance, his impossible shallowness, but Winston kept his eye on the boat.

The boat moved through the water. It didn't matter how it moved, by nature or magic or the ripples sent out by a metaphorical storm, it moved beneath the water of a swamp-lake in eastern Arkansas.

It moved past cypress and gum, past a grove of walnut and pecan. It moved past a cross that once was burned on the Winter Quarters side of the lake, it moved past Mrs. Hightower's lakebank where the Methodists held the annual picnic, past the spot where a one-man band made music a long time ago and caused the children to dance, it moved past a brown and white cow drinking knee-deep in the Ebeneezer Church's baptizing pool. It moved past Harper's woods and a sunken car and a washed-away boat dock. It moved past the Indian mound and past some flooded chicken houses, it moved past the shack where Mr. Lang shot himself, it moved past the Kingfisher Café.

And then it stopped. Still twelve inches beneath the water, the boat stopped its movement and rested against the pilings of a narrow bridge above the lake. On the bridge Winston could see two boys—himself one of them—naked and laughing in the sun. Winston did not avert his eyes.

The boys' clothes were piled beside them in a heap. One of the boys—himself, as Winston knew it would be—left the railing of the bridge.

It was part fall, part dive—a fall he would make the most of. It lasted, it seemed, forever. Slow-arching and naked, spraddle-legged, self-conscious, comic, bare-assed, country-boy dive.

There was no way for him to miss the boat, of course. He hit it. The other boy, the terrified child on the bridge, climbed down from the railing and held his clothes to his bare chest and did not jump.

He only had to see it once.

*A*nd yet it was not quite over.

Winston's life was being saved, like cavalry arriving in the nick of time. This was not an hallucination, this was real. There was an ambulance team in the little apartment, two men in white uniforms. It was hard to believe, but Jesse was there as well—Jesse the boogieman, repentant and returned, still explaining himself, just as he had in the hallucinations. "Boogie is my *life*," he said, as the ambulance team began their work.

Then it began to happen again, the opening of the magical eye. It was focused on Jesse. Through it he saw, as he always saw, even without magic, the bright exterior of Jesse's physical beauty—his slenderness and sexuality and strength and straight back and perfect limbs, and also, somehow, beyond his beauty, which before this moment had been always a perverse mirror in which to view only his, Winston's, own deformity and celibacy and loss, beyond the mirror of his physical perfection and, with clear vision, even in this real but dreamlike room, filled with a hellish blue-flashing light from outside, and with IV bottles and injections and an inflatable splint for his leg and the white of sheets and uniforms and the presence also of the apartment manager who had come, a large oily man named Sooey Leonard, he saw past Jesse's beauty to the frightened, disorganized, hopeless boy that Jesse was. Winston understood, at last, the pain in what Jesse told him. Boogie is my life. It was not a thing to be mocked, as Winston had so recently thought. It was not a lame excuse for failure. What was terrifying and painful was that Jesse knew exactly what he was saying, and that he meant, in despair, exactly what he said. It was acknowledgment and confession, not excuse, a central failure of intellect and spirit that Jesse understood in himself, was cursed to know, and to know also that he could not change, a doom he had carried with him since his conception and could look at, as if it belonged to someone else. The knowledge that Jesse knew himself so well and, in despair of it, could prophesy his future, with all its meanness and shallowness and absence of hope, swept through Winston like a wind of grief. He wanted to tell Jesse that it wasn't true, that he was not doomed, no matter the magnitude of the failure here. He wanted to remind him of the table he had built and of how they felt together that night it was finished, when they had sat at home alone together and not turned on the television but only sat and looked at the table and talked about it and then made small talk about other things, both of them knowing they were talking about the table. He wanted Jesse to know that the table proved him wrong.

He could say nothing. The ambulance team bumped and jolted him onto a stretcher-table and held the clanking IV bottles above him.

The sunlight was momentarily blinding as he was wheeled out the door of the apartment and onto the sidewalk. For a moment Winston could see nothing at all, only a kaleidoscope of colors and shapes behind his eyelids.

And yet in the kaleidoscope, by magic he supposed, he

found that he could see Jesse and himself. They stood—
somehow Winston could stand—in the landscape of another
planet, with red trees and red rivers and red houses and red
farm animals, and through all the atmosphere, as if in a red
whirlwind, flew the small things of Winston's life: the typewriter and the failed poem in it, the battery charger for his
chair, and the water mattress and the sheepskin, the chair
itself and the leather strap that held him in it, his spork—the
combination spoon-fork utensil he ate with—and the splint
that fitted it to his hand, the leg-bag and the catheter and the
stoma, his trousers with the zipper up the leg, his bulbous
stomach, the single muscle in his shoulder, the scars of his
many operations, the new pressure sores that already were
festering on his backside from so long a time in the chair, his
teeth, the bright caps that replaced them when his real teeth
decalcified after the spinal break, his miniature arms and
legs, the growing hump on his back, his hard celibacy and
his broken neck. And the thought that he had, in this red
and swirling landscape, was that they were not hateful things
to gaze upon, and not symbolic of anything, but only real
and worthy of his love. Twilah was there in all the redness,
the long-lost girl with the freckles and the orange hair, who
for so long had been only a symbol of everything Winston
had missed in life and who now was only Twilah, a girl he
never knew and could scarcely remember. It was a gentle red
whirlwind that harmed no one. His father was there with a
duck call, his mother washing dewberries. The ambulance
door slammed shut and the siren started up. Winston hoped
he could make Jesse understand.

Part iii

Sugar Among the Chickens

I had been fishing for an hour and still hadn't caught anything. I was fishing for chickens. Mama wouldn't let me walk to the town pond by myself. What else was I going to fish for?

I looked back over my shoulder through the torn-out screened door and tried to see Mama in there. I said, "Mama." I was using the voice that says you're being real good and not fishing for chickens.

Mama said, "You better not be fishing for chickens, Sugar Mecklin, you going to get switched." She's got this ability.

She was out in the kitchen, that was good anyway. I put a fresh kernel on my hook and scattered shelled corn on the slick dirt yard below the porch and dusted off my hands on my white blue jeans. A handful of old hens came bobbing and clucking up to the corn and poked at it with their heads and then raised their heads up and looked around, and then started poking at it again.

I dropped the baited hook in amongst them. I wished I could figure out some way to use a cork. The chickens bobbed and pecked and poked and scratched. I moved my baited hook into the middle of the chickens and eased it down onto the ground and waited. I still didn't get a bite.

My daddy didn't much care whether I fished for chickens or not. My daddy knew I never would catch one, never had, never would. It was my mama who was the problem. She said it would ruin your life if you fished for chickens.

I wasn't studying ruining my life right now. I was thinking about hooking and landing some poultry.

I wasn't using a handline, which is easy to hide if your mama comes up on you. I was using a cane pole and a bream hook, little bitty rascal of a hook. I liked a handline all right, I wasn't complaining. Nothing better for fishing in real tight places, like up under your house on a hot day when the chickens are settled down in the cool dirt and have their neck feathers poked out like a straw hat and a little blue film of an eyelid dropped down over their eyes. A handline is fine for that. A cane pole is better from off your porch, though.

Or I guessed it was. I never had caught a chicken. I had had lots of bites, but I never had landed one, never really even set the hook in one. They're tricky, a chicken.

I really wanted to catch one, too. I wanted the hook to snag in the beak, I wanted to feel the tug on the line. I wanted to haul it in, squawking and heavy and beating its wings and sliding on its back and flopping over to its breast and dragging along and the neck stretched out a foot and a half and the stupid old amazed eyes bright as Beau dollars.

I dreamed about it, asleep and awake. Sometimes I let myself believe the chicken I caught was not just any old chicken but maybe some special one, one of the Plymouth

Rocks, some fat heavy bird, a leghorn, or a blue Andalusian. And sometimes, as long as I was making believe, I thought I might catch an even finer specimen, the finest in the whole chickenyard. I thought I caught the red rooster itself.

The red rooster was a chicken as tall as me. It seemed like it, I swear, when I was ten. It was a chicken, I'm telling you, like no chicken you ever saw before. It could fly. There was no half-assed flying about it. It could fly long distance. Daddy said it could migrate if it had anywhere to go. It couldn't do that, but it could fly fifty times farther than any other chicken you ever saw. This was a chicken that one time killed a stray dog.

I dreamed about that rooster. The best dream was when I caught it not on a handline and not on a cane pole. I dreamed I caught it on a limber fine six-and-a-half-foot Zebco rod and spinning reel, like the ones in the Western Auto store in Arrow Catcher. That's the town I used to live right outside of when I was little, in the Delta. The line on that Zebco spool was almost invisible.

I watched the chickens. There was a fine old Plymouth Rock I would just love to catch. She dusted her feathers and took long steps like a kid wearing his daddy's hip boots. I moved the bait closer to her and held my breath. She started poking around at the corn. She hit the bait once but didn't pick up the hook. My line was taut, so I felt the strike vibrate through the line and down the cane pole to my hands, which I noticed were sweating. I thought, If she hit it once, she just might . . . But she didn't. She stopped eating corn altogether and scratched herself with her foot like a dog.

I tried to listen for my mama. Mama couldn't be expected to stay in the kitchen forever. I needed to say something to her in my I-ain't-fishing-for-chickens voice, but I couldn't. The Plymouth Rock pecked the earth a few times, but not the bait. Then, all of a sudden, she shifted position a little and pecked right down on the corn with the hook in it, the bait. For the second time that day I felt a strike vibrate through my hands. But the chicken missed the hook again and I jerked the bait out of her mouth. She didn't know what happened to it. She looked like, What in the world?

I repositioned the bait, and the hen started pecking around it again. I had to say something to Mama. I held real still and tried to talk in a voice that maybe a chicken couldn't hear. In my head I invented a voice that seemed like it was going to be all throaty and hoarse and animal-like when it came out, but when it did come out, it didn't make any sound at all, not even a whisper, just a little bit of released breath and a wormy movement of my lips. I said, "Mama, I ain't fishing for chickens." Nobody heard it, not even me. The Plymouth Rock hit the bait a third time.

It wasn't possible to catch a chicken. I knew that. My daddy had convinced me. He said, "A chicken is dumb, but not dumb enough." So I knew it was impossible. But I also knew it had happened. I had the Plymouth Rock.

I jerked my pole skyward and set the hook hard in the chicken's beak.

The sound that rose up out of the chicken's throat was a sound that nobody who has never caught a chicken on a hook has ever heard. It sounded like chicken-all-the-way-back-to-the-beginning-of-chicken.

I was anchored to the porch, with the butt end of the pole dug into my groin for support. The heavy flopping squalling bird was hanging off the end of my line in midair. The sound didn't stop. The sound was like the fire siren in Arrow Catcher. As beautiful and as scary as that. It was like a signal. I thought it signaled danger and adventure and beauty.

I was screaming too, along with the chicken. I didn't even know I was screaming. I heaved on the heavy bird. The pole was bent double. I wanted to land the chicken. I wanted the Plymouth Rock on the porch with me.

I couldn't pick it up high enough. It was too heavy for me. It was up off the ground, all right, but I couldn't get it high enough to sling it onto the porch. The chicken was beating its wings and spinning in a wild circle. I held it there.

I heaved on the pole again. The bird swung up and around but was still not high enough. It hit the side of the house and then swung back out into midair.

Mama came out on the porch and stood behind me. I knew she was back there, because I heard the door slap shut.

At first I didn't look back. I just stopped hauling on the chicken. I was still holding it up off the ground, though. I couldn't give it up yet, not all of it, even though I had stopped trying to land it.

Finally I did look back. The face of my mama, I thought, was the saddest face on this earth. It just had to be. I said, "Hey, Mama," real subdued, trying not to provoke her. I was still holding the chicken off the ground, and it still hadn't stopped making its noise. I said, "I been fishing for chickens." No use lying about it now.

I expected my mama to say, "I swan," like she always said when she meant "I swear." What she really said surprised me. She said she was a big failure in life. She said she was such a big failure in life she didn't see why she didn't just go off and eat some poison.

I eased the chicken down onto the ground. It got loose and scooted off toward the garage with its feathers sticking out.

Mama cut a switch off a crape myrtle and switched me good on my bare legs and went back inside the house. She lay across her bed on the wedding-ring quilt my grandmama Sugar gave her when she got married, with hers and Daddy's names sewed in a corner and a heart stitched around the names, and had herself a long hard cry. And so that part of it was over.

Some time passed. Some days and, I guess, some weeks. I watched my mama around the house. At night, after supper, and after she had wiped the table, she would do what she liked best. She would lay out on the table a new piece of cloth from Kamp's Low Price Store and pin to it a tissue-paper Simplicity pattern. She would weight the pattern down all around with pieces of silverware from the dark chest lined with green felt. The silver came from my mama's grandmama who lost her mind and threw away the family Bible and almost everything else and so left only the silverware, which she forgot to throw away. Mama would get the pattern all weighted down, and she would look around for a minute, in her sewing basket or in a kitchen drawer, and say, "Has anybody seen my good scissors?" She would find the scissors and bring them to the table and cut through the paper and the cloth. She would poke through her sewing basket. I saw the faded pincushion and the cloth measuring tape and a metal thimble and about a jillion buttons and the pinking shears.

She would lay down a towel to keep from scratching the dining room table and then heft the heavy old portable Kenmore onto it. She might have to thread the bobbin. She might lift the cloth to her nose and breathe its new-smell before she put it into the machine, under the needle, and on the shiny metal plate. She would touch the pedal with her foot.

Before any of this would happen, before supper even, my daddy would come home from work. I could hear the car pull into the drive and head around back of the house. He would get out of the car, and he would be wearing white overalls and a paper cap with the name of a paint store printed on it. He would smell like paint and turpentine and maybe a little whiskey.

Daddy would shoo the chickens back from the gate in the fence where the chickens would flock when they heard his car. He would open the gate and ease inside, real quick, before anybody could get out. I would watch him.

The chickens were gossipy and busy and fat and fine. Daddy would scatter shelled corn from a white metal dishpan and pour out mash for those that needed it and run well water into the troughs.

I always wished Mama would watch him do this. I thought that if she did she would stop thinking she was a big failure in life.

I went down the steps and into the chickenyard with him. He let me reach my hand into the fragrant dusty corn and pelt the old birds with it.

Then there was the part where the rooster attacks you. Every day I forgot it was going to happen, and then it would happen and I would think, Now why didn't I remember that?

It happened today, this particular day, I mean, a Tuesday and just before sunset. The rooster was on top of us. It hadn't been there before, and now it was all I could see, the red furious rooster. Its wings were spread out and its bones were creaking and clacking and its beak was wide open and its tongue was blazing black as blood. And the rooster's eye—it looked like it had only one eye, and the eye was not stupid and comical like the other chickens.' It seemed lidless and magical, like it could see into a person's heart and know all his secrets and read his future. And the feet—they were blue-colored but blue like you never saw before except in a wound. And the spurs.

And then it was over. Today, like other days, Daddy kicked the chicken in the breast with the toe of his work shoe and it flopped over on its back. It righted itself and stood up and started pecking at the corn on the ground. Daddy walked over to the rooster and petted its neck. The bird made a stretching motion with its head like a cat.

Then there was the next part. We watched the rooster eat. Without warning, as we knew it would, it stopped eating. It stood straight up and cocked its head so far that the comb flopped over. It looked like somebody who has just remembered something real important.

Then the rooster took off. Any other flying chickens you see are all hustle and puffing and heaving and commotion and getting ten feet maybe, no matter how hard they work at it. This chicken could fly like a wild bird, like a peacock, maybe, or a wild turkey. There was nothing graceful about it, nothing pretty. It was just so amazing to watch. When the rooster flew, it looked like some fat bad child who has rung your doorbell and is running down the street away from your house, slow and obvious and ridiculous, but padding on anyway, uncatchable. It flew out and out, over the chickenyard fence, over a little side yard where Mr. Love kept a goat, over the trailer the midgets lived in, out farther like a kite, over a house, and finally into the branches of a line of hardwood trees across the railroad tracks.

We went inside the house then, and Daddy went into the bathroom and came out after a long time with his new smells of Wildroot and Aqua Velva and his wet combed hair. The whiskey smell was a little stronger, a little sweeter.

After supper, and after the sewing machine was turned off and put away, Mama said, "Now all I have to do is hem it, and it'll be all done." She was on the sofa, so she sat up straight and held the dress up to her front and pretended like she was modeling it. Daddy was moving out of the room. He was weaving a little when he walked, on his way to the kitchen.

I looked at Mama. She had a pleased look on her face that made me think she thought she looked pretty. She did look kind of pretty.

I picked up the package the pattern came in. There was a color picture of two women on it. I said, "Where do these ladies live, Mama?"

She took the package out of my hand and looked at it with the same look on her face. She looked off somewhere away from my eyes and said, "I think maybe these two ladies live in New York City. They live across the hall from one another in a penthouse apartment. I think they just met up downtown by accident." She looked at me and smiled and handed the pattern package back to me.

I said, "What are they talking about?"

Mama said, "Hm." She took the package from me again and looked at it, serious. She said, "I think maybe, well, maybe the lady in the red dress is saying why don't we go somewhere real nice today. She's saying why don't they shop around a little and then maybe go to a picture show. They might even be talking about going to the opera, you don't know."

I tried to think about the opera, men in turbans and women in white-powdered wigs. The men carried sabers at their sides, and the women had derringers in their purses. I said, "I ain't studying no opera."

Mama laid the package down and put the new dress aside

too. She started poking through her sewing basket for something, but then stopped without finding it. She had lost the look she had before.

I said, "Are you going to the opera?"

She said, "No."

I said, "When you put on that dress, you know what?"

She didn't answer.

I said, "You ain't going to look like neither one of those ladies." I don't know why I said that.

Mama got up from where she was sitting. She said, "Don't say *ain't*, Sugar. It will ruin your life." She got up off the sofa and went into the bedroom and closed the door.

Daddy came back into the living room. He was wobbly and ripe with whiskey. He said, "What happened to Mama?"

I said, "She's lying down."

He eased back into his chair and started to watch *Gilligan's Island* on the television.

I went to my room. I sat on the bed and let my feet hang off. I had to do something. I felt like I was working a jigsaw puzzle with my family. I saw my mama and my daddy and the chickens and the midgets and Mr. Love's goat and I thought I could never get it worked.

I started to fish for the rooster. Sometimes I fished with a handline, sometimes with a cane pole. The rooster never looked at my bait.

I fished every day, and every day I got older and the rooster didn't get caught. School started up again and I got new shoes. The leaves finally fell off the trees and I helped Mama rake them up in the afternoons. The rooster hated my bait. He couldn't stand to look at it.

I changed bait. I used raisins. I used jelly beans. I used a dog turd. You got to want to catch a chicken to bait a hook with dog turd. Chickens eat them all the time, no reason it wouldn't work. It didn't though.

I threw the cat in the chickenyard. I had ten hooks dangling off the cat, feet and tail and flea collar, everywhere you can put a hook on a cat. The rooster killed the cat, but it didn't take a hook. Too bad about the cat. You're not going to catch a rooster without making a sacrifice or two.

After a while fishing for the rooster and keeping Mama from knowing about it became like a job, like an old habit you never would think about breaking. All that mattered was that I fish for him, that I never give up, no matter how hopeless, no matter how old or unhappy I got.

$\mathcal{S}$omething happened then that changed things. It was Saturday. I got on my bike and pedaled from my house to the picture show in Arrow Catcher. There was always a drawing at the matinee.

Mrs. Meyers, the old ticket-taker-upper with the white hair and shaky hands and snuff-breath—she would do the same thing every time. She would take your ticket out of your hand and tear it into halves and tell you what a fine young man you were growing up to be and to hold on to your ticket stub, you might win the drawing.

I walked down the aisle and found me a seat up close to

the front. I looked at the torn ticket in my hands, and the other seats filled up with people.

Mr. Gibbs owned the picture show, called it the Strand Theater. The lights were all on bright and Mr. Gibbs climbed up on the stage by a set of wooden steps around the side. He was huffing and sweating, waving his hands for everybody to be quiet. Like he said every Saturday, he said, "Be quite, boys and gulls, be quite, please." We laughed at him, and the underarms of his white shirt were soaked with sweat.

I watched Mr. Gibbs crank the handle of a wire basket filled with Ping-Pong balls. Every ball had a number on it. Mr. Gibbs would draw them out, one at a time, and put each one on a little cushioned platform with the number facing out to the audience, until he had four of them. He would draw them out slow and teasing and smiling. It was something he loved to do, you could tell. He would call out each number in its turn, real loud and exaggerated. He would say, "Fo-urrr," or "Nye-unn," and he would hold up the white ball and show everyone he wasn't cheating, and then he would put the ball on the cushioned stand. You had to like Mr. Gibbs.

Then it started happening. The first number he called out was the first number on my ticket stub. And then so was the second. It seemed impossible that the number in my ear was the same number as in my eye. It kept on being the same number, digit by digit, right down to the end. I had won the drawing.

I had never won anything before. One time I won a pink cake in a cakewalk. It tasted terrible and I hated it, but I ate all of it anyway, same night I won it. I had never won anything except that cake, so it was impressive enough to win the drawing.

But winning was nothing compared to the prize I was going to take home. I had won the Zebco rod and spinning reel from the Western Auto.

Mr. Gibbs was standing up on that little stage like a sweaty fat angel. He was giving his heartfelt thanks to the Western Auto store, home-owned and home-operated by Mr. Sooey Leonard, and to all the other fine local merchants of Arrow Catcher who donated these fine prizes and made these drawings possible.

I went up on the stage. I climbed the same dusty wooden steps that Mr. Gibbs had climbed. I showed Mr. Gibbs my ticket stub. I was trembling. He shook my hand, and my hand was sweaty and slick against his manly palm and fingers. Mr. Gibbs asked me if I didn't think every single person in this fine audience ought to take his patronage to the Western Auto store and all the other fine local merchants of Arrow Catcher.

I said, "Yessir," and everybody laughed and clapped their hands.

Mr. Gibbs said what was I going to do with my fine prize.

I said, "Go fishing," and everybody laughed again.

Mr. Gibbs said why didn't everybody give this fine young fisherman another round of applause, and so everybody did.

I don't know what was on the movie. I sat through it, and I watched it, with the fishing rod between my legs, but I didn't see it. I remember a huffing train and some wreckage,

I remember an icy train platform and taxicabs and a baby growing up rich instead of poor. Barbara Stanwyck married John Lund, I remember that. Whatever was on the movie, one thing was all I was thinking about and that was that I was definitely going fishing, no doubt about it. The fish I was going to catch was as tall as me and had red feathers and was big enough and fine enough to ruin the life of every soul in Arrow Catcher, Mississippi.

I look back at the day I caught the rooster. I see the familiar yard, the fence of chicken wire. I smell the sweet fresh fragrance of grain and mash and lime and chickenshit and water from a deep well poured through troughs of corrugated metal. I smell creosote and the green pungent shucks of black walnuts under the tree. I see the trailer the midgets lived in and the goat next door. I see myself, a boy, holding the Zebco rod I won at the Strand Theater. The Zebco moves back, then whips forward.

The line leaps away from the reel, from the rod's tip. It leaps into S's and figure eights. It floats like the strand of a spider's web. At the end of the line I see the white fleck of sunlight that covers the hook: the bait, the kernel of corn. I watch it fly toward the rooster.

I look ahead of the corn, far down the chickenyard, and see the rooster. It seems to be on fire in the sunlight. For one second I lose my mind and believe that the rooster means something more than a rooster. I don't believe it long. I come to my senses and know that the rooster is a chicken, that's all. A very bad chicken. He is the same miserable wretched

193

mean bad son-of-a-bitch that my daddy has called him every day of the rooster's life. I remember that the rooster is smarter than me, and faster and stronger and crazier. I remember that I am in the chickenyard with him and that he doesn't like me and that my daddy ain't home from work to protect me and my ass is in trouble, Jack.

I understand, at last, what the rooster is going to do. He is going to catch the bait in the air, like a dog catching a Frisbee. I can't believe what I am watching. The rooster has positioned itself, flat-footed, with its mouth open, its head cocked to one side. Until this moment I have not believed I would catch the rooster. I have meant to catch it, but the habit of fishing for it is all I have thought about for a long time. And now, in the presence of an emotion something like awe, I understand that the rooster is about to catch me.

It happens. The rooster, at the last moment, has to lurch a step forward, it has to duck its head, but it does so with perfect accuracy. The bird might as well have been a large red-feathered frog plucking a fly from the air. He catches the baited hook in his mouth.

I do not move to set the hook. There is no point. The rooster has been fishing for me for three years, and now it has caught me. I have become old enough to believe that doom will always surprise you, that doom is domestic and purrs like a cat.

The bird stands quiet with the bait in its mouth. The line droops to the ground from his chicken lips. I stand attached to him by the line. It is no help to remember that the rooster is a beast and without humor.

Then it does move. At first I thought the creature was growing taller. Nothing could have surprised me. I might have been growing smaller. Neither was true. I was watching what I had watched many times. I was watching the rooster take flight.

It left the ground. The hook was still in its mouth, attached to nothing. The rooster was holding the hook in its mouth like a peanut.

More than ever the bird seemed on fire. It flew out and out, away from me. The nylon line trailed it in flight. The sun shone on the rooster and on the line and told me that I was in big trouble and had not yet figured out how.

It flew over the chickenyard fence, over the goat, over the midgets. It gained altitude. I watched the line be stripped in coils from my open-faced reel. The bird flew and flew, high as the housetops, and then the treetops, out toward the railroad tracks. I was a child flying a living kite.

It took me a minute to see what the rooster was up to. I had never seen him do this before. Just when he was almost out of sight, out over the railroad tracks and ready, I thought, to light in the hardwood trees, the bird seemed to hang suspended. It seemed to have hung itself in midair and to have begun to swell out like a balloon. I was holding the fishing rod limp in my hand and studying the rooster's strange inflation. The rooster, above the treetops, ballooned larger and larger. It grew large enough that I could distinguish its particular features again, the stretched neck and popped-out eyes, the sturdy wings and red belly feathers. Nothing about the appearance of the rooster made sense.

And then everything did. I was not looking at the bird's tail feathers, as I should have been. I was looking him in the face. He was not growing larger, he was coming closer. I looked at my reel and saw that the line was still. The rooster had turned around in flight and was coming back after me.

I looked at him. The rooster had cleared the goat and the midgets. It was big as a goose, big as a collie. Its feet were blue and as big as yard rakes. I dropped the fishing rod into the dirt. I turned to the gate and tried to open the latch. I could hear the rooster's bones creaking and clacking. I could hear the feathers thudding against the air. My hands were clubs, the gate would not come unlatched. I pounded at the gate.

I heard the rooster set its wings like a hawk about to land on a fence post. The rooster landed on my head. It didn't fall off. I thought it might, but it did not. It clung to my scalp by its fierce toenails. I clubbed at the gate with my useless hands. The bird stood on my head, and its wings kept up their motion and clatter. I could not appreciate the mauling I was receiving by the wings for the fire the feet had lit in my brain. I tried to climb the gate, but my feet had turned to stumps.

The chickenyard was in hysterics, the Plymouth Rocks and leghorns and blue Andalusians. I clung to the gate with the rooster on my head. I imagined flames the shape of an angry chicken rising from my head.

I screamed, and still the rooster held on. It drubbed me with its wings. My eyes were blackened and swollen, my nose ran with blood. I didn't care, so long as someone put out the fire in my scalp.

I got the idea that it could be put out with water. I gave up at the gate and ran stumbling across the chickenyard. Layers and pullets and bantams, all the curious and hysterical, fanned away from me in droves. The rooster hung on.

I reached the hydrant hopeless. There was no hope of putting my head under the spigot while wearing the chicken. There was a garden hose in the old garage, but it was of no use. If I could not open the simple latch of the gate, there was no chance I could retrieve the garden hose from its wall hook and screw it to the spigot.

My mama was standing on the back porch watching. I longed for the days when I was young enough to be switched with crape myrtle. I saw her start to move toward me. She was moving toward me but I knew she would never reach me in time. Blood and chickenshit ran down the sides of my face and into my ears. The wings kept up the pounding, and the rooster's bones and ligaments kept up the creaking and clacking and clicking.

I had not noticed my daddy drive up, but now I saw his car in the driveway. He left the car and was headed toward me. He also moved in slow motion.

I left the spigot. My motion and my parents' motion had become the same. They stood at the gate and pounded at it. Their hands were clubs too and the gate would not open for them.

I motioned for them to stay where they were. They saw that I knew what I was doing. Something had changed in me. I was not running now. The rooster was still riding my head. I walked, purposeful, like a heavy bear through the chickenyard.

And yet my steps were not heavy. My life was not ruined.

I could wear this chicken on my head forever. I could bear this pain forever. In a year no one would notice the chicken but myself. Then even I would not notice. My mama had believed that spending your life in the place of your birth, absorbing its small particulars into your blood, was ruination. I looked at my parents beside the gate. My daddy held my mama in his arms as they looked at me. My daddy had gotten the gate open now but again I held up my hand and stopped him. I knew now what I could give them. It was a picture of myself that I would live the rest of my life to prove true: they watched their son wear this living crowing rooster like a crown.

They were proud of me. I knew they were. They were frightened also but pride was mainly what I saw in their faces as I kept them from helping me. They believed that my life would not be ruined. They believed that a man who has worn a chicken on his head—worn it proudly, as I was beginning to do—would never be a fool to geography or marriage or alcohol.

I stood tall in the chickenyard. My parents looked at me from the gate and I felt their love and pride touch me. They believed that a man and his wife with such a son could not be ruined either, not yet, not forever.

The rooster had stopped flapping its wings. It was heavy on me, but I straightened my back and did not slump. Now it balanced itself with more ease, it carried more of its own weight and was easier to hold. It stood on my head like an eagle on a mountain crag. I strode toward my parents and they toward me. The three of us, and the rooster, moved through the chickenyard in glory.

The Talker at the Freak-Show

The summer I was eleven a freak-show followed the Arrow-Catcher Fair into town. The Fair itself was an annual event and very popular; motels filled up for miles in every direction. It was not uncommon for various sideshow-type attractions to set up in the shadow of the Fair to catch the overflow. A wild animal cage, a caricaturist, a boomerangist, two men and a horse who dived from a high platform into a vat of water—all at one time or another found space beneath the spreading cottonwoods and pecan and black walnut trees of the fairgrounds. Evangelists sometimes set up a tent or a booth, and once a gospel singer of great talent and pain stole the attention and hearts of spectators at the Fair.

Mama was opposed to my going to any such event, even a gospel singer or boomerangist, so a freak-show seemed out of the question.

After supper I didn't wait, I did what I knew would please Mama. I went around the table and stacked the plates and took them to the kitchen. Mama said, "Why, Sugar-man, *thank* you."

We had used paper napkins, but there was a stack of linen napkins in the sideboard. I took one from the top drawer and snapped it out smartly and held it draped over the open palm of my hand. With the other hand I brushed crumbs off the table into the napkin until the table was clean and then I stepped smartly past Mama to the trash can in the kitchen and shook the crumbs into it. I recreased the napkin and put it back in the sideboard.

Good linen reminded Mama of trains, and the thought of trains would sometimes soften her mood. She was thinking of black porters in starched white jackets, of Pullman cars flashing across snow-fields and through tiny nameless train stations at dawn and into great cities. She was thinking of soiled linens—sheets piled in the aisles of sleeper cars—and of tablecloths in the diner embossed with the Illinois Central emblem, or with the name of some train on the IC line, the City of New Orleans, the Panama Limited, the Loozianne. She loved to speak the names of those trains. She sang them to me in the night sometimes, sad sweet songs she made up about them. It was my lullaby since the beginning of my memory.

I closed the drawer of the sideboard and knew that she was thinking of the sweet noisy Amtrak from Chicago still carrying—in her mind, even though it was July—a skim of ice on its front cars and nosing southward to New Orleans and the Gulf of Mexico, and riding in one of its staterooms, some beautiful lonely woman brushing her hair before a mirror. I wiped off the table with a damp sponge and had done all I could do.

I sat in the living room at one end of the sofa, where Daddy was watching TV. He left the room for a minute to go to the linen closet in the bathroom where he kept a bottle and came back smelling sweet with whiskey, ripe in fact, since he had been sweetening himself all afternoon.

He sank into the other end of the sofa. After a while he said, "Have you seen this one before?" He meant the TV show that was on. It was called "A Special Musical Edition of *The Love Boat*."

I said, "Nosir."

Then as each actor crossed the screen he would tell me the actor's name. "That's Eddie Albert," he would say. "See that one?—that's Ann Miller. She used to be a great dancer."

There seemed to be dozens of them. He pointed out Ethel Merman, Pearl Bailey, even Duke Ellington. He said, "Each one of those fine actors is actually a great musician in his own right." He said that not a single one of them needed to be on television. "It's just a lark," he said. "They don't even need the money. For them the Love Boat is just one big party, like a vacation they get paid for taking." (In a strange way Daddy seemed sincerely to believe everything that happened on television, at least that all the places were real, the geography. He was convinced that Gilligan's Island and Fantasy Island were charted on maps by those names, that Mayberry was a real town in North Carolina. He was sure that the Love Boat was a commercial ship on which a person could book passage.) He said, "I wish I could afford to take that cruise someday, the one with the musicians. I would like to shake each and every one of those artists by the hand personally." He said he was a lot like each of them, that he would tell them he knew their hearts.

I said, "Can I go to the freak-show?" It was a mistake, I should have waited for Mama.

Daddy looked at me. He said, "Did you hear one single solitary word I spoke?"

Mama came into the room drying her hands. She said, "I wish you wouldn't go to the freak-show, Sugar."

Daddy said to her, "Sugar here tells me he never heard of Duke Ellington. Seems impossible, don't it? I guess Sugar is just too busy talking about freak-shows to listen and maybe learn a little something. Sugar's not aware of what all you can learn by paying attention to conversation for once in his life."

Mama said, "You don't want to go to the freak-show, Sugarman. Those pathetic souls . . ."

Daddy said, "When I was your age I knew how to listen to television and learn a few things. When I was your age I one time slipped off from the house on a Saturday morning and took the bus to Memphis. All by myself. And do you know why?"

Mama said, "Gilbert . . ."

He said, "To see the late great W. C. Handy, that's all. I expect you never heard of the late great W. C. Handy, did you, Sugar."

I said, "Not for a while."

He said, "I expect you never heard of Beale Street either, did you."

Mama said, "The trash a sideshow like that will attract . . ."

Daddy said, "W. C. Handy was the Father of the Blues, that's all W. C. Handy was. Just the Father of the Blues, for God's sake."

Mama said, "Gilbert . . ."

Daddy said, "And the brilliant Sugar Mecklin never heard of him. Eleven years old and never heard of the late great W. C. Handy."

Mama said, "Gilbert . . ."

Daddy said, "And do you know why you never heard of him? Because you don't know how to watch television." He said, "Do you want me to tell you who W. C. Handy was? In your infinite wisdom are you willing to learn one more little thing?—like the identity of the Father of the Blues?"

I said, "You bet."

He told me that when he was a boy—Mama rolled her eyes, she couldn't stand this story—the late great W. C. Handy had a fifteen-minute television program from Memphis on WMCT at noon. "Alive and in person," he said. He said he would stay home from school pretending to be sick so he could watch the old man and listen to him play trumpet. "Me!—alive and young and in love with music, and W. C. Handy not even dead!"

Mama said, "You won't go to the freak-show will you, Sugar?"

I said, "All by yourself?"

Daddy said, "Eleven years old. All alone. All the way to Memphis. On the Greyhound bus."

Mama said, "I don't want you at that freak-show. I mean it."

I said, "*Beale* Street?"

He said, "Never heard of it, did you?" He went to the linen closet again and came back sweeter than ever. He told me the story of how he walked Beale Street like a king.

Mama gave up. She got up from her chair and walked to the big wardrobe in the hallway and came back with a large cardboard box filled with clothes given to her by a rich old Cajun woman who was dying.

Daddy didn't like for Mama to accept used clothes. He stopped telling me about his trip to Memphis. He said, "Mamzelle Montberclair is a hundred years old, Mama."

Mama took out a black silk dress with a huge black silk rose at the breast and held it up to her shoulders to model it.

Daddy said, "You don't want to wear the clothes of a woman a hundred years old." He added, "I don't care *who* she is."

Mama was sitting in an overstuffed chair that she liked. The box was in her lap and she had her feet tucked back under her. You could tell that she felt pretty. Was trying to feel pretty.

She said, "It's not *who* she is. Look at this dress, it's lovely. You could wear a dress like this to . . . why, anywhere on earth."

Daddy said, "*If* you was a hundred years old."

Mama put the black dress aside and pulled another, heavier piece out of the box. It was a cloth coat with a fur collar.

Daddy said, "It's an insult to me. I don't want to be seen with my wife wearing hundred-year-old-woman clothes."

I didn't like the turn the conversation had taken. I was willing to forget about the freak-show.

Mama smoothed the fur collar with her hand and then picked at something invisible in the perfect fur with her fingers.

Daddy said, "It looks like something Mamzelle caught under her sink."

Mama stopped fooling with the collar. She put her hands in her lap and sat still for a while. She said, "I wish you wouldn't talk to me that way, Gilbert."

I didn't know what to say. I said, "Beale Street?"

Daddy turned to me angrily. He said, "You going to *think* Beale Street. I'm going to Beale Street your bare butt you open your smart mouth to me one more time." He said to Mama, still in his angry voice, "Talk to you in what way?"

It didn't get much worse. There was no screaming. Daddy watched the rest of the special musical edition of *The Love Boat*, but I could tell he didn't enjoy it. He got up and snapped off the television and left the room.

On the way to my room I passed the bathroom and saw that the door was open. Daddy was standing in front of the bathroom mirror with a glass of whiskey in his hand.

He knew I was there, watching him, but he didn't stop, he played it out anyway. He raised the glass slowly and held it in front of him. He kept one eye on the mirror and touched the glass to his lips and drank. He lowered the glass and watched himself feel the bite of the whiskey. He said, "Uhh." He was tragic and handsome. He rinsed the glass and put it back on the sink.

He turned to me and said, "So my young man wants to go to the freak-show, does he?"

I wished I had never heard of the freak-show. I wished I hadn't watched him drink the whiskey.

He said, "So you would like to go to the freak-show with your ole daddy, would you. Would you like that, Sugar-man? Would you like for your daddy to take you to the freak-show?"

I said, "Bye, Mama," when we went out the door, but Mama didn't answer.

We entered the fairgrounds by the main gate, beneath the usual long banner with red lettering: WELCOME TO THE ARROW-CATCHER FAIR. I kept close to Daddy.

There were crowds of people milling around the grounds, but not much activity. We pushed through a line of people buying hot dogs and Pepsis and cut past the bandstand and across the area where the Great Spit would be held, a tobacco-spitting contest. Men were stretching out rolls of butcher paper for accurate marking of the distance of the farthest propelled droplet. We went on, past booths and games of chance, through a roped-off area where the arrow-catching events were held, past the ass-kicking booth, which was deserted except for Wiley Heard, the one-legged coach of the local football team. (I don't know what he was doing there.) Another booth was being decorated with crepe paper streamers by ladies from St.-George-by-the-Lake, the Episcopal chapel near the fairgrounds.

And then we came to the freak-show. I had no heart for a freak-show, not even a good one. I thought of Mama at home, picking at the fur collar of Mamzelle Montberclair's coat and dreaming of trains crossing through the forests of Canada and China and all the other places where snow fell and geese flew and danger heightened and refined lives. And this freak-show was not a good one.

Mama had been right about who would be in the audience, violent stupid men some of them, with Mama's-boy names—Precious Mahoney, who weighed four hundred pounds and carried a kitchen chair and a pistol and a dogwhip with him wherever he went, like a lion-tamer, who sat on the kitchen chair now before the freak-show platform, like a wise fat sunfreckled toad, the sleeves of his sweaty shirt rolled up over his red arms; Brother Hot McGee, who smelled like a fried-chicken shack and once accidentally killed a man in an argument over whether a willow was actually a tree or a weed; Dr. Pudd'n DeBlieux, whose last name was pronounced "W" and who was drunk beyond belief, Arrow Catcher's only physician. There were also the Bunkies and Tooties and Bubbas and Alicks and a brainless blockhead of a child my age named Joseph of Arimathea who was at the freak-show with his blind granddaddy, who carved soap.

The freak-show itself was no better than its audience. For one thing it was situated near the old trestle that crossed the lake, down on the gray hard mud-flats. It was a dry year, so the lake was low, and the platform and the tent and the spectators stood on land that usually was covered with water. "Those pathetic souls," Mama had said, and she was right. No one but a person of that description could have exhibited himself on this unholy ground, which smelled of mussels and rotten shellfish and the regular stink of gumbo land.

And yet the scene—the freak-show and, I suppose, its spectators—brought to Daddy a life and vitality that could not have been predicted. Before, he had been tramping and dogged and determined to do this thing, to take his son to the freak-show in spite of a wife who was forever knowing best and advising sensibly. Now he was alert and amazed and humble before what he considered the wonder and the glamour and the magic of show business.

I looked at him in surprise; he had changed in appearance. He had been small and weasly and drawn and petty in his drunkenness and anger, and now he was childlike and beautiful and new in his small stature. His eyes, like his mouth were literally wide open. I saw him in the shape of the child he must have been at my age, in Memphis, on Beale Street, in the clash and glare and dark beauty of whores and the dangerous black men he must have braved to walk that wide now-extinct street in search of a man I'm sure he never found, old tan man Handy, the Father of the Blues, and held in his child-hand only a return bus ticket and in his child-mind danger and distance and courage and strange honor. I looked at him in love.

I looked at the freak-show and tried to see it through Daddy's eyes. Without having words for this, I tried to see the spectators of the Fair as he must have seen them, doomed and tragic men, romantic as explorers for their hidden pistols and whiskey-ruined, sun-ruined faces and lives. I could almost see them through Daddy's eyes, almost know some true bad value in their lives—Alick, whose business was the Hocus Pocus Liquor Store, which had a straw-hatted spook on its electric sign, Tootie, whose car lot had a sign that flashed a giraffe and a dachshund—HIGH QUALITY, LOW

PRICES; W, the physician, who saved lives. I could almost believe in their reverse beauty as he believed in it.

I looked hard at the freak-show and tried to see what he saw.

The freaks had done what they could to make the show a gay and interesting-looking affair. The wooden platform was securely built, with new two-by-fours here and there to replace those that must have broken or rotted. The tent behind it, a long shallow rectangular affair, was ancient and faded and water-stained—and yet it too had been the object of someone's special care.

Along its front wall had been painted large caricatures of the freaks inside—Jo Jo the Dog-faced Boy, Fanny the Fat Lady, the Alligator Woman, Mitzi Mayfair (a midget lady), a fire-eater, a four-legged man (who I learned later was not traveling with the show). The original caricatures were old-fashioned things, but they had been touched up with fresh paint.

There was a podium at the left side of the stage with a large roll of bright yellow tickets on top of it and, on the front of the podium, a hand-lettered sign that said, Show Time Dusk Come One Come All One Dollar.

A line of lightbulbs had been strung around the top of the canvas and were blazing with yellow light. There were flood-lights at the foot of the platform. A million bugs had been attracted to the light. There were also three faded banners that must have been red at one time, drooped down on the canvas from the tops of three of the tent poles.

Daddy said, "Look at it, Sugar! Just look!"

Suddenly I was afraid to imagine the wonders he saw in this tacky spectacle. I saw only bugs and bare bulbs and faded flags, old-timey cartoons on stained colorless canvas.

Then a man stepped through the folds of the tent and walked, aimlessly I thought, onto the platform and stood scratching himself as if he were alone. The suit he was wearing was formless, made of silk the color of snuff. I am sure it had never been washed or cleaned in any way. Wearing it, he looked like a man who has been dashed with brown paint that is sheeting from him in bags and tatters.

For a long time he made no movement at all except the slow motion required to smoke a cigarette. He stood slumped with his hands in his pockets. He drew on the cigarette until the tip was red and then exhaled the smoke, which rose into his right eye and caused him to squint hard. When the butt was tiny he took it from his mouth with his left hand and field-stripped it in his slow casual precise way and then scattered the tobacco bits on the platform beneath him. He stood slumped again in his snuff-colored suit.

At last he began to move. He shook his head like a man waking up on a park bench and remembering where he is. As he came more to life, he moved forward to the front of the platform and started to speak.

He said, "I am *honored* . . ." For a while he spoke in his incredible, lethargic way, nasal and northern, of some vague wonderment which was his own to possess, or that possessed him, that seemed responsible for his presence on this platform, in this suit, which now I saw (with of course no words to say this) as the filmy material of himself, his real flesh, and beyond flesh.

He talked on, sweat poured off his face, and more and more the suit seemed a fluid and essential thing. The bugs in the floodlights had multiplied into the billions. They soared around the lighted area. They converged on the floodlights and rose up into the dark sky. They formed a haze between the talker—which is what we called him later—and his audience, as thick as a beaded curtain, and the curtain rippled and changed and rattled as if it had been shaken.

He spoke of the humanity inside the tent behind him. "Jo Jo," he said, "Ohyeah ohyeah, Jo Jo the Dog-faced Boy"—he was singing now—almost a song, his voice—singing to us in the sweltering Mississippi evening in a sweat-soaked silk suit the color of snuff and the shape of bad rain—"found, oh Jesus, in the wilds of Australia, continent of gentleness and punished sin, and raised by a friendly band of marsupials, ohyeah ohyeah." It was a song that rattled (seemed to rattle) the limbs and fruit of the pecan trees around us.

And then he stopped. He took a snuff-colored handkerchief from his pocket and mopped at his face. He did not look at us now. He did not move, only looked at the platform beneath his feet. Sweat formed again on his face and dropped to the boards in a pool.

We stood waiting on him, men and boys in our sweat-soaked shirts, women (there were a few) with sweat caking the talcum powder to their necks.

The talker turned sidewise to the audience and looked away from us, back at the cartoons on the tent. I thought—

or think now anyway—that he looked like a trainer who, confident and heedless, turns his back on a troupe of performing animals and is not afraid.

When he began again he said that inside this tent behind him, for the sum of a single paper dollar bill, we would see Fanny the Fat Lady, that the bikini she wore was a bedsheet, that once she had been thin as a wisp, "as lithesome," he said, "as smoke" and lovely, that she had loved, unwisely, a traveling man and now ate to soothe the pain of her loss, that her fat was a measure of her love. Honesty throbbed in his voice like a musical saw.

Belief and disbelief were the same creature in me. My eyes suddenly saw lights blazing and banners whipping, the wonderful parade, elephants and hooves and bright horns, tightrope dancers and jugglers and clowns, all that Fanny and Jo Jo and Mitzi Mayfair stood for in my daddy's mind, dark dangerous bright Beale Street in Memphis, the whores and knives and pointy-toed shoes and Panama suits and pink convertibles and blue-plumed pimps and, somewhere, probably asleep in his old-man bedroom with a slop jar beside the bed and flowered wallpaper on the walls, and lying beside a gray-haired shriveled old wife in a flannel gown, the brightest most dangerous apparition of all the amazing street, the Father of the Blues!—ancient and foolish and toothless and blind, W. C. Handy, live and in person, with snuff-colored skeleton fingers to touch the valves of a sweet oiled horn, DeBlieux C. Handy in the same city, on the same street, and not even dead.

The talker was singing again, every sentence. He described

the Alligator Woman—alley-gay-tor, he pronounced it, sang it—her mossy scaly skin; he described the Giant—sad and gentle, tragically born in Lapland where, when he was a child, there was not one lap large enough for him to sit in, not even his own mama's; the hermaphrodite ("Lord," he said, "the embarrassment, born of the union of brother and sister, twin children, Hermes and Aphrodite Johnson of the Hill District of Pittsburgh, Pennsylvania, Lord I say don't look, for God's love, do not, when you walk inside that tent, do not cast eyes on what is too private, too sacred, too sad to be seen, one dollar, a single paper dollar bill"); and he sang of someone else, I forget who, *ee wolnks ee tolnks ees almos chewmann ee crawlzonisbelly like a rep-tile*

The magic of his song made me know, or believe, that the Love Boat was, in some way, an actual ship that carried a crew of actors and sailed from ports where my daddy might book passage and board and embark and find love. I thought he did know the hearts of Ethel Merman and Eddie Albert and the others, that if he shook them by the hand they would somehow recognize him as their own kind and welcome him aboard, that the world on shipboard was a world made for him, with music and dancing and kisses, and that because he had entered it, so could I, all good men and women could, where Mama could wear silk roses and fur-trimmed coats and speak with strangers of train rides across the frozen Ukraine.

Men in the audience were paying their dollars to go into the freak-show. I was frightened but ready to walk inside too, to view a spectacle that would mark me forever with some sign, outward and visible, as my father's child and thereby make known to all the world that I too might shake the hand of Pearl Bailey and Duke Ellington and be recognized and received into their company.

I saw Daddy fumble excitedly in his pocket. He pulled out a small roll of bills and peeled one off and stuck the others back.

Suddenly I knew he was not going to let me go into the freak-show. Daddy said, "Go on home." I said, "Let me go in." He said, "Go home, you don't want to see no morphodite." I said, "Joseph of Arimathea is going in, let me go in, Daddy." He said, "Joseph of Arimathea has got to describe it to his blind granddaddy. I ain't blind."

Daddy paid his dollar and took a ticket from the man in the snuff-colored suit and went inside without me.

For a minute, maybe longer, I stood by the platform in disbelief and shame. People pushed by me and paid their dollars and followed Daddy inside the tent, even the blind soap-carver and his blockhead grandson.

At last I left the Fair, alone and running, past the arrow catchers and the ass-kickers and the tobacco-spitters and the Episcopalians.

*A*t home I took off my clothes, down to my underwear shorts, and pulled back the covers of the bed. I lay in the darkness beneath a sheet and a bedspread I didn't need in the July heat.

Mama came up the stairs and into the room and stood beside the door with the light behind her. She was wearing

Mamzelle's coat—in this heat, a winter coat!—why not just the silk dress? I turned on my side away from her.

She said, "Is everything all right, Sugar?"

I said, "Yes." I tried to make my breathing sound normal.

She said, "How was the freak-show?"

I said, "Okay."

She said, "Are you sure you're all right?"

I was tired of trains through winter forests, of romantic cruises and silk and fur and alcohol, the misery of false geographies and populations of misfits.

Mama sat on the bed beside me and touched my bare back beneath the covers with her fingers. She said, "What happened?"

I said, "Nothing."

I thought of the talker at the freak-show. I hoped he would say to Daddy, "Eddie Albert wouldn't know you. Ethel Merman wouldn't shake your hand."

Mama said, "Don't be too hard on your daddy, Sugar."

I said, "Did he really go to see W. C. Handy? Did he really walk down Beale Street like a king?"

She said, "Oh, Sugar-man . . ."

I turned over on my back and looked at her. She was sweating in Mamzelle's coat. Her face was covered with sweat and her hair was stuck to her neck and forehead.

She said, "Daddy thinks that all the world's magic is almost evolved out."

I thought of Roebuck Lake, its swamps and sloughs and loblollies and breaks of cypress and cane, its sunken treetops and stobs and bream beds and sleepy gar rolling over and over and over, its baptizing pools and bridges and mussels and mosquitoes and turkey vultures and, now in the drought, the gray flaking mud-flats and logs crowded with turtles and sometimes a fat snake yawning its tame old cottony mouth like a well-fed dog in a pen.

I said, "Is that what the freak-show is?"

She said, "Dirty miracles."

I said, "What about Mamzelle's coat?"

For a long time neither of us spoke again. I may have slept, I'm not sure. Then Mama was singing to me in a dry dead voice, sweating in the dry Mississippi evening. She must have been singing some made-up song about trains, but in my ears it was the voice of the talker at the freak-show, a song about friendly roving bands of marsupials, of giants in Lapland, of Hermes and Aphrodite, of wonderful geographies.

I said, "Mama, it ain't worth it."

She said, "I know, Sugar. I know. But, Lord, I just love him so."

Sugar, the Eunuchs, and Big G.B.

One time when I was eleven—this was fifteen years ago, soon after my daddy first told me that wild bands of eunuchs run amuck in the Mississippi Delta—I spent the night with a friend named G.B. Junior. His daddy's name was Big G.B., and his mama was Sweet Runa, rhymed with tuna. Big G.B. had a houseful of guns, all kinds, pistols and rifles and muzzle-loaders and shotguns, even a blunderbuss with a bell-shaped barrel, and an illegal thing or two, grenade launchers and automatic rifles. He loved to show them to G.B. Junior's friends.

In fact, the guns were about the only reason G.B. Junior had any friends. He was fat and had a round snoutish nose with prominent nostrils. He would wrestle you to the ground and hold you with his fat and put his face into your neck or bare belly. He would make a grunting, rooting sound with his mouth and nose against your skin. He called this "giving pig." G.B. Junior was a mess.

Big G.B. would show us boys his guns and treat us grown-up. He'd say, "I wouldn't show you men these here firearms if I didn't know I could trust you." Sometimes he would tell us, "Always remember, it's the *un*loaded gun that

217

kills." He would look me and G.B. Junior in the eye and say, "Now do each and every one of you men get my meaning?" Sweet Runa, his wife, might holler out from the kitchen, "Explain your meaning to them, Big G.B." He'd give us a manly wink.

So it was a bunking party and I was in a big bed with G.B. Junior. I don't know why I couldn't sleep. I felt lonely all the time, that's one reason. I wanted to be home where I could hear my mama and daddy in the kitchen. I could stand anything I could hear—that's what I thought. Anyway, I couldn't sleep.

I lifted the comforter and sheet off me and slid my legs from under the covers. It was January and cold in the room. I sat on the edge of the bed and pulled on blue jeans and a T-shirt, no shoes.

I eased out of the room and down the hall toward the bathroom to take a leak. When I was finished I stopped outside the bedroom where Big G.B. and Sweet Runa were sleeping. There were no lights on in the house, but the moonlight was bright and I could see the two of them beneath the covers sweet as whales.

I went into the room and prowled a little. I poked through some bureau drawers and didn't find much. I found a box of rubbers in Big G.B.'s bedside table and took one to keep; it couldn't hurt.

There wasn't much else to do. I walked out of the bedroom and down the hall.

I started to go back to bed, but on second thought walked

down to Big G.B.'s gun room and snapped on the light at the wall switch.

Guns were on every wall, most of them behind glass locked up. The dark bright oiled woods of the stocks and butts made me love Big G.B. and Sweet Runa. The room seemed orderly and under control and full of love. There were deer heads and goat heads and a bearskin on the walls. The face of Jesus was made out of Indian arrowheads and spearpoints. There were boxes of dueling pistols on a low table and a great gray papery hornets' nest hanging on a hook from a ceiling beam.

I went to a chestlike table topped with rose-veined marble and opened the drawer. I knew what was in it. There were two green felt bags, heavy with their contents. I took out the first and loosened the drawstring and put my hand inside and ran my fingers through the bullets like a pirate through coins in a treasure chest.

I set it on the marble top. The second bag was heavier, the pistol Big G.B. called his three-fifty-seven.

I took it out of its bag and held it in my right hand and measured its weight. It was nickel-plated and had a hand-carved grip with a nickel ring at the bottom. I pressed the release near the trigger guard, the way I had seen Big G.B. do a hundred times, and the cylinder swung out with a soft metallic sound.

It was loaded with six cartridges. Daddy said one time Tex Ritter performed live and in person right here in Arrow Catcher, Mississippi, on the stage of the Strand Theater. Tex

Ritter would sign your program. Daddy said he was just a little boy at the time and he asked Tex Ritter if he had any
advice for somebody who wanted to break into show business. (I wondered why Daddy would ask a question like
that.)

I snapped shut the cylinder of the pistol with one hand,
like a policeman, and it clicked into place. I used both
thumbs to cock the hammer. I pointed the barrel at the
bearskin on the wall and said, "Blammo," and then eased the
hammer back down. (I don't know what Tex Ritter answered.)

I stuck the big revolver inside the front of my pants and
walked out the gun-room door. I walked down the hallway
and into the kitchen and right out the kitchen door and let
the screened door slap shut behind me. It was freezing cold.
Before I could get down the splintery frosty steps and out of
the stiff grass of the backyard, my feet were numb.

Nobody was on the streets. I felt invisibility grow in my
freezing bones.

I walked past the gin and past Runt Conroy's house. I
walked past the lightplant and past the firehouse where
Hydro Chisolm, the marshal's grown son, shot stray dogs
and blew the fire whistle, fire or no fire, and sometimes
chased cars. I walked beneath the legs of the water tower and
past a blind man's house, Mr. O'Kelly, who was sitting on his
porch in the middle of the freezing night carving soap. A
ventriloquist's dummy was sleeping in his lap. I crossed the
railroad tracks at Scott Butane and from there I could see my
house. The lights were on, as I knew they would be, no matter how late.

I walked into the side yard, outside the kitchen window, and stood beside a line of fig trees. I was out of sight of the midgets, in case they were awake. They lived in a trailer on the other side of the house and worked construction on the pipeline. Mavis Mitchum, a lady who sucked her skirt, lived on this side. My bare feet were numb, and I could scarcely feel the frozen dirt beneath them.

I could see Mama and Daddy in the kitchen. Mama was wearing a quilted robe and looked like a witch, the way she looked when Daddy was drinking. Daddy wore white painter's overalls and a billed cap all day and then got dressed up to drink. He was wearing his salt-and-pepper suit and a fresh starched shirt and his favorite tie, with a horse-head painted on it, which he got long years ago when he was a boy and visited the winter circus in Sarasota, Florida, and fell in love with a woman who swallowed things, swords and fire.

Daddy had propped a square mirror in the kitchen window. On the counter were four half-pints of Early Times and four shot glasses. (He called this "shooting fours.") Mama was saying something to him, I knew what. She was saying to him that he was an artist, that he was special and perfect and magic that his pain was special. She was telling him she wanted to carry his pain for him. I had heard it a hundred times, she meant every word. In front of the bare fig trees I grieved and celebrated my invisibility.

Daddy was looking into the mirror. Sometimes he would cut his eyes to it, quick, and glimpse himself there by surprise. Then he would stare at himself full face and turn his head, real slow, to catch another angle. He was tragic and handsome. He was dreaming of the woman who swallowed things. Mama was telling him that if his heart had to break she wanted it to break inside her own chest.

Daddy filled one shot glass from one bottle and then the next from the next bottle, and on to the end, until four drinks had been poured from four bottles into four glasses. He filled a larger glass with Coca-Cola from a quart and put it on the sink too.

He lifted the first shot in his hand and checked the mirror. Mama looked a hundred years old in her love for him. He drained the whiskey from the glass and set it back on the counter. He chased the drink with Coca-Cola. He looked into the mirror again. He was handsome and manly and tragic and fine. He was the Marlboro Man of alcoholism. He drank each of the four shots of whiskey in the same way.

I took Big G.B.'s three-fifty-seven out of my pants and pulled back the hammer with my aching cold thumbs and held the pistol in both hands.

The sound of the gun might as well have been Niagara Falls, it was so permanent and loud and useless.

A column of fire a foot long jumped out of the pistol's muzzle. The window I had shot through disappeared in one piece, glass and wood. Even the screen dropped straight down in front of me. When I fired the second shot I looked at my mama and believed that she was all women in the world, beauty and grief, and at the same time nobody at all, as shadowless and invisible as myself beside the white bare limbs of the fig trees. Then the lights were out and I was alone in my invisibility.

I walked out of the yard with the pistol still in my hand, swinging at my side, and went back to Big G.B.'s the same way I had come. The blind man was still carving soap, the dummy was awake now, had opened his eyes. Joseph of Arimathea was the dummy's name.

Neither of the shots had hit my daddy. I had missed him both times. I heard the siren of Big'un Chisolm's car just as I stepped inside Big G.B.'s back door and felt my feet start to thaw out. I put up the pistol and the cartridges and I slipped back into bed beside G.B. Junior. My body and my heart were saying, crying, *I want I want I want I want*

*J*oseph of Arimathea told the marshal I was the one fired the shots. The soap-carving blind man agreed with him. I heard this from the men talking at the Arrow Cafe. They were big talkers and big laughers and they acted like it was a joke and told me what a fine boy I was and don't worry about a thing, they all knew better than to believe a word those two dummies said, but there was nothing funny about it to me. I'll tell you why. Mavis Mitchum—the neighbor who sucked her skirt— she told on me too. She said she was up late watching for eunuchs and saw me. (She agreed with Daddy about the eunuchs. She said they sing and dance at Episcopal baptizings. Mavis Mitchum was a mess her own self.) Hydro saw me too, said he did. Hydro had a big head and wanted to be believed. He swore to his daddy he would never chase another car if somebody would please believe him, it was Sugar Mecklin who did the shooting he said, he saw me.

Big'un, the marshal, didn't believe any of them, least of all his own poor son Hydro. Big'un apologized to Daddy, and even to me. He made Hydro apologize. Big'un said it was bad enough to live in a town full of freaks (oh, he was hard on Hydro), let alone be accused by them. Daddy said, "It don't matter, Big'un." Big'un said, "I just wouldn't want you to think a whole townful of freaks has turned on your boy." Daddy said, "I know that, Big'un, it ain't everybody who's against us." Big'un was relieved. He said, "You so right, Gilbert. The midgets, for example, ain't said a word."

I was sick with grief. I cried all the next day and Mama held me and told me Daddy was fine, just fine, you hush, Sugar, he's not hurt one bit. It didn't help. I still couldn't stop. I lay on my bed in my room, but I couldn't lie still. I walked out in the yard and threw corn to the chickens. Nothing helped.

I wanted to confess to Daddy. I walked through our house and looked at all the things that told me he was alive. I looked at the closet full of empty whiskey bottles, I stirred them with my hand and made them rattle and clank. I read their labels and fondled their shapes. I held them up to the light, one and then another, and looked at the small drops of amber fluid that collected in the corners when I tilted a bottle to one side. I unscrewed the caps and tasted the fluid on my tongue and knew that this was the only magic that kept him alive and in love with the sorry likes of me.

People were in the kitchen. A party started that day

around the bullet holes and lasted a month. People loved Daddy for being shot at. The Communists did it, somebody said, the Klan did it, jealous husbands and heartbroken women and politicians and "the money men" did it—the law, the church, the blacks, the Indians, even the Iranians— no suggestion was too outlandish—and Daddy and Mama didn't deny one possibility. There were a million good reasons a man as fine as my daddy might be shot at.

I went in Daddy's bedroom and opened the drawers of his chest. I looked in his shirt drawer and picked up a shirt and held it to my face and breathed in the smell, the fragrance of Daddy's flesh that could never be washed out. It was whiskey and paint and Aqua Velva and leather and shoe polish and wool and peppermint. I closed that drawer and opened others. In the deepest drawer I reached in and searched with my hand, behind the underwear and the rolled socks—I knew what I was looking for—until I found the candy, the peppermint puffs that he hid there, the light unbelievable airy candy that melted on the tongue, as if it had never been there, and left only the taste, the sweet aroma that was always with Daddy. I don't know why he hoarded peppermint.

I looked between his mattress and box springs and found the cracked leather folder with the brass zipper. I opened it and took out the old Tex Ritter program with the faded-ink autograph. There was a full-face picture of Tex on the front, a black-and-white drawing of him wearing his big hat and smiling his big smile. "For Gilbert Mecklin, your friend, Tex Ritter," the autograph said. There was also a ticket in the folder, faded, torn across the center, with the words Ringling Brothers Circus on the stub. And there was a picture of Elvis Presley, an eight-by-ten glossy with Elvis's signature in the corner. There was a triangular tip of steel—it might have been a swordpoint. I believed that it was, I believed it had belonged to the woman who swallowed things. I put the swordpoint in my pocket and stuck everything else back in the folder.

I went to Daddy's closet and knew where to look for the suit. Not even Mama knew about the suit. I had found it by accident a year before.

Deep in the closet, back behind his shotgun, behind the rubber hip-waders and the canvas jackets, behind the croquet set with its wire wickets and slender-handled mallets and wooden balls with bright stripes, which he had bought drunk and had never taken out of the box or allowed Mama to set up, behind the box of souvenirs from the junior high school he had dropped out of—a script from a play called "The Beauty and the Beef," a boutonniere he had worn to a dance—lay the suit-box I was looking for.

I lifted the box out of the closet—white sturdy cardboard—and put it on the floor of Daddy's bedroom. The house was full of people, more and more of them, looking at the bullet holes and congratulating Daddy. People were laughing and happy, whiskey bottles and ice and glasses were clinking. I lifted the top off the large rectangular box and laid it aside. I knelt on the floor in front of the box and lifted out the airy tissue paper, a piece at a time, away from the cloth of the suit.

The suit was cheap—thin and shiny, almost brittle, and there was no lining. There were a million loose threads in the seams. It was a suit jacket studded with rhinestones. The pants had a double row of rhinestones down either leg. I lifted the jacket from the box and held it in my fingers to test its incredible light weight.

I learned to cry with no sound. I could hear Daddy in the kitchen, with Mama and their friends. I could tell by the way he talked and laughed that he was dressed in his Sarasota tie with the painted horse's head. I knew that Mama was glowing with pride and joy and grief.

I put on the jacket and stood looking at myself in the door-length mirror on the closet. I thought of the woman who swallowed things. I thought of trapeze dancers and jugglers and freak-shows. I thought of Tex Ritter and of lariats and spurs and chaps. I thought of a man my daddy had known when he was a boy, who carried with him a saddlebag full of knives and another saddlebag full of harmonicas. He told me, "Sugar, I would die to play Orange Blossom Special on one of those harmonicas on stage." He said his favorite musicians were a group called the Harmoni-cats, which featured a dwarf with a harmonica three feet long. He said, "I would live forever if I could throw those knives." He said, "If I could throw those knives, I would name them, each one. I would name one Boo Kay Jack, I would name one Django. I would throw them and I would watch the bright brave frightened face of a beautiful woman as it sailed end over end toward her—one knife and then the next and the next—until every knife was quivering in the board next to her sweet bare body and her perfect figure was outlined in steel." I was wearing the rhinestone-studded coat of my daddy, which was too big for me, and I was looking at myself in the mirror. The coat-tail hung down to my thighs, the sleeves covered my hands. Rhinestones ran the length of the sleeves, they outlined the lapels. I turned my back to the mirror and looked over my shoulder. I read the words spelled out in rhinestones on my back: *Rock 'n' Roll Music*. I thought—dreamed, somehow, although I was awake—that knives were being thrown at me, that harmonica music was being played. I thought I was riding horseback, behind somebody else, a man, that I was holding on to him, my arms around his waist, and that the horseman was insane and smelled of peppermint and whiskey and that he dug the horse's bloodless sides with sil-ver spurs and was Death made flesh and was somehow also my daddy and mama and Tex Ritter and everybody else in Arrow Catcher, Mississippi, and that there was a voice in the wind and in the horse's hooves and it told me that we lived, all of us, in a terrible circus geography where freaks grow like magic from the buckshot and gumbo, where eunuchs roam the Delta flatscape looking for Episcopalians. I didn't know why I had shot at Daddy. I only knew I wanted to confess to him, to have him know that I knew he was magic and that I loved him, that I wanted to drink whiskey and be like him, to find a woman who swallowed swords and fire, to marry a woman like my mama, who could grow ugly with love. I wanted to confess my betrayal of Daddy to the midgets, so the last freaks in town might know and not think well of me. Nobody caught me that day, nobody came into the bedroom from the kitchen. I took off the jacket and replaced the tissue paper and folded the suit and hid it away again in the box, far back in the closet.

⚘
I was insane until April, when the eunuchs came to Arrow Catcher looking for St. George. I poached pigeons in the belfry of the Baptist Church (it was Daddy's favorite kind of hunting) and with a tennis shoe swatted down the warm fat feathery ovals, with amazed eyes and all their bustle and clutter and complaint, purple and gray and brown and white and with glittery heads. I peeled off their feathers and skin and took out their insides and spread them in front of me. I wanted to live in my daddy's skin, behind his rib cage, to share his heart and lungs and liver and spleen. I wanted to confess to Daddy, but I could not. I cooked the pigeons over fires in the woods near Roebuck Lake, and ate them, mostly raw. I chanted *I want I want I want I want*. I squatted on the lake-bank, or in the pigeon-fragrant dark of the church loft and imagined wild bands of roving eunuchs galloping the Mississippi roads and flatwoods, clattering across bridges and through pastures, skirting the edges of small towns. I thought of farmers with rifles on the lookout for them like wild dogs among the livestock. I looked for my own face among the eunuchs.

I ran a low fever every day for months, and frightened my mama with my crying, which I could not stop. She was afraid for me, and Daddy drank, and I spent the night almost every night with friends, and finally with only one friend, G.B. Junior—and not really with G.B. Junior, with his daddy. I spent as many nights as I could with Big G.B. It may have been Mama's idea, to get me away from the drinking and the loud bullet-hole parties—I don't know whose idea it was. Big G.B. invited me to go places with him, especially out to his farm, which he called Scratch-ankle. He let me drive his pickup through the cattlegaps, we shot a .22 pistol at dead tree stumps. I was not afraid of the pistol. I shot accurately and he congratulated me on my aim. G.B. Junior was never invited to go with us.

Sometimes Sweet Runa would make Big G.B. take him with us, but it never worked out. G.B. Junior said he hated the stupid farm, he said the pistol shots hurt his ears, he said the pickup made him carsick. Big G.B. said, "Well, Runa, if he don't *want* to go . . ." So it was always the two of us. Sometimes we would check the horses, sometimes Jabbo Deeber, the black man who ran the farm, would take us to a honey tree and we would scoop out honey in the comb and suck it off our fingers and dodge the angry bees. Sometimes the three of us—Jabbo and Big G.B. and me—would pinch Red Man out of a foil pouch and I would end each day dizzy with joy.

Big G.B. knew who shot at my daddy. He didn't tell Sweet Runa, he didn't even tell me—I just knew he knew. He started keeping me, like I was his child. I wished I was his child.

On the first day of turkey season, in April, I was spending Saturday night with Big G.B. to go hunting early the next morning. Even Mama believed I was getting better in Big

G.B.'s care. I had stopped crying and running fever and poaching pigeons. I had put back some of the weight I had lost after the shooting. Daddy was still the town hero for getting shot at. People bought him drinks, gave him tickets to football games, asked his advice on things he knew nothing about. He dressed up more and went to work less. He drank whiskey in front of the mirror and spoke of taking a trip to see the winter circus, which he said had been moved to Venice, Florida. I held on to the swordpoint, I ate from his stash of peppermint, I wore his Rock 'n' Roll suit.

And then, on that Sunday morning, the first day of the season, when the rain was lashing the windows and the abelia hedges and I was awake at four o'clock and sitting at Big G.B.'s kitchen table eating Rice Krispies and milk while Sweet Runa and G.B. Junior slept, I brought out Daddy's swordpoint and laid it on the table. I laid out a few peppermint puffs. I told him about the Tex Ritter program and the Rock 'n' Roll suit. I told him about Django and Boo Kay Jack and the saddlebag full of knives and the one full of harmonicas. I told him about the woman who swallowed things and about shooting fours and Mama's housecoat and the pigeons. I told him Daddy was magic.

Big G.B. said, "Your daddy ain't magic."

I said, "He ain't?"

He said, "Naw, there ain't any magic."

I said, "What about the blind man's dummy? Is Joseph of Arimathea magic?"

He said, "Get your shotgun, Sugar."

I went to the corner near the stove and took my shotgun

231

by the barrel. I got my shell bag and looked at Big G.B. to see what he was thinking. His face didn't tell me. I stood by the kitchen door holding the shotgun and shells. I said, "Is Joseph of Arimathea magic, Big G.B.?"

He said, "There ain't no magic. Magic is the same as sentimental. Scratch the surface of sentimental and you know what you find?—Nazis and the Ku Klux Klan. Magic is German in nature and evil and not real. Scratch magic, Sugar, and you're looking for death."

I said, "You already know, don't you."

He said, "No man is going to get mad at his boy for taking a shot at him, Sugar."

This was the first time the shooting had been spoken between us. He said, "Shooting to kill is what a boy is supposed to do to his daddy, Sugar-man."

We went out the kitchen door together into the morning darkness, both of us carrying unloaded shotguns and the shell bag clicking between us. The rain was whipping through the porch screens and the floor was slick. We ducked out the screened door and down the steps and into the pickup. We slammed the doors and wiped rainwater off our faces. Sweet Runa and G.B. Junior were awake, trying to get G.B. Junior dressed to go with us.

Big G.B. didn't want to take him. He started up the engine. He said, "Sweet Runa is not a bad woman, Sugar. I want you to know that." Sweet Runa was shouting something to us from the back door, but we couldn't hear. Big G.B. shifted into first gear and we pulled out of the yard. I didn't say anything. He said, "And your daddy is not a bad man. He truly ain't." He was going through the gears of the truck now and his feet in the big boots covered his whole side of the cab floor. I looked back through the rear window and saw Sweet Runa and G.B. Junior standing in the yard in the rain. I said, "Big G.B., sometimes I hate myself so much." He slowed the truck and pulled to a stop. He started turning around to go back to the house. He said, "I just try to keep an open mind about Joseph of Arimathea."

So now G.B. Junior was in the front seat of the pickup too, surly and sleepy and unhappy and silent. Big G.B. and I were wearing the two camouflage ponchos and G.B. Junior was wearing a Day-Glo yellow slicker his mama had put on him. Big G.B. told him he couldn't wear a yellow raincoat in the woods, he would look like a fool. G.B. Junior said don't worry he wouldn't wear it to a fucking dog fight and said he hadn't brought his shotgun, he wasn't going hunting. Big G.B. said don't use that word and what did he mean he wasn't going hunting, what was he doing in the truck if he wasn't going hunting. When we parked near the Arrow Cafe, G.B. Junior opened the truck door and stepped out into the rain and took off the Day-Glo raincoat and threw it into the bed of the pickup. Big G.B. said what did he want to do that for. I knew none of us would see the turkey woods that morning.

Hunters from all around Arrow Catcher were in the Arrow Cafe. Everybody was in camouflage and hip-waders and raingear, a dozen or more men. The linoleum was slick with rain that had blown in and had been tracked in, and Miss

Josie, who ran the cafe, had thrown a couple of blue towels on the floor to soak up the water. Some of the men were at the counter and others were at tables or in booths, eating sausages and eggs and biscuits. Miss Josie was bringing extra gravy. A couple of men were having shots of whiskey with their coffee. The rain was lashing the streets and blowing like sheets on the line across the streetlights. G.B. Junior was soaked through, because he had taken off the raincoat. It was hard to think of a child as lonely and unhappy as G.B. Junior, or one as happy as I was. There were guns and ammunition belts everywhere, propped against the counter, leaned in corners, draped across tables and barstools. I thought of Tex Ritter on the little stage of the Strand Theater in Arrow Catcher, the way he looked on the program and the way Daddy had described him. I thought of my daddy as a boy in that audience, sitting on a hard chair down front and looking up at the big horse and the lariat and Tex Ritter's six-guns and boots and spurs and hat. I believed that my daddy and I were somehow the same person, that I had visited Florida and loved the woman who swallowed things. I believed that when I cried in my heart *I want I want I want I want* that I was speaking, crying, in my daddy's voice, saying what he meant to say when he dressed in secret in his Rock 'n' Roll suit and watched himself drink whiskey in the mirror.

We looked for a place for three people to sit in the Arrow Cafe. Big G.B. made Runt Conroy change to another seat at the counter so there were two empty stools together near the rear. I sat on one of the stools and could see through the low window into the kitchen. A large black woman in an apron was flipping hotcakes and cracking eggs into a bowl. I loved the turkey hunters in the Arrow Cafe. I loved Miss Josie, who owned it. I loved Big G.B., who gave me love without pain. Big G.B. told G.B. Junior to sit on the other stool at the counter with me, but G.B. Junior wouldn't do it. He said he wanted to sit on the floor next to the jukebox. Big G.B. said, "Oh, gotdog, son," and went over and tried to talk him into sitting at the counter. He still wouldn't. He wouldn't even look at his daddy. He was fat as lard and shivering and drenched and angry and cold but he would not come up to the counter. I knew how much he hated me. I didn't care. I was glad he wouldn't sit at the counter. Some people in a booth told G.B. Junior come on over here, they had plenty of room if he wanted to sit with them. He wouldn't do that either. Big G.B. said, "Well, don't meddle with the jukebox." G.B. Junior said, "I ain't studying no fucking jukebox." Big G.B. pretended not to hear.

Big G.B. came to the counter and sat beside me—this was why I was glad for the empty seat. He put his big hand on my left shoulder and squeezed it. Miss Josie poured me a cup of coffee, because I was with Big G.B., and then looked in the direction of G.B. Junior on the floor and decided against asking if he wanted a cup, it was too much trouble. I felt like a king. In the midst of these men and their camouflage and, in my nostrils, the smell of coffee cooking and breakfast and whiskey and the fragrance of wet rubber raingear and canvas and in this room full of breached firearms and the click-click of ammunition in the pockets of these men—in my own pockets—and the fine low sound of manly laughter and good southern whiskey voices, I felt for the first time free of my daddy, his magic if there was magic. I felt it even now, when it was hardest to know which was Daddy and which was me, when I wasn't sure just who had sat in the Strand Theater and heard a whiskey-voiced cowboy sing rye whiskey rye whiskey rye whiskey I cry if I don't get rye whiskey well I think I will die. Even when it was hardest to believe that it was my daddy and not myself who remembered Sarasota and longed for Django and Boo Kay Jack and loved the music of Spike Jones and the Harmoni-cats and the dwarf with the three-foot harmonica, and Daddy who dressed in secret (as I did now myself) in a rhinestone suit and ate peppermint puffs—I felt free of him, free to feel hatred if that came to me, and resentment and pure anger where I thought there should be acceptance and awe and love. I was free of Daddy's shooting fours, would never have to aim a pistol at anyone ever again, never have to know or care why I shot at him in the first place, never have to confess to him those evil seconds and know the pain it would inflict in his heart and in mine.

I was sitting beside Big G.B. and he was pouring milk into my coffee and a drop of whiskey from a flat bottle into his. I looked out the big window and saw the rain lashing at everything, at the steel awning in front of the Arrow Cafe, the sidewalks gleaming with reflected light, the pickups with gun racks and STP stickers and water standing in the beds, and the alley, its slick brick street where somebody had piled mattress boxes, and I saw the van drive up. I could see it out the window, blue and extra long, with lots of seats in it. It was filled with grown-up men in suits—I could see them already—eight or nine of them lined up in rows in their seats. The lights of the van shone through the sheeting rain, yellow and wonderful and unexpected in the dark morning. I watched the van park and sit with its motor running and the lights still on. Nobody got out. Nobody was looking at it but me. I kept watching, felt strange and frightened. I leaned on my stool far to the side so that my shoulder touched Big G.B.'s sleeve and allowed my heart to fill up with love for this big man, and for all these men who were not my daddy.

G.B. Junior had gotten up from his place on the floor and had pulled the jukebox out from the wall. He was groping around in the oily dust behind it for the cord, he wanted to plug it in. Miss Josie saw him and walked from behind the counter to where he stood. I could tell she didn't want to scold him in front of everybody, especially not in front of his daddy, or in front of me. I could almost feel sorry for G.B. Junior. He was trying to stick the plug into the wall socket.

A spray of rainwater and cold April wind caused Miss Josie and everybody else to look at the front door, which had opened. G.B. Junior went ahead with what he was doing and plugged in the jukebox. He started going through his pockets for a quarter, but he didn't have one. I looked at the door too. I expected to see whoever had been out in the van, the men in suits, but it was not them.

It was Daddy who came in the door. He was a little out of breath, not from running. His face was streaming with rainwater. He was wearing a plastic raincoat and a billed cap, so wet it stuck to his head. The men in the cafe cheered when they saw him, Runt Conroy and Red Goodlook and Grease Foley and Bubba Corley and Jimmy Scallion, everybody. He was still the town hero for getting shot at.

He was looking around the room, looking for me. I made myself small so he might not see me. Men slapped him on the back, offered him coffee and whiskey, which he didn't notice just now. G.B. Junior stopped meddling with the juke-box and looked at Daddy, with love I thought. I wondered why G.B. Junior and I couldn't swap daddies.

Only Big G.B. didn't look up. He seemed to know it was Daddy and that Daddy knew something or had something or disproved something that might change everything. Miss Josie's smile lighted up the room when she saw Daddy. He didn't notice. He walked across the blue towels on the floor and stopped and looked around until he found me.

I could see through the cheap plastic raincoat of course, to the paint-stained overalls and the flannel shirt. And yet I half expected to see that Daddy was wearing the Rock 'n' Roll suit. He looked handsome and certain and hopeful, the way I thought he might look in the rhinestones. I looked at his face and saw that he was not drunk yet, maybe still sick with a hangover, it was hard to tell. We faced each other and I felt emotions come into my heart that I didn't want. I saw myself with Daddy when I was six years old. I was sitting in a low tree in our yard, maybe six feet off the ground, and Daddy was painting the tree blue. He dipped carefully into the paint can with a brush and then spread the bright enamel evenly over the bark, trunk, and branches. There was sweet magic in the combined fragrances of enamel paint and mimosa blossoms. The limb I sat on swayed and threatened to give way. I loved the danger and the blue tree. Daddy said "I hope this don't kill it. The yard needs the color, though." I had believed in the Arrow Cafe that I had become another man's child, that because I had fired his .22 pistol into tree stumps and had driven his truck through the cattlegaps and fished his ponds and lain on his floor in his den in front of his television set and fallen asleep and been carried in his arms to a warm bed and had loved him that all my terrible past had not really happened, that I had never been born into the family of a drunkard, handsome and tragic and fine as any man who ever walked across a movie screen, and that I had never learned from my mama that Daddy was magic and should be worshipped until she and I and everyone else who loved him grew ugly and pure and mad with love, and that the only control we could expect in our lives was exactly what we needed most, blue trees and pigeon suppers and lonely secrets in the backs of drawers and closets.

I turned on the barstool and held Big G.B.'s arm with both my hands. I knew Daddy had come for me. I didn't want to go. I was afraid to love him again, and yet I already did love him, I had never stopped loving him, even when I hated him. I held on tight to Big G.B. I cut my eyes toward G.B. Junior and read his hatred of me. No one else in the Arrow Cafe cared about hatred; everyone else was in love with my daddy. They loved him—not, as I had thought, simply because he had been shot at, but because he truly was in some way pure, in some way perfect, as they knew they would never be—as I knew I would never be—in some way special, as Mama had known he was and had given up her life and beauty in wonder of, and that nothing he had ever done—his drunken violence and self-pity, his bullying and meanness and pettiness—was unforgivable, nothing too terrible to embrace. I had no words for any of this at age eleven, I hardly have them now, fifteen years later.

All the men wanted Daddy's attention. All asked about him, asked to do things for him. He did not ignore them, but he was not interested either. I was still clinging to Big G.B., and Big G.B. had laid his big hand over both of mine.

Daddy came squishing and squelching and squeaking across the linoleum in his rubber boots. He stood beside me at the barstool. He said, "Sugar, those men out in the van— do you know who they are?" He might have been giving me a gift, might have been afraid I was too young to know its value, too small to accept it. I shook my head to say no. He said, "It's the eunuchs. I called Sweet Runa and she told me y'all were down here. I wanted to let you know."

I let go of Big G.B.'s arm. I didn't know what to do with my hands. I put my face in them and put my head down on the counter, the way Daddy put his on the kitchen table sometimes after he had been shooting fours. I didn't know whether I would faint or cry or become invisible or explode, anything seemed more likely than that I would feel this chaos of strange love well up in my blood. I felt as if Daddy had shot me from ambush and that I was mortally wounded and that the gaping great bloody hole in my chest and heart was the dearest prick of pain and forgiveness and loss of hope that ever touched the purest part of man or child.

I said, "Daddy, I shot at you through the window. It was me."

He said, "You'll never guess who told me."

I said, "About me shooting at you?"

He said, "No, about the eunuchs."

I said, "Mavis Mitchum?"

He said, "Nope."

I said, "The midgets?"

He said, "No, of course not the midgets, that's silly."

I said, "I know who it was then. I know exactly who it was."

He was proud of me for guessing. He said, "He's a smart little bugger, ain't he?"

I said, "How does he do it, Daddy? Is it really Mr. O'Kelly who knows these things? Is it really the blind man?"

He looked surprised that I would say such a thing. He said, "Mr. O'Kelly?—that poor thing?" He said, "Mr. O'Kelly don't know much of nothing, Sugar. Poor Mr. O'Kelly wouldn't last the night, if he didn't have Joseph of Arimathea to wait on him hand and foot."

I said, "Did you talk to them—the eunuchs?"

He said, "Let's go outside, I'll introduce you."

I left Big G.B.'s side without really even a thought. I don't know what he felt, or what G.B. Junior felt or did, whether he moved onto the stool where I had been sitting and took the place he should have had all along, or whether he found a quarter and played the jukebox against everybody's wishes. I just don't know, didn't think to look, didn't think to ask, even later.

Daddy held the door and we went out into the lashing rain. Daddy said, "They are looking for St.-George-by-the-Lake, the little Episcopal chapel Dr. Hightower built out of the old Swiftown depot. We'll ride out and show them where it is."

I said, "Is it a baptizing this morning?"

He said, "The Barlow child."

The eunuch who was driving the van wore a short haircut and no mustache or sideburns. He rolled down his window and said, "I sure appreciate your help in locating the place, Mr. Mecklin. It's some kind of weather we're having this morning."

Daddy said, "This is my boy Sugar. Y'all just get behind us, we'll lead you out to the church."

The rain slacked up some, though it didn't quit yet. The turkey hunters—one or two of them—had already started out to their trucks. The woods were flooded, there would be no hunt today. Me and Daddy led the eunuchs out of town toward St. George, the old converted depot down by Roebuck Lake.

The All-Girl Football Team

Dressing in drag was not new to me. I had never worn a dress myself, but my father had.

My father was all man. His maleness defined him to me. Evenings, when he came home from work, I loved to hug him and to feel the rasp of a day's growth of beard against my face and neck. I loved to smell him, a fragrance of wool and leather and whiskey and shoe polish and aftershave.

Drag was not a frequent thing, only twice a year. Halloween, of course. Kids in costume would come to our house and ring the bell and Father would answer it in women's clothes. "Trick or treat, Gilbert," the children would say, and my father would try to guess who was behind each mask. He would drop candy into the plastic pumpkins or paper sacks and send the children on to the next house.

The other time was the Womanless Wedding. It was an annual affair, a minstrel show in rouge instead of blackface. The Rotary and the Lions—all the solid male citizens of Arrow Catcher, Mississippi—would put on a raucous play in drag and donate the money to charity. One year Mr. Rant got drunk and fell off the stage in a floor-length gown.

My father loved the Womanless Wedding. He took a different part each year: bride, mother of the bride, flower girl, maid of honor, whatever was available. He shaved his legs and Naired his chest and bleached the hair on his arms and plucked his eyebrows and rouged his lips and mascaraed his lashes and he was ready. He owned wigs. With a pedicure and a close shave, my father was a pretty good looking woman for his age.

So dressing in drag was not new.

In my junior year of high school, my class got the idea of putting on an all-girl football game. We were raising money for some worthwhile project or other—a new scoreboard for the gym, I think. The idea was for the junior and senior girls to put on uniforms and helmets and to play football against each other. The school principal agreed to let us use the stadium. We would charge admission and sell hot dogs and Cokes at the concession stand.

It seemed like a good idea.

The idea seemed even better when I first saw the girls in uniform. They were beautiful. Hulda Raby had long legs and boyish hips and large breasts, and when she was dressed in our school colors and was wearing pads and cleats and a rubber mouthpiece, I thought no one on earth had ever had such a good idea as the all-girl football team.

The girls were enthusiastic. They found a senior boy who agreed to coach them, Tony Pirelli, whose Aunt Josie owned the Arrow Cafe.

Positions were tried out for and assigned. Plays were drawn up and mimeographed and passed out to the players and carried around in notebooks and memorized. A wide-hipped girl named Tootie Nell Hightower learned to snap the ball, and Nadine Johnson learned to take the snap from center.

I stood on the sidelines and watched Nadine hunker into position behind the center's upturned rear end and put her hands into position. *Green forty-two . . .* My heart jumped out of my chest.

Pads began to clash, helmets to clatter. Nadine was a natural at quarterback and could throw the bomb. Ednita Prestridge could get open. I saw these girls through new eyes. I feared them and I loved them.

The days passed. No one except the players was allowed inside the locker room, of course, not even Tony Pirelli, the kid who coached them. But each day after practice I hung outside in the parking lot and imagined them in there. I saw them unlace their cleats and fling them into a corner. I saw them strip dirty tape from their ankles and remove the Tuf-skin with alcohol. I smelled the pungency of their skin. I watched them walk through the locker room wearing only their shoulder pads, nothing else, the padding stained with sweat. I watched them soap up in the shower and play grabass and snap each other with towels. I saw them stand under the shower and let the water pour into their upturned faces and I watched one or another of them relax her bladder and allow the urine to run down her leg and swirl away in the drain.

Never before in the history of the whole wide world had anyone ever had such a good idea as the all-girl football team.

I wanted to be near the girls. I hung around the parking lot to watch them. At first a few other boys did the same, and we punched each other's arms and made jokes, but my interest outlasted theirs and soon I was the only boy in the parking lot.

My favorite part of the day was when the girls came out of the locker rooms after practice, after their showers.

Nadine Johnson came out, the quarterback. She had short hair and it was still wet and slicked back like a man's. Hulda Raby had blonde hair that hung down to her hips. One day she stepped out of the gym into the late afternoon sun and bent over and allowed her wet hair to hang down over her face, almost to the ground. She toweled it roughly with a white locker-room towel and then flung her hair back over her head so that it hung down her back again. She dropped the towel behind her, arrogant, and she seemed to know that someone would pick it up for her. It was my joy to rush across the lot and place the towel into a bin of soiled linens.

Hulda Raby did not notice me, of course. My reward was to be close to the locker-room door when the others came out.

Tootie Nell Hightower, the center—I could not look at her without seeing her bent over the ball, its leather nap gripped in her certain hands. Lynn Koontz—I heard the beauty of her name for the first time. It was a football player's name. You could play tight end for the Steelers with a name like Lynn Koontz. The twins, Exie Lee and Nora Lee Alridge. The Buell girls, Marty and Ruby. Ednita Prestridge, the wide receiver. I heard Nadine say to her, "Nita, honey, you got a great pair of hands."

I envied them their womanhood.

☀
I watched them on the practice field each day after school. Tony Pirelli, their coach, seemed to me the luckiest boy in the world.

I insinuated myself into their midst. I volunteered to act as a flunky for the team. I helped line the field. I asked parents to act as referees and scorekeepers, and I made sure everyone had clean socks. I carried equipment and water bottles and the first aid kit. I saddlesoaped footballs and replaced broken elastic. I dealt with the high school principal, who was worried about the light bill, since the game was to be held at night.

It was springtime and the Mississippi Delta was Eden to me. I saw it as I had never seen it before, the whippoorwills and coons and owls and little bobwhites. Mornings the pecan trees outside my window were heavy with dew and smelled like big wet flowers.

In my dreams I listened to the music of *green forty-two hut hut hut* . . . It floated on the air like a fragrance of wisteria. I knew why men married, as my father had, and were true to the same woman over a lifetime. I thought of my father's mortality.

I went into my father's room and found his revolver and broke it open and poured its cartridges onto the chenille bedspread. I thought of my own mortality. I understood for the first time the difficulty of ever knowing who I am. I longed to be held as a lover by a woman in a football suit.

The all-girl football team idea got out of hand. It became elaborate.

Somebody suggested that we should have boy cheerleaders, dressed up in girls' cheerleading costumes. It would be hilarious, everybody said. What fun. Somebody else thought it would be just great if we made it homecoming as well. You know, with a homecoming court. Everyone agreed, Sure! Oh boy! It would be like the Womanless Wedding, only better. We'll hold the ceremony at halftime. We'll crown a homecoming queen!

I didn't like the idea. I said, "I'm against it. It's a silly idea. I vote no."

Everybody else said, "It'll be hilarious. Let's do it, sure it's great."

I wanted to say, Are you insane? We have discovered what makes women beautiful. The girl-children who were our classmates three weeks ago are now women—they are constellations! Do you want a constellation walking in a parade with some goon in a dress?

Instead I said, "No way. I'm not doing it. I've got to line the field. I've got to pump up the balls. Count me out, brother."

I did it anyway. I was elected cheerleader. That's small-town high school for you. It was a big joke. I didn't want to do it, so everybody voted on me. No try-outs, nothing. One day I get the news and a box with a cheerleader costume in it. I said, "Forget it."

Everybody said, "Be a sport."

Right up until the night of the big game I still wasn't going to do it. I wasn't even going to the game. Why should I? Nobody was taking the game seriously—nobody but me and the girls who were knocking their heads together.

Maybe this will explain it: One day after practice I saw Ednita Prestridge get into her father's pickup alone. She yanked open the door and, as she did, she put her fingers to one side of her nose and blew snot into the gravel driveway of the schoolhouse parking lot. The door banged shut behind her and she drove away.

Do you understand what I mean? It was not Ednita I loved. Not Tootie Nell or Lynn Koontz or Nadine Johnson. It was Woman. I had never known her before. She was a presence as essential and dangerous as geology. Somehow she held the magic that could make me whole and give me life.

That's why I wasn't going to the all-girl football game.

I said all this to my father in his room at the back of our house. In this room I could say anything. I could smell my father's whole life in this room, the guns in the closet, the feathers of birds he had killed, the blood of mammals, the mutton that greased the line of his fly-casting equipment.

I said, "It would take a fool to dress up like a girl, when there are women—women, Daddy, not girls—dressed in pads and cleats."

What do you suppose my father said to me? Can you guess? Do you think he said, "Don't be silly, it's a school project. I want you to participate." Do you think he said, "It's up to you, of course, but I just want to tell you, you're going to be missing out on a whole lot of fun."

My father was a housepainter. He went to sixth grade and no further. He said, "I will dress you in a skirt and a sweater and nice underwear and you will feel beautiful."

I said, "Uh . . ."

He said, "You have never felt beautiful."

I said, "Well . . ."

It was near dark. The fall air had turned cold. In two hours the all-girl football game would begin. My mother was still at work.

Father drew my bath and put almond oil into the water and swished the water back and forth with his hand until it foamed up. He hung a green silk bathrobe on a hook on the bathroom door. He set out bathpowder and a powder puff he had bought new for me. He showed me how to shave my legs and underarms. It didn't matter that no one else would be able to see.

When I was clean and sweet-smelling, I came into his room wearing the robe. He gave me the clothes I would dress in.

I said, "Dad, is this queer?"

He did not answer.

I took the box with the uniform in it, and a small bag with new underwear.

I slipped into the lacy underpants, and then into the pantyhose.

I let him show me how to hook the bra, which he did not stuff with Kleenex. He gave me tiny false breasts, cups made of foam rubber, with perfect nipples on the ends. When I slipped on my sweater with the big AC on the front, you could see my nipples showing through.

I put on a half-slip and the skirt. He showed me how to apply my makeup. I could choose any wig I wanted. He spritzed me with Windsong.

I did not feel beautiful. I felt like a fool. I looked at myself in the mirror and saw that I looked like a fool as well. I stood like a boy, I walked like a boy, I scratched myself like a boy. I had a dumb boy-look on my face. My hands were boy-hands. My dick, for no good reason, was stiff and aching.

The masculine smells of my father's room—the rubber raingear and gun oil and fish scales stuck to his tacklebox—reached me through my false femininity and mocked me.

My father said, "How do you feel?"

I said, "Like a fucking fool."

I said, "I've got a hard-on."

He said, "Do you know any cheers? Can you do one cheer for me before you go?"

I said, "I don't think so, Dad."

He said, "Well, I'll have my eyes on you the whole game. I'll be watching you from the stadium."

I said, "I wish there was a Book of Life, with all the right answers in the back."

He said, "Do 'Satisfied.' Just once, before you go. 'Satisfied' is my favorite cheer."

There was something about that football field: the brilliant natural carpet of green grass, the incredible lights, the strong straight lines of chalk dust, the serviceable steel bleachers filled with cheering people and the little Arrow Catcher High School marching band in uniform—there was something in

251

all that scene that told me who I was. I did not feel beautiful, as my father had predicted. I was the same person I had always been, and yet the bass drum, with its flaking bow-and-arrow design and the words ARROW CATCHER, MISSISSIPPI, printed in faded letters around the perimeter of the drum-head, told me that the worst things about myself were not my enemies and that the Womanless Wedding held meaning for my father that I might never understand and did not need to understand.

I had come to the game late. The referees in their striped suits had already taken the field. The opposing teams, in black-and-gold uniforms, had finished warm-up calisthen-ics. Steel whistles sounded and drew the players from their final huddle and prayers.

The captains walked like warriors to the middle of the field. They watched the toss of the coin.

I watched it also, from the sidelines. The coin went up and up. It seemed suspended in the air beneath those blaz-ing lights, above the green table of Delta land. The coin seemed forged of pure silver and big as a discus. It turned over and over, as if in slow motion. It hung for a century.

I jumped up and down in my wool skirt and saddle oxfords. I was a cheerleader at the center of the universe. I waved my pom-poms and clapped my hands and kicked my heels up behind me. I tossed my hair and fluttered my lashes without knowing I knew how to do these things. The coin that I was watching was a message of hope and goodness throughout the land.

It was a land I loved, this fine ellipse in a crook of the

Yazoo River—its alligators and mallards and beaver dams, its rice paddies and soybeans and catfish farms.

Suddenly I knew that my father was right, that I did feel beautiful, except that now beauty had a different meaning for me. It meant that I was who I was, the core of me, the perfect center, and that the world was who it was and that those two facts were unchangeable. Grief had no sting, the future was not a thing to fear, all things were possible and personal and pure.

I watched the opening kickoff. It was a short grounder that scooted between the legs of the front line of girls in uniform.

By the time someone in the backfield picked it up, my small breasts had become a part of me, not rubber but flesh. My cock, beneath the lacy underpants, was what it had always been, this odd hard unpredictable equipment I had been born with, and yet it was also a moist opening into the hidden fragrance of another self that was me as well. My arms were woman-arms, my feet woman-feet, my voice, my lips, my fingers. I stood on the sweet sad brink of womanhood, and somehow I shared this newness with my father.

The game had begun, and I was the cheeriest cheerleader on the sidelines. One team scored a touchdown. Hulda Raby sustained a serious knee injury. Nadine threw the bomb to Ednita but had it intercepted. The band played the fight song, and we went through all the cheers.

My father and mother were in the bleachers, far up, and I could see the pride in their faces. I was a wonderful cheerleader, and they knew that I was.

We did "Satisfied," and in my heart I dedicated the cheer to my father.

I went to the principal, we cheerleaders called out, with our hands on our hips, sashaying as we pretended to walk haughtily into the principal's office.

Satisfied, came the refrain back from the cheering section, including my father and mother.

And the principal said, we called out, shaking our finger, as if the principal were giving us a stern talking-to.

And again the loud refrain, *Satisfied*.

That we couldn't lose . . .

Satisfied . . .

With the stuff we use . . .

Satisfied . . .

You take-a one step back . . . Here we put our hands behind our backs and jumped one step backwards, cute and coy, as if we were obeying the principal's stern order.

Satisfied . . .

You take-a two steps up . . . Here we put on a look of mock surprise, as if we just could not understand what the principal was getting at with all his complicated instructions, but we put our hands on our hips and took two cute steps forward anyway.

The principal's final line is: *And then you strut your stuff, And then you strut your stuff, And then you strut your stuff*. Which we did, by wagging our sexy hips and prankishly twirling our index fingers in the air.

Sat-isss-fied!

The Mississippi Delta air was the Garden of Eden, filled

with innocence and ripe apples. The blue of the skies shone through the darkness of the night and through the glare of the stadium lights. I smelled fig trees and a fragrance of weevil poison and sweet fishy water from the swamp.

The game went on. The huddles and the time-outs, the sweat and the bloody noses and the fourth-down punts.

And then halftime. I had literally forgotten all about halftime.

My whole world exploded into ceremony and beautiful ritual. The band was on the field in full uniform. The goalposts were wrapped in black and gold crepe paper, and streamers were blowing in the autumn breeze. Boys with shaven legs strutted past the bleachers wearing majorette costumes. They carried bright banners on long poles. The band marched in formation, and then it formed a huge heart in the center of the field. It played "Let Me Call You Sweetheart," and I felt tears of joy and the fullness of nature well up in me. I knew that the world was a place of safety and hope and that my father was a great man. I knew that I was a beautiful woman and that because of this I had a chance of growing up to be as fine a man as my father. *Let me call you sweetheart I'm in love with you, Let me hear you whisper that you love me too*. I loved the girls in uniform; I would always love them. They were lined up under the home-team goalposts with the maids of the homecoming court. *Keep the lovelight burning in your eyes so true . . .*

Nadine Johnson was the captain. She led the beautiful slow processional of players and maids toward the center of the field. The band played. There was a sweetness of Mow-down in the air from the rice paddies nearby.

I knew the meaning of love. I thought of my father, the way he had looked on the day of his wedding, the first of his weddings that I was old enough to attend. He had been the bride and had worn a high-bodice floor-length gown, antique white, with a train and veil. He carried a nosegay at his waist. When the minister asked whether any person here present could show just cause why this couple should not be joined in holy matrimony, a drunken pharmacist named H. L. Dewberry, wearing a print dress and heels, jumped up out of the audience and fired a pistol in the air. My father fell into a swoon.

It was all part of the show, of course—and although I knew it was only a play and that my father was only an actor in it, I wanted to leap from my seat in the audience and make known to all the world that he was my father and that without him my own life was without meaning.

On the football field Nadine Johnson turned to a tiny boy-child, three or four years old, who was a part of the home-coming ceremonies. He was wearing a ruffled dress with stiff petticoats and was standing beside Nadine with a satin pillow in his hands. There was a silvery crown on the pillow. The homecoming court was assembled around them, arms hooked in arms, smiles bright.

Nadine took the crown from the pillow, as flashbulbs went off.

A boy named Jeep Bennett was standing beside Nadine. He was wearing a yellow evening gown and had only three fingers on one hand. He had been in a hunting accident the year before and this year had been elected homecoming queen.

Nadine placed the crown on his proud head, and the flashbulbs went off again. The bleachers roared with applause and cheers and approval. Nadine kissed Jeep, and Jeep was demure and embarrassed.

I had wanted—dreamed!—of this moment, dreaded it in a way, because I had believed I would envy Jeep this perfection, this public kiss of a woman in a football suit, which I had believed for three weeks was the completion of love and sex and holy need.

And yet now that it was here, it was oddly meaningless to me. There was no jealousy in my heart, no lust for Nadine in all her sweaty beauty.

And yet there was lust in my heart, sweet romance. My breath caught in my throat, my tiny breasts rose and my nipples hardened. (Seemed to harden, I swear!)

I looked down the line of suited-up women and their male maids. Tootie Nell, wide-hipped and solid; Hulda, with a damaged knee; Lynn Koontz, her magical name. I looked at the drag-dressed boys who clung violetlike to the certain arms of these beautiful women. And yes there was lust and even love in my heart, but not for the women in black-and-gold. The person I loved was wearing a business suit with a back-pleat in the skirt, so that when he walked you could see a triangle of his gray satin slip and the back of his beautiful knee. Tony Pirelli, the kid who coached the team, was an Italian boy with dark skin and dark eyes and a nut-brown

257

wig that caressed his shoulders. He wore a soft gray silk blouse with ruffled sleeves and, at his throat, a ruffled ascot. His shoes were patent leather sling-back pumps with two-inch heels, and the girls had given him a corsage, which he wore on his breast.

I hated my thoughts and my feelings. I was certain my father could read them all the way to the top of the bleachers.

I had never seen anyone so beautiful as Tony Pirelli. He never smiled, and now his sadness called out to me, it made me want to hold him and protect him from all harm, to kiss his lips and neck, to close his brown eyes with my kisses, to hold his small breasts in my hands and to have him touch my own breasts.

I believed I was a lesbian. What else could I call myself? I felt like a fool for not having noticed before. I was a fool for having strutted my stuff during the cheers, for having loved the Mississippi Delta and the sentimental songs played by the band.

I didn't see the rest of the game. The band played and the crepe paper rattled and the banners whipped and the crowds cheered, and I ran away from the sidelines and through the gate and away from the football field and the school grounds.

This happened in the autumn I was sixteen years old. Now I am forty-five years old, and all of it seems too fantastic to be true. Maybe my memory has exaggerated the facts, somehow.

I remember what happened afterwards very accurately, though.

I ran through the little town of Arrow Catcher, Mississippi, toward my parents' home. I don't know what I wanted there, the safety of my father's room, I think, the fishing rods and reels with names like Shakespeare and Garcia, the suits of camouflage and the rubber hip-waders. I was still wearing my cheerleader costume and my makeup and false breasts and even the wig.

And then something happened, by magic I suppose, that stopped me. The southern sky seemed to fill with light—no, not light, but with something like light, with meaning, I want to say.

I stood in the street where I had stopped and I listened to the distant brass of the Arrow Catcher High School marching band. It sounded like the blare of circus horns. I took deep breaths and exhaled them into the frosty air.

I took from my skirt pocket the lace handkerchief my father had put there for me, and I dabbed at my eyes, careful not to smear the mascara more than it was already smeared.

I began walking back toward the football field. I was not a woman. I did not feel like a woman. I was not in love with a boy. I was a boy in costume for one night of the year, and I was my father's child and the child of this strange southern geography. I was beautiful, and also wise and sad and somehow doomed with joy.

The gymnasium was decorated in black and gold. There was a table with a big crystal punch bowl, and other tables with ironed white tablecloths and trays of sandwiches and cookies. Around the walls of the gym our parents had placed potted plants and baskets of flowers. The girls had changed to their party dresses, the boys had put on the trousers and sport jackets our parents had brought for us. We were proper boys and girls, and our costumes were stuffed into bags in the locker rooms where we changed.

A phonograph blared out the music we loved.

I danced close to Nadine Johnson and imagined, as I felt her cool cheek against mine, that I could see the future. I imagined I would marry—not Nadine but some woman like Nadine, some beautiful woman, faceless for now—and that together we would have sons and that we would love them and teach them to be gentle and to love the music we were dancing to and to wear dresses and that, in doing this, we would somehow never grow old and that love would last forever.

Sugar Among the Freaks

I knew I had made a mistake when the iced tea came with a spoon sticking out of it. I was in the Skelly truck-stop restaurant in Alma, Arkansas. It's got a sign that says HOME COOKING and a glass case full of slabs of coconut pie and chocolate pie with real dilapidated meringue on them and a couple of flies crawling around on the inside of the glass.

Meringue and flies don't mean a thing compared to tea. You can scoop that meringue off and sling it up under some furniture and never see it again, and there's not a nickel's worth of taste in a fly, even if you do happen to eat one. It's the iced tea in a place that predicts what the food is going to look like when it comes out. I learned that from my mama, who served instant potato sandwiches on light bread. She also pronounced *meringue* as "merry-gew," if you want some idea of what kind of cook she was.

In fact, I've got to tell you about my mama. She used to cut a magnolia blossom off the tree in our side yard and put it on the dining room table for decoration. "Big as a dinner plate," she would always say, which made it sound kind of sickening in the first place, if you see what I mean. It was so

261

sweet-smelling it would give you cavities. Not really, of course. That was my grandmama's joke, Sugar Mecklin. I wanted to live with Sugar, but nobody would let me. The magnolia wouldn't cause cavities, but it would give you Excedrin Headache Number 57, if you remember your TV commercials at all, before you could jerk a cat in two. That's the one where two ram goats are butting each other in the head.

The worst thing was she would leave it on the table so long. She would leave it there a month, seem like. She would leave it there until it was all black and horrible and runny before she would throw it out. Even if she'd been a better cook you couldn't have eaten in the presence of that magnolia. Nobody could. My daddy could, of course. But not any normal person, no way, José, which is something else my Grandmama Sugar used to say.

I took one look at that tea and I said, "Instant!" right out loud, couldn't have stopped myself if I tried. Some customers looked over at me. I said "Instant" another couple of times real loud, and clapped my hands together when I said it. They might think *instant* means waitress in German or some other language, you don't know. Some people will believe anything.

You're going to say, "Now he sounds a little crazy to me," and I don't blame you a bit. I am crazy, I act that way. I start acting crazy whenever I'm under the influence of Winston Krepps.

Winston is this guy I help out whenever he asks me. He's a full-time quadriplegic, got him a motorized wheelchair and everything. I was supposed to meet Winston at this truck stop and help his attendant drive him out to west Oklahoma to some kind of conference he was going to.

Winston jumped off a bridge when he was a boy and hit a submerged boat, broke his neck pretty as you please. I said, "I bet you won't be jumping off any more bridges any time soon, will you," and Winston said he had to agree. He said he learned his lesson the first time. I lived with Winston for a while a couple years ago, helped him out. He says I ought to get a more realistic view of life, and other helpful advice. I have to agree.

I get along fine with Winston. The trouble is, I've got this personality flaw. That's what Winston told me. I'm ashamed to tell you about it, but here's the truth. Deformed people make me go crazy. You're going to say, "Uh-oh, look out, he's a mean one." It's not true. Winston'll tell you that himself. I'm as sweet a guy as you ever want to meet—Sugar Mecklin, named after my grandmama. Twenty-four years old, high school equivalency diploma—I mean what else do you want, Burt Reynolds, or what?

But I never can treat deformed people or crippled people like they're real. To me they're just a bunch of freaks, not much better than a midget. And don't get me started on the blind. I took work out at the School for the Blind in Little Rock for a while, so I know what's on a blind man's mind. They've got this good sense of smell, though, I'll give them that.

Anyway, it's a problem I've got. Winston says it doesn't matter to him; he likes me anyway, which I appreciate. Oh, I get along fine with Winston. I wouldn't go so far as to say I like him. No sense lying about that. You can't go around having a passel of freaks as your friends. No way, José.

Part of it is I run into so many of them. In the Safeway, squeezing cantelopes, look out!—somebody's going to sneak up behind you and hand you a deaf-mute card and cost you a quarter and make you think for about the one-millionth time that you might try to learn sign language off the hand illustrations on the back.

Or you're down at Roger's Ozark Pool Hall, shooting a little snooker, hold on!—here comes a man with one leg shorter than the other, and he's wearing one of those built-up shoes, rocking his way around the table, rocka rocka rocka, while he chalks his cue and takes you for every nickel you got in your pocket. How are you going to shoot snooker with a rocker?

I went out with a girl one time who showed me a glass eye she wore around her neck on a gold chain. I never asked her whose eye it was, I just drove her home. I counted myself lucky I hadn't made a big hit with her. Think about taking a girl's blouse off and finding an eye staring out at you. What kind of life can you live when you keep meeting people who might do that to you.

And you try applying for a job in Fort Smith, second largest town in Arkansas. Just try it and see what happens. A third of the men you shake hands with will have two fingers missing on their right hand, and the rest of them will be wearing a hearing aid. They wear those flesh-colored rascals that fit behind your ear and look like you've got a disease. I can't stand a hearing aid. One of those big curved horns you used to see in pictures would be all right, but not something that looks like ear disease.

Deformed people are attracted to me, see. I'm a lightning rod and they're a big dark cloud just rubbing his old hands together he's so happy.

Wait till I tell you what happened to me when I was a child growing up in Mississippi. A pipeline for natural gas was being put through the Delta and had everybody all excited. A lot of new work opened up. Transient workers from all over the country piled into our little town in trailers. My daddy, trying to latch on to some of the new money that was flowing through, rented out our side yard with the magnolia tree. It was a good place for a mobile home hook-up, he said. You probably already know what happened. A family of midgets moved in. You wouldn't think there would be many midgets in the construction field, would you? But there they were, a whole trailerful of them.

I used to be Winston's attendant. That's the kind of job I'm always getting myself into. I lived with him for about six months before he moved to Hot Springs to teach in the Rehab Center there. He's a poet, and they tell me he understands the problems of the handicapped and is well appreciated for his good work. I don't doubt it a bit.

Here's the thing, though. It was a relief to me when he moved down there. When I was living with him I had this unhealthy compulsion to be the best attendant the world has ever known. Winston says I ought to try to break myself of that. He says I'm just a generous kind of guy and I take everything too far, even generosity.

I didn't catch on to what I was doing at the time, but I think I see it now. I would do anything in the world that Winston told me, and I mean anything. My goal was to give Winston the freedom to do anything he would have done if he never had jumped off that bridge in the first place.

He said, "Okay, what if I told you I couldn't stand you? What if I said I'd shoot you dead if I could hold a gun and pull the trigger?" I swear, it scared me. I didn't know the answer. I knew it wouldn't come to that. Winston wouldn't do that to me. But you see what I mean. It's a question you want to know the answer to.

I did plenty of other stuff though. If Winston was dead drunk and wanted more whiskey, I poured it down him, brother, no questions asked, forget about tomorrow. Next day he'd be sick and I'd be holding the pan he was gagging into and he'd catch his breath for a second and he'd say, "Use your goddamn brain, man! Don't feed a drunk man whiskey!" Too late, and just don't tell me to do it again, we'll both be smelling vomit in the morning. That's what I would think; I wouldn't say it. I make it a rule never to disagree with a freak.

If he wanted to blow the horn in traffic, I blew it, forget about rude, forget about unnecessary. If Winston wanted to stay late at a party that everybody else had already left and the host wanted us the hell out of his house, we stayed. "Christ, don't let me do that again," he'd say when he caught on to what had happened. Same thing—don't ask it again.

Plenty of times I drove down roads I knew were the wrong road, because Winston had misread the map. I made wrong turns into one-way traffic, because Winston had his directions mixed up.

I understand it better now. Winston explained it to me. He said it was a way of redressing the wrong in myself, what I knew was wrong. He said I felt guilty for thinking he wasn't real. He said I was trying to act like he, Winston, was the real person and that I was the one that was something else, something less. He said it would suit him fine if I was to disagree with him sometime. He said it would beat hell out of driving into one-way traffic.

It didn't help. I still do whatever a freak tells me. When I'm under the influence of Winston, even nonfreaks can control me.

Like the tea, for example. I can't stand instant tea. My mama, who was the worst cook you ever want to meet up with, used to make instant tea when I was little. They say the product has been improved since then but it's a lie, it's the same.

My mama wasn't deformed, but she was a kind of freak. My daddy actually called her a freak one time, right to my face. We were sitting out on the porch swing, and Daddy was shooting out the Christmas lights around the porch, still up in August, with a Red Ryder BB gun, manufactured at the plant right out here in Springdale, with a leather thong hanging off the side. He said, right out of the clear blue, like when a daddy decides his boy ought to be told some important thing that he'll need to know about for the rest of his life, like about tail or something, he said, "Sugar, your mama is a first-class freak. It has not escaped my attention." What's a child going to do with that kind of information, I ask you? He was telling me he loved my mother. He might just as well have said, "I have been cursed with premature ejaculation, but I love family life anyway." What's a child supposed to say? What's he supposed to think about for the rest of his life? And anyway, who arranged for the midgets to live in the side yard with the magnolia tree? Not Mama. I remember she did introduce me to a clubfooted Latvian girl, and she kept giving us that look that says she's just dying for us to like each other right away and get married and have her a passel of little clubfooted Latvian grandchildren, but she doesn't want to seem pushy so just go right on and take our time.

I knew I was going to drink that tea the minute I saw it. I caught a couple of flies with my hand, just to calm down. I took the tea from the waitress and said, "Donkey shane, honey." I was using my German accent to deal with her; couldn't hurt.

The reason was, this waitress had a mean look. She was old and had heavy biceps and old-fashioned heart-shaped lips painted over her regular lips. I didn't look to see if she had her stockings rolled down to her ankles or was wearing white socks, but I bet it was one or the other. She wasn't wearing any kind of waitress uniform, just a plain blue dress with a broad collar. She looked like somebody who was having to work on her day off, so just watch out, Jack, don't mess with her.

I wasn't wrong about the tea. I looked down in the glass.

There was a solid brown mass at the bottom. I pushed it around and around until it broke up and an amber foam floated up to the top. Presweetened and lemon flavored, same as Mama used to make, you could smell it.

And I wasn't wrong about the food either. It was as bad as Mama's. In fact, I've got to tell you about Mama's cooking. The scariest meal she fixed was spaghetti. The recipe was real simple. For the sauce she dumped a couple of quarts of canned tomatoes into a big skillet, along with an onion chopped into four pieces. That was all. There were no other ingredients. No garlic, no salt, no meat, no oregano—nothing. Listen to this. When the tomatoes were bubbling, she stripped the cellophane off a package of noodles and, without separating them, jammed them up under the hot tomatoes like a short baton. They just sat there and cooked until they were a solid gummy rod of pasta.

My daddy, he was a little red-faced man with webbed toes on both his feet and went around barefoot all the time. He claimed this was his favorite dish. He would clean his plate. I mean he really liked it, he wasn't just being nice. He'd finish up and he'd say, "Whew!" He'd push his chair back from the table and stretch out his little short legs with his old duck toes hanging off the end, and he'd pat his stomach with both hands. He'd say, "I ought not, I'm going to get fat if I do, but, honey, if you'd be kind enough to slice me off another three four inches of that spaghetti, I do believe I could find a place for it." Do you see what I mean? It's no wonder I've got some personality problems.

I played it safe with the waitress. I wrapped the Salisbury steak up in a paper napkin and stuffed it inside the torn plastic lining of the chair I was sitting in. I let the mashed potatoes get cold and stiff enough to stick to the underside of the table. I hoped they would hang there long enough for me to make my getaway. I didn't know what to do with the cole slaw, so l scooped it up in the palm of my hand and looked around the room. When I thought nobody was looking, I lobbed it onto a table nearby. Nobody was sitting at the table, and the dishes from the last customer hadn't been bused yet. I had hoped it would hit one of the plates. It didn't, but it looked okay where it did hit, mostly in one of the ashtrays.

When the waitress brought the check, she noticed I had cleaned my plate. For a second there I thought she was going to tell me what a good boy I was, but she didn't. She just gave me one of her suspicious looks and slapped the check down in front of me. I think I know why she was mad at me. I got the impression she could tell I hitchhiked in here. I got the impression she knew I had caught two rides to get here, the first one to Winslow with a college boy in a 280Z and the other one with a man in a twenty-five-year-old Cadillac. I got the impression she knew he told me he was driving to Waco to kill his brother-in-law and showed me the pistol he was going to use. I got the impression she was thinking, You're batting . 500 already, sonnyboy, don't try nothing smart with me. I got the impression hitchhikers are on an especially low rung of the social ladder in a truck stop, especially those who can't do any better than an Arky college boy and a murderous Texan. She didn't say a word about it, but I've got this ability.

Just then Winston and his attendant drove up. The attendant's name was Floyd, Winston had told me on the phone. I recognized the van right away, when I saw it out the window. It's a white Ford with a hydraulic lift on the back. I thought about Winston and remembered he would be in his old heavy humming buzzing chair. I couldn't stand that thing.

Old Biceps looked in my direction from the next table. She had found the ashtray full of cole slaw and didn't act happy about it. I checked the mashed potatoes and thought they had started to lose their grip.

I eased away from the table and went outside in the parking lot to meet Winston and Floyd. I didn't know Floyd, just his name, which sounded a little sissified to me, if you want the truth. The waitress was still busy with the slaw problem and didn't see me leave.

Now here is the way things can turn on you. I had been worrying about dealing with Winston being a freak. There was a bigger problem with Floyd. He wasn't the pretty-boy I had expected. In fact, he was extra ugly. He was ugly enough to qualify for a full-time freak, if you ask me. Sugar Mecklin would have said he was ugly enough to strike you blind. I shook hands with him out in the parking lot and went blind.

It's the truth, I couldn't see him. The only thing I noticed about him before I lost my sight was that Floyd was a black man. I wouldn't want you to think I'm prejudiced against

271

black people. You might think so, since you know I grew up in Mississippi. But it's not true. In fact, I grew up thinking my family was part Negro. My Grandmama Sugar told me ever since I can remember that she was one-quarter black. She'd say, "One-quarter black, and it had to be the hind quarter."

Her right leg and hip weren't black exactly, they were more purple. It was a birthmark, I guess. I don't know what age I was before I finally caught on that she was making a joke. I used to roll around on the linoleum floor of her kitchen and try to look up Sugar's dress to see how high her blackness went. She'd kick me away from the sink, real playful, and she'd say, "You little freak."

Anyway, Floyd was black and I couldn't see him; I looked, but he just wasn't there. It turned out, though, that I wasn't blind after all. Floyd was invisible. I could see everything around him. I saw the parked tractor trailers, I saw the greasy asphalt and the diesel pumps. I could see Winston just fine. He looked all right, too, as good as he ever looks. But Floyd wasn't there. He was too ugly to be seen.

Winston said that before he ate he wanted to be taken into the souvenir section of the truck stop. He said he was collecting material for a poem. I knew what he wanted to look at. He wanted to look at the Bowie knives and billy clubs and Confederate flags and bumper plates that say I JUST BARFED and I'M GLAD and oil paintings of Jesus riding shotgun in a Kenworth hauling logs.

Floyd said, "Nah, we don't have time."

272

Do you think I'd ever say such a thing to Winston?

Winston said, "I'm going in there, open the door."

Floyd wouldn't do it. Floyd said, "What you want me to get you to eat?"

Winston dropped the subject of the souvenirs and rolled into the restaurant. He said, "I believe I'll have a beer."

Floyd said, "You don't want any beer."

I thought, I like Floyd pretty good, invisible or not. It was an odd thing to be thinking, if you see what I mean.

All during the meal I spoke with this exaggerated British accent. It tickled Winston and Floyd to death, but I was serious. You can't go into a restaurant with a pair of freaks and not do something to protect yourself. I used words like *bloody good* and *old chap* and *amusing*. Partly it was to throw the waitress off my trail. We had Lady Biceps again, and I didn't know whether she had found the Salisbury steak or not.

The funny part is, she didn't recognize me. I'm terrible with accents, and I never fool anybody, but with her it was working perfect. She looked at me like I wasn't there at all. She could see Floyd just fine, you could tell, but she couldn't see me. It scared me a little, to tell the truth, even though I always thought it would be kind of nice to be invisible.

One time I paid a woman at a carnival five dollars to make me invisible, and do you think she would do it? Why, no. She tried to give me the five dollars back. She said I reminded her of her poor little sweet nephew who was a harelip (which I'm not) and why didn't I just run on and

273

spend my money on something else. I said, "Uh-unh, honey, we made a deal. I got a signed contract." She said, "I ain't a real gypsy. I was just lying to you. I can't make nobody invisible. You scat." You talk about mad, that was me. I tore that contract up right in her sassy face. Her name was Sister Medium Jackson, and she could have done it too, if she'd tried.

Right now I had this waitress problem. I made some squawking and hooting noises at her, like jungle birds and monkeys. I stretched out the features of my face with my fingers. It didn't faze her a bit. She didn't bat an eye. She wasn't faking either. She didn't give me that look that says she really does see me and she knows what a bratty little jackass I am and wouldn't my mama be ashamed of me if she knew the kind of fool I'm playing in a public place but just you wait and see how long it takes her to bat an eye she doesn't care how crazy I act. That wasn't her. She really couldn't see me, just like I couldn't see Floyd. I thought invisibility wasn't all it was cracked up to be. I thought Sister Medium Jackson was a pretty nice old girl after all, back in that sawdusty old horse lot they called a carnival in Mississippi, trying to save me five dollars and a hard time.

But mostly I felt all alone and left out. I hated being invisible, even to just one person. I felt awful that I had probably made Floyd feel the same way. I looked at him again and hoped I'd be able to see him, but I couldn't. Still invisible. These are strange times we are living in, I'm telling you.

I wanted out of the Skelly station. I kept looking at the black hole of Floyd, trying to see him in there somewhere, peeking out or something. The blackness didn't have anything to do with his race. Floyd was like watching an eclipse of the moon, except there was no light around the rim. I wondered if anybody who could be invisible could be real, even myself. But that wasn't it. It wasn't a blackness of Floyd's not being there. It was like he was too much there, like a real black hole in space you hear so much about, like he's pure there, not like most everybody else, who are only half-assed here. I got the feeling Floyd's ugliness was only just the tiniest little bit of his real ugliness, like it had been distilled down to this and maybe could be bottled in a little glass decanter and sold on the open market for a million dollars an ounce for real pretty women to put behind their ears before they go out on a date to calm down some of that prettiness and get a little bit ugly like the rest of us so we won't feel uncomfortable when they come around.

I said, "I've got to get out of here. I'm going crazy."

Winston and Floyd said they had to agree.

The drive to Oklahoma was long and hard, but I didn't mind. I was happy to be in the van, behind the wheel. Sometimes cars would pass us, and one time a child in the backseat caught a glimpse of Floyd and had a conniption fit and his mama and daddy probably wondered what in the world, but mostly nobody even looked. We drove until it got dark, and we kept on driving.

It was real late. The traffic through Oklahoma City was fierce. Every cowboy and Indian in the state was out driving around in pickups. We kept on going.

After a while we pulled off the road for gas. It was the

middle of the night by now, and the station we stopped at was deserted except for us. We pulled up alongside the pumps and I saw the station attendant come out of the little lighted office and head our way. He was just a boy.

I could see that his name was sewn on his shirt, up over the Exxon patch, but I didn't read it. I knew his name already. I have this mental ability. His name would be Jimmy, and his last name would be Fish. I looked around for his daddy, whose name would be Ellis, then I realized his daddy wouldn't be working in a service station. He would be assistant manager of the planing mill.

Jimmy Fish was in his late teens. He was a skinny boy with a big adam's apple and pretty good teeth. He looked tired and friendly. I watched him come up to the van on Floyd's side. Floyd turned toward him, and they met face to face.

Here's the thing. One time when I was Jimmy Fish's age, I had a temporary job in the complaint department of a big store. It was the day after Christmas, and I was making exchanges on Christmas presents that were being brought back. It was a pretty good job too, tissue paper in your hands all day and the smell of cardboard in your nostrils. Where are you going to get a better job than that? I was sitting framed behind an open window at a counter. I waited on a long line of polite dissatisfied customers. Look up, smile, inspect the merchandise, do the paperwork, look up again, next customer. Nothing to it. Then I looked up into the face of a monster.

It was a woman with no face. There was no nose, only a

wet hole to breathe through. There were no lips, only teeth. There was a wild caged tongue that was roaring for freedom from behind its bars. There was one eye, wide open and hairless as a fish eye. The other eye was sealed shut. There was no hair, only a badly fitted wig that couldn't hide the fact that she didn't have any ears. There were sermons that might have been preached on that good woman's suffering. No sermons came to my mind. I screamed. A loud horrible out-of-control scream.

Everybody in the line of customers hated me for noticing her deformity. The store manager sent me home. People comforted the monster, who couldn't cry because her tear glands had been blown away in the explosion along with everything else. I was not proud of that scream.

I expected Jimmy Fish to scream like that when he saw Floyd. I was wrong. Do you know what Jimmy Fish said? He said, "Unleaded?"

I wanted to be like Jimmy Fish. I wanted to be anybody but myself. I wanted to blame my crazy mama and daddy for making me so crazy. I wanted to blame Winston and Floyd. I couldn't. Blame had never seemed so out of place. I looked at Floyd and hoped I might be able to see him. I thought if I could see him I wouldn't hate myself so much.

He was still invisible, but he had changed. A dim halo had formed around his eclipsed face, his eclipsed self. I looked at Jimmy Fish. I admired him. I admired his innocence. I admired him for never having lived in Mississippi with a yardful of midgets. I admired these dark Oklahoma plains. I loved the people of this moony land. I knew that nobody in

Oklahoma would ever scream into a woman's face, no matter how ugly she was.

I stopped myself. I made a couple of jungle noises, to test the air. I placed my right hand inside my shirt, in my armpit, and blew off a couple of quick bilabials. It was love. Love is what I was up against. I fought it.

I resisted the easiness of love you feel when you meet a boy in the middle of the night and you think he reminds you of yourself and yet you know he represents everything you could never have been because you had midgets and he didn't, and you were once invisible and he wasn't, and you couldn't see Floyd and had screamed in a woman's face and learned to eat spaghetti by the slice. I resisted loving anyone for the reason that he was not deformed and that his family was not crazy and that he fit, anyway, into a world of deformity better than I did.

I looked out the window on my side of the van. The boy was pumping gas. I made a sound like a siren at him, and he only looked up and smiled. He made small talk. He told me about a man he saw on *Real People*, the TV show, who called himself the Human Siren. I barked at him and snarled at him, and he started telling me the plot of a werewolf movie. I loved him, but I didn't want to love him.

I resisted love because I knew that Jimmy Fish was not the thing I loved. The love I felt had no object. It was flying loose everywhere in a whirlwind; it had no place to light. Jimmy Fish was the first scrap of bark it came to and clung to by its toenails. I remembered a time when my mama invited the midgets into our home for dinner.

She served them her unbelievable spaghetti. The midgets thought a cruel joke was being played on them. The father of the little family took a deep breath. He got up, with dignity, from his chair. He jerked the napkin back through the napkin ring and put it beside his plate. He said, "We will go now. I understand now." With his tiny wife and three midget children squeaking and peeping and cheeping behind him, he made his lofty exit and never entered our home again.

I was a child at that table. I felt as embarrassed and as alone and as different as the midgets. I ran out of the house by the back door. I hid in the ditch under the chinaberry tree and watched them. I dreamed of finding words to apologize to them. I never did. I could never bring myself to speak to any of them again.

When the pipeline was finished and they moved out of our yard, I was the loneliest person in the world. I felt like a child who dies before it gets baptized, like somebody told me, and has to wander around all through eternity by himself and so lonesome he can't stand it. I was on a journey too, always had been, and I'm not off it yet, maybe never will be. Winston told me the kind of journey it is. He said I was on a Journey Through the Land of the Flat Characters. I know what he means now. It means that all my life I've been on an excursion through hell, and at every gate a new freak is crouched to jump out at me and scare me and refuse to let me get back up to the light. I want to get out, but I can't find my way.

I resisted love, I clawed at it, I scratched it with my fingernails. I bit off its nose. But it was still there. It was love, and it was real. When Jimmy Fish did not scream, love swept through me like a sudden wind. I felt it. It felt like the breeze made by the wings of a million bats swarming up out of a cave, squealing. I thought I was one of the bats in the swarm. This was love to me. Behind us a million tons of bat shit on the floor of the cave, and all around us nothing but a blaze of starlight and a million piercing shrill cries to be read with our pained ears like a million tiny white canes with red tips tap-tap-tapping along a sidewalk looking for the curb.

I was in love, but not with Jimmy or Winston or Floyd or myself. I was in love with America. The love I felt—crazy, diffuse, bat-out-of-hell love—was patriotism. I loved America. I loved Exxon. I loved the Ford Motor Company, who built the van that brought me to Oklahoma and this insight. I loved America's golden indifference to deformity. I loved American parents, who could name the ugliest child to be born in modern times with a pretty-boy's name. I loved American consumers, who hated me for screaming at a monster. I loved American politicians, who treated Floyd to a free education at the Rehabilitation Center Trade School for the simple reason that he was ugly as hell and had applied for a scholarship on those grounds. America the beautiful! I almost sang it. Land of the freaks and home of the strange.

I looked at Floyd. I smiled my brightest smile into his invisibility. Out of his eclipse he said, "Are you okay, man?"

I said. "Floyd, I am proud to be an American!"

Winston looked at me, and then at Floyd. They both seemed worried about me. Winston said, "We're all tired. We're all getting punchy."

I tried to curb my enthusiasm. They were probably right. I probably did sound a little wild. I went inside the station and gave Jimmy Fish Winston's credit card.

I said, "Fine night, Jimmy, just *fine!*" Jimmy didn't say anything. I was sorry I had had to make the noises at him, happy he had not seemed to notice. I wanted to ask about Ellis, but I decided against it. Maybe people in Oklahoma aren't named Ellis. Maybe there are no planing mills in Oklahoma.

Jimmy Fish handed me the credit slip to sign. He said, "Write down your tag number."

I made up a number and wrote *Arkansas* in the block marked "State."

He took the slip and read it over, real careful. I was afraid he would know I was lying about the license number. He didn't care about the number. He said, "Arkansas," reading from the slip. His voice didn't have much expression. He didn't hand back the credit card or my copy of the bill yet. He said, "Whereabouts in Arkansas."

I said, "Hot Springs." Not much of a lie.

He said, "My granddaddy used to live in Arkansas."

I said, "Is that right."

He said, "Yep."

I took the credit card from him and slipped it into my shirt pocket. He held on to the charge slip. He wanted to read *Arkansas* a little longer.

I said, "Well . . ." I shifted to the other foot. I said, "Time to get back on the road."

He said, "Texarkana."

I said, "Oh, your granddaddy. I see. Texarkana."

He said, "He's dead now."

I said, "I'm sorry to hear it," and put my hand on the doorknob. I didn't need the receipt slip. And yet when I tried to leave, I couldn't. I looked at the boy, whose name might not have been Jimmy Fish at all. He seemed even younger than before. My patriotism was gone, it seemed silly now. I felt very calm, and I began to see this boy in a way I had not been able to see before. He looked human to me for the first time. I thought maybe it was not just freaks I saw as less than human. Maybe it was everybody.

He said, "He died last weekend."

For some reason I had thought his grandfather had been dead much longer. I didn't answer right away. I said, "Just this last weekend."

This time he didn't answer.

I said, "Were you able to get over for the funeral?"

He said, "They didn't have a funeral."

I didn't know what to say. His grandfather had been left unburied for a full week.

The boy said, "His house burned down on him. Mama's still hunting bones." He handed me my receipt. He said, "Mama said no use burying him till we've got the whole thing."

I let a second or two pass. I said, "What's your granddaddy's name, Jimmy?" I wasn't reading his shirt. I said, "What did people call your granddaddy?"

He said, "Ellis."

I said, "Nice talking to you," and walked back out to the van.

Floyd was sitting in the shotgun seat ready to go. Winston was still in place in his chair.

I remembered something about my Grandmama Sugar. In the last two weeks of her life, she believed a band of Mexican midgets, with sombreros and ammunition belts, was camped in her bedroom. She thought they were playing cards and gambling at the foot of her bed at night. The day before she died she called me to her bed. She said, "They're not really there, Sugar. Don't pay any more attention to them than you have to."

I said, "All right, Sugar."

She said, "Muldrow was my youngest brother. You never knew him. He got a brain tumor and went blind and couldn't see anything but the inside of farm implement companies."

I said, "All right, Sugar, you rest now."

She said, "It's the same with these midget banditoes. They're not here either. No more than Muldrow's tractors and disks and haymows."

I said, "You rest."

She said, "Nothing is real." She said, "Nothing you see is ever really there."

I said, "All right."

She pointed to the Mexicans playing cards. Her voice was tolerant and loving. She said, "They're cute little buggers, but you can't understand a blessed word they say."

I got in the driver's seat. I said, "Winston, this is a long drive."

Winston said, "We're almost there."

283

I looked over at Floyd. The eclipse had passed. I could see him now, quite clearly. I said, "Floyd, how about you driving for a while."

Winston said, "I want you to drive, Sugar. You're a much better driver than Floyd."

I started up the engine.

Floyd got out and walked around to my side anyway. He stood outside the window.

I said, "It's okay, Floyd, I'll drive."

He said, "You start letting a cripple push you around, you're going to have a problem."

I looked out of the car at Jimmy Fish, where he stood in the fluorescent glare. I had never seen such a picture of loneliness.

Winston said, "Sugar, you start letting a cripple *and* a man as ugly as Floyd push you around, you've got a bigger problem."

They were right. It was time. I let Floyd slip behind the wheel and we pulled out. I wished we could take Jimmy Fish with us. I know he wanted to go. But there was no way it could be done. Just no way.

Sugar Mecklin was not right about one thing though, my grandmama. People *are* really there, every one of them. They definitely are. I swear, these are strange times we are living in.